CW01558682

797,885 Books

are available to read at

www.ForgottenBooks.com

Forgotten Books' App
Available for mobile, tablet & eReader

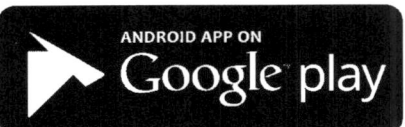

ISBN 978-1-330-82735-2
PIBN 10110642

This book is a reproduction of an important historical work. Forgotten Books uses state-of-the-art technology to digitally reconstruct the work, preserving the original format whilst repairing imperfections present in the aged copy. In rare cases, an imperfection in the original, such as a blemish or missing page, may be replicated in our edition. We do, however, repair the vast majority of imperfections successfully; any imperfections that remain are intentionally left to preserve the state of such historical works.

Forgotten Books is a registered trademark of FB &c Ltd.
Copyright © 2015 FB &c Ltd.
FB &c Ltd, Dalton House, 60 Windsor Avenue, London, SW19 2RR.
Company number 08720141. Registered in England and Wales.

For support please visit www.forgottenbooks.com

1 MONTH OF
FREE
READING

at

www.ForgottenBooks.com

By purchasing this book you are eligible for one month membership to ForgottenBooks.com, giving you unlimited access to our entire collection of over 700,000 titles via our web site and mobile apps.

To claim your free month visit:

www.forgottenbooks.com/free110642

* Offer is valid for 45 days from date of purchase. Terms and conditions apply.

English
Français
Deutsche
Italiano
Español
Português

www.forgottenbooks.com

Mythology Photography **Fiction**
Fishing Christianity **Art** Cooking
Essays Buddhism Freemasonry
Medicine **Biology** Music **Ancient
Egypt** Evolution Carpentry Physics
Dance Geology **Mathematics** Fitness
Shakespeare **Folklore** Yoga Marketing
Confidence Immortality Biographies
Poetry **Psychology** Witchcraft
Electronics Chemistry History **Law**
Accounting **Philosophy** Anthropology
Alchemy Drama Quantum Mechanics
Atheism Sexual Health **Ancient History**
Entrepreneurship Languages Sport
Paleontology Needlework Islam
Metaphysics Investment Archaeology
Parenting Statistics Criminology
Motivational

VERDICT
in
DISPUTE

EDGAR LUSTGARTEN

526633
6 . 9 . 51

ALLAN WINGATE

LONDON AND NEW YORK

122 East 55th Street New York

*Set in Linotype Granjon
and printed in Great Britain by
Billing and Sons Ltd
Guildford and Esher*

PREFACE

Six famous murder trials are examined in this book. All six verdicts are open to dispute. Three, in my belief, are demonstrably bad.

I have tried not only to analyse the facts but to recreate the atmosphere in which these trials were fought, so that the reader can determine the dominating influences that led to their unsatisfactory result—shortcomings of counsel, ineptitude of judge, prejudice of jury, or any other weakness to which the human race is constitutionally prone.

There is reason to suppose that, in British and American courts, miscarriages of justice are relatively rare. But however infrequent, they still affront the conscience, and study of those that disfigure the past will not be profitless if the knowledge thereby gained lessens the chance of repetition.

CONTENTS

FLORENCE MAYBRICK

1

PLANNED, deliberate killing is no drawing-room accomplishment. It needs callousness of heart, insensitivity of mind, indifference to suffering and contempt for human life. These are grim qualities; repulsive in a man, in a woman against nature. The calculating murderer is vile but comprehensible; the calculating murderess is an enigmatic paradox.

Hence the compelling fascination of those cases where a woman stands charged with a premeditated murder. Reasoning and logic no longer seem sufficient. The onlooker is swayed by imponderable factors: imagination, instinct, the gulf of incongruity between the crime and the accused. He gazes on the figure in the dock; he notes the slight form, the gentle manner, the appealing face. Is it *possible*, he asks himself, that the Crown case is well-founded? Did Edith Thompson *really* instigate that crime and lead her victim, unsuspecting, to the appointed place of death? Did Lizzie Borden *really* slay her stepmother with a hatchet and then calmly wait her chance to slay her father likewise? Was Florence Maybrick *really* a systematic poisoner who did her beastly work for weeks and watched her husband die?

Mrs Thompson, Miss Borden, Mrs Maybrick: in the same dread setting, for the same dread reason, their names have achieved unenviable immortality. And indeed, though widely separated by both time and space, the three women have many things in common. Up to a point, their stories coincide: the charge of murder, the long dramatic trial, a verdict ever after in dispute. Up to a point, their backgrounds coincide: the quiet home, the decent upbringing,

9

the orderly, respectable routine. Up to a point, their very natures coincide : each had a strong and forceful personality, determined to preserve its independence, and rebelling, in one form or another, against the bondage of domestic life.

Only in the last analysis do the three part company, but this final break is radical and sharp. Edith Thompson had passion but no breeding. Lizzie Borden had breeding but no passion. Florence Maybrick had both and therein lies her own peculiar and poignant tragedy.

2

The Maybrick story, with its disastrous denouement, opens in America in 1881.

In that year Mr James Maybrick, a Liverpool cotton broker, paid a business visit to the United States. He was in his early forties; a well-to-do bachelor of vigorous physique and sporting inclinations. In the course of his travels he met Miss Florence Chandler, the daughter of a substantial Alabama banker. Florence Chandler was then only eighteen; vivacious, handsome and sexually magnetic. James Maybrick promptly lost his heart and when he returned to England she came with him as his wife.

The couple ultimately settled down at Aigburth, where they lived in conditions of considerable affluence. They had a fine large house; they maintained several servants; nothing was wanting for their two children or themselves. On the surface, at any rate, the union seemed happy and the May-brick ménage, like a million others, firmly based upon mutual content.

Then, in the early part of 1889, Mrs Maybrick embarked on an intrigue.

She had formed an attachment to a man named Brierley, and for a time there is no doubt she supposed herself in love. Brierley's attractions are a matter for conjecture; he hovers in the shadows of the case, represented only by a chilly, frightened note written some weeks after his conquest was complete. ('We had perhaps better not meet until late in the autumn.') But the simple fact remains: having given her husband a plausible excuse—an aunt, she said, was to undergo an operation—on March 21st Mrs Maybrick went to London, where she stayed with Brierley for three nights at an hotel.

It should be recalled—for enlightenment, not in extenuation—that her husband was now fifty and she was twenty-six.

There are strong grounds for believing that James Maybrick had preceded her in a marital offence. But the eighties were the heyday of the sacred Single Standard and his lapse —if lapse there was—passed straight into oblivion. Hers, when it came to light, outraged the prim Victorian conscience and seriously prejudiced her chances when she came to be tried by a jury of her peers.

Mrs Maybrick in due course returned from London and resumed her place as the lady of the house. Mr Maybrick still did not know of her daring escapade. It is doubtful whether he ever did, although Mrs Maybrick later said that, on the day before his death, she made 'full confession' and received 'entire forgiveness'. These expressions, however, are ambiguous.

But if there were gaps in Mr Maybrick's knowledge, he was well aware that Brierley paid attention to his wife. Moreover he resented it, and on March 31st he upbraided Mrs Maybrick in very bitter terms. A violent quarrel followed, in the course of which it seems he struck her more than once and gave her a black eye. Mrs Maybrick was indignant and distressed; she threatened to leave home, but there were the children to consider, and, through the family doctor's tactful mediation, the discord was resolved and the partners reconciled.

Less than a month later—on April 27th—Maybrick showed the first signs of an illness that proved fatal. .

From that point the scenes flicker like an early film, gathering evil momentum as they pass. Maybrick stricken with vomiting and pain; Maybrick better; Maybrick ill again; Mrs Maybrick nursing him herself; doctors; more doctors; an uncertain diagnosis; Maybrick worse; Maybrick better; Maybrick worse than he had ever been; trained nurses summoned; Maybrick's brother arriving down from London; Maybrick sinking; Maybrick dying; Maybrick dead.

And then—the searching of the house and the discovery of arsenic; in jars, in packets, in tumblers, in pans, in bottles, on garments, on rags, on pocket handkerchiefs. This sinister search assumed still graver significance when a quantity of arsenic was found in Maybrick's corpse.

Maybrick had died on Saturday, May 11th. The postmortem took place on Monday, May 13th. On Tuesday, May 14th, Mrs Maybrick was arrested.

3

The accused's reaction to a charge of murder largely depends on the individual temperament. Some are goaded to hysterical activity, some are incredulous, some are stunned.

It makes no difference in a prison cell. There is nothing you can do except rely on those outside. Relatives and friends must rally to your cause; organising sympathy, combating rumour, giving reassurance and preparing your defence.

Mrs Maybrick was devoid of such support. Her relatives were in a distant land, and those whom she had counted among her English friends were mostly nosing round in search of evidence against her. Sympathy was scant, rumour raged unchecked, and no one was at hand to offer comfort or advice.

In her extremity Mrs Maybrick wrote to Brierley. 'I am writing to you', she said, 'to give me every assistance in your power in my present fearful trouble. I am in custody without any of my family with me and without money.'

This letter found its way not to Brierley but to the police. Forsaken and alone Mrs Maybrick remained until Messrs Cleaver, a firm of Liverpool solicitors, took up the defence of the unhappy lady and briefed Sir Charles Russell to appear on her behalf.

Russell was, by common consent, the greatest advocate of his generation. One is tempted to go further and roundly declare that the Bar has never known his equal. But in advocacy, as in acting, it is hard to measure the giants of the past. You can read descriptions of a dead actor, but that is not the same as seeing him on the stage. You can read the speeches of a dead advocate, but that is not the same as hearing him in court. The force of a character, the magic of a presence, cannot be distilled at second hand.

Irving or Garrick? Russell or Erskine? No reply can ever be conclusive. But of Russell at least this much may be said. There have been those who, as young men, saw Russell in action and who haunted the courts thereafter for another fifty years. They thus covered what I once heard Quintin Hogg describe as the Golden Age of the English Bar. And though many remarkable counsel followed—Carson, Isaacs and F. E. Smith among them—more often than not the veterans would agree that Russell was the greatest of them all.

He was an able but not outstanding lawyer; as Lord Chief Justice—an office he accepted six years after his defence of Mrs Maybrick—he had only mild success. But then Russell's disposition was the converse of judicial. By nature he was a fighter, who loved battling for a cause, and no forensic fighter ever carried stronger weapons. Here was no smooth charmer, trading in fair words, and seeking victory by ingratiation. Russell's gift was *power*: the overwhelming influence of a giant personality. One judge called him 'an elemental force', and he must often have appeared to his opponents in this guise. His bearing was fearless, his oratory direct, his cross-examination raking and implacable. 'He was no respecter of persons,' says his biographer, Barry O'Brien. 'His blows fell indiscriminately on leaders and on juniors, and even, when the occasion warranted it, on judges. There was a bigness about the man that all appreciated.'

Russell was not primarily a criminal defender. His path had lain more among the fashionable 'society' suits which were such a signal feature of his time. But in any kind of court this masterful advocate was equally at home. His enlistment on the side of Mrs Maybrick accorded her the champion of whom she stood in need.

4

The coroner's inquest and the hearing by the Bench poured fuel upon the rising flames of local indignation. Mrs Maybrick's lapse with Brierley was the chief talk of the town and coloured every comment on the murder charge itself. She was a loose, foreign woman who had betrayed her English husband; who could be surprised that she had poisoned him as well?

Few were disposed to wait for the full facts. Rigid in

righteousness and fierce with hate, Liverpool made up its mind. It did not trouble to conceal this prejudging of the issue. At the police court Mrs Maybrick was hissed by a gathering of ladies who, in dignity and moral sense and delicacy of taste, must be historically regarded as rivals of the harlots who danced in the streets at the trial of Oscar Wilde.

The English law, to guard against such fits of mass hysteria, permits a trial to be transferred from the area of prejudice. The merits of this course were carefully weighed by Mrs Maybrick's lawyers. She herself was clear upon the point; she wanted to be tried in London. 'I should receive an impartial verdict there,' she wrote, 'which I cannot expect from a jury in Liverpool.' But after due deliberation the lawyers recommended otherwise and Mrs Maybrick yielded to their view.

Russell was to mention this matter in his final speech. 'This lady', he said, 'has elected to take her trial in Liverpool before a Liverpool jury, in the community with which her husband lived, in which he was known, and in which upon a bare recital of the supposed facts of this case it was inevitable that, to ill-informed and imperfectly informed minds, great and serious prejudice must have been caused. If she had desired to shrink from meeting a jury drawn from this community she would not have had any difficulty interposed by those who represent the Crown. But she comes before you, asking from you nothing, save that you will willingly grant a careful, an attentive, and a sympathetic hearing to her case.'

She might ask, but would she get it? Were the twelve men of the neighbourhood who formed the jury—three plumbers, two farmers, a wood-turner, a baker, a painter, a grocer, a provision merchant, a milliner and an ironmonger—likely to be capable of putting from their minds the campaign of denigration amid which they had been living?

Russell, notwithstanding, began the case with confidence. As he walked to the court on the first morning, he met a friend and entered into conversation. Not unnaturally he was asked what he thought about his chances. 'She'll be acquitted,' Russell said.

5

The trial of Florence Maybrick opened at Liverpool Assizes on July 31st, 1889. The court was packed with an intently listening crowd, and, far beyond the confines of the courthouse and the city, millions followed the proceedings as if personally concerned. Seldom has the battle for an individual's life been fought out in an atmosphere of such continuous tension.

Leading counsel for the Crown was Mr Addison, Q.C. He was a popular Northern Circuit silk; not in the highest flight perhaps, but a thoroughly sound advocate of ripe experience. If he could not match Russell's stature, at least he was not the man to be put off or overawed. Through the five days of conflict that went before the summing-up, Addison never failed to make a valid point.

It early became apparent that, though there was much detailed evidence in prospect, the prosecution rested on three main pillars. There were the fly-papers, there was the meat-juice, and there was a letter written by the prisoner to Brierley only three days before her husband died.

In his opening, Addison dealt with each in turn and explained the interpretation placed upon them by the Crown.

The fly-papers—and, be it noted, the fly-papers alone—were put forward as the source from which the prisoner procured arsenic. On April 24th Mrs Maybrick had bought a dozen; on the 29th, from a different chemist, she had bought

16

two dozen more. Some were seen by servants in the May-bricks' bedroom, soaking in a basin which was covered by a towel.

Addison linked these purchases with James Maybrick's illness which, he recalled, began on April 27th. Maybrick was very bad indeed that day and the day following, but on the 29th he was considerably better. 'It is an extraordinary thing', Addison remarked, 'that when her husband was just recovering she should have bought these further fly-papers.'

That was the extent of the evidence on the fly-papers. It showed that Mrs Maybrick had had them in her possession; it gave ground for suspicion that she had tried to extract arsenic; but there was nothing to prove that any arsenic *was* extracted, or for what purpose any such arsenic had been used.

The evidence on the meat-juice went a good deal further.

During the greater part of his illness, as Addison pointed out, Mrs Maybrick had 'regulated' all her husband's medi-cines. Then in the closing stage the trained nurses appeared. One of these asserted that she saw Mrs Maybrick tamper with a meat-juice bottle before a dose was due. The nurse took care not to give it to the patient and it was subsequently found to contain half a grain of arsenic. This Addison de-scribed, with laudable moderation, as 'one of the serious features of the case'.

Although, in kind and sequel, this was the gravest charge of 'tampering', it is necessary to add that it did not stand alone. According to the nurses and to Mr Maybrick's brother, Mrs Maybrick's conduct was generally suspicious. She didn't behave 'openly', she changed the contents of the bottles, she caused the dying man to say she was giving him wrong medicines.

The prosecution's third prop, Mrs Maybrick's letter to

Brierley of May 8th, worked up into a major issue of the trial. Dashed off hurriedly by a tired and harassed woman, it was examined at the time and has been debated since with a meticulous precision more appropriate to a statute.

This letter (like the other previously mentioned) never arrived at its intended destination. Mrs Maybrick, tied to the sick room, handed it for posting to a servant, Alice Yapp. Yapp, by her own account, dropped it on the ground and opened it, intending to replace the dirty envelope. But having opened it, she read it; having read it, she retained it; and subsequently she passed it to Mr Maybrick's brother, with consequences that cannot be computed even now. Russell went so far as to declare that, but for this letter, no charge would have been made.

DEAREST, [it ran] Your letter under cover to John K. came to hand just after I had written to you on Monday. I did not expect to hear from you so soon, and had delayed in giving him the necessary instructions. Since my return I have been nursing M. day and night. He is sick unto death. The doctors held a consultation yesterday, and now all depends upon how long his strength will hold out. Both my brothers-in-law are here, and we are terribly anxious. I cannot answer your letter fully today, my darling, but relieve your mind of all fear of discovery now and in the future. M. has been delirious since Sunday, and I know now that he is perfectly ignorant of everything, even of the name of the street, and also that he has not been making any inquiries whatever. The tale he told me was a pure fabrication, and only intended to frighten the truth out of me. In fact he believes my statement, although he will not admit it. You need not therefore go abroad on that account, dearest;

but, in any case, please don't leave England until I have seen you once again. You must feel that those two letters of mine were written under circumstances which must even excuse their injustice in your eyes. Do you suppose that I could act as I am doing if I really felt and meant what I inferred then? If you wish to write to me about anything do so now, as all the letters pass through my hands at present. Excuse this scrawl, my own darling, but I dare not leave the room for a moment, and I do not know when I shall be able to write to you again. In haste, yours ever,

FLORIE.

No question but that this gave indications of misconduct. Did it go further and breathe a hint of murder? So the prosecution claimed, laying special stress upon the passage : 'He is sick unto death. The doctors held a consultation yesterday and now all depends upon how long his strength can hold out.'

It is perfectly true that, at the time this note was written, the doctors did not take a pessimistic view. They thought James Maybrick was seriously ill; they did not think he was at all likely to die.

'On May 7th', said one of them in the box, 'I formed a hopeful prognosis and thought he would soon recover. On the 8th I found him better.'

'His condition was still as hopeful?' enquired counsel.

'Yes.'

'Did you say to Mrs Maybrick or use any words to the effect that all depended on how long he could hold out?'

'No.'

'Did you say that he was sick unto death or any words to that effect?'

'No.'

'Had he been in any way delirious since the Sunday?'

'No.'

So the Crown could and did legitimately argue that, whatever prompted Mrs Maybrick's dire forebodings, it was not the opinions of her medical advisers.

These, then, were the questions confronting the defence. Why did Mrs Maybrick buy and soak the fly-papers? How did arsenic get into the meat-juice? What was the foundation for the statement in her letter·that on May 8th her husband was sick unto death?

Here, in fine and stripped of inessentials, was the case on which the Crown relied to send her to the gallows.

6

In his opening Addison refrained from lengthy comment and contented himself for the most part with a recital of the facts. Occasionally Russell growled out a correction. For the rest, he sat as he always did when not himself in action—stern, glowering, infinitely formidable. . . .

The first witness was Michael Maybrick, brother of the deceased, who had arrived from London on the fateful 8th of May. In his own words, he was 'dissatisfied with the case', and he criticised the treatment that his brother had received. In fact, Michael Maybrick had promptly made up his mind that his brother was being poisoned and that it was Mrs Maybrick who was poisoning him.

One can understand, if not excuse, this precipitate conclusion. Minds, too, can be poisoned, and events had conspired to work on Michael Maybrick's. He had been summoned by a telegram that said 'strange things are happening'. He had heard about the fly-papers in the cab going out to Aigburth. He had seen the captured letter as he stepped inside the

house. Add to all this the shock of his brother's serious illness, and it may well be that his state of mind did not con-
duce to calm assessment.

Certain it is that he engendered among the nurses grave
suspicions that did not exist before.

Russell brought this out in a sharp cross-examination.

'Had you from the first a strong suspicion in the case?'

'I had.'

'And you expressed this suspicion openly to Mrs Maybrick
and the nurses?'

'Not to the nurses.'

'Did you not, sir?' The ring of Russell's voice echoes down
the years. 'Did you not, sir? Are you not aware that instructions were given to the nurses?'

Michael Maybrick fenced.

'Oh, you mean the hospital nurses.'

(There were no others, bar the children's nurse, inquisitive
Alice Yapp.)

'I said, the nurses.'

'Yes, I was aware that they had been given instructions.'

Instructions which would convey the idea that there was
felt, by those interested in the case, considerable suspicion?'

'Yes,' admitted Michael Maybrick, 'that is so.'

Russell was not merely attacking Michael Maybrick. He
was undermining in advance the evidence of other witnesses: those who 'saw' Mrs Maybrick 'tampering' with
bottles. It is notorious that people see what they expect to see;
primed observers are as dubious as spies.

7

Having thus set the stage Russell got to grips with the funda-
mental questions. Presently he was driving hard and deep
into the prosecution's case.

The second witness was a Dr Hopper; he had not attended Maybrick during his last illness but had treated him on and off for many years. (It was Hopper, incidentally, who had acted as peacemaker between Maybrick and his wife.)

'When did you first attend Mr Maybrick?' Russell asked.

'As far back as 1882.'

'Were his complaints always the same?'

'Generally.'

'To do with the liver and digestive organs?'

'Yes.'

'Was he given to dosing himself?'

'Yes, he was.'

'Had he a habit of taking larger doses than were prescribed?'

'Yes.'

'Did he know arsenic as a nerve tonic?'

'I believe so.'

'Did he tell you that he had taken arsenic when he was in America?'

'I gathered as much from his conversation.'

'As early as June 1888 did Mrs Maybrick speak to you about certain habits of her husband's?'

'In June or September.'

'What did she say to you?'

'She told me Mr Maybrick was in the habit of taking some very strong medicine which had a bad influence on him, for he always seemed worse after each dose. She wished me to see him about it.'

'To remonstrate with him?'

'Yes.'

Here was laid down the foundation of a substantive defence which Russell built up, brick by brick, as opportunity arose. Here was a plausible alternative explanation of the presence of arsenic in James Maybrick's body. Here too—though not so instantly apparent—was a plausible explanation of its presence in the meat-juice. (In cross-examination Russell never denied that it *was* Mrs Maybrick who had put arsenic in the meat-juice. This meant that she herself did not deny it. The question therefore was: in what circumstances and with what motive was it done? The defence at a later stage tendered an explanation with which James Maybrick's habit was intimately linked.)

There was no dramatic set-piece on the first day of the trial, no outstanding single coup in cross-examination. But as one Crown witness followed on another, Russell kept extracting valuable admissions. It was agreed by the chemist who sold the first lot of fly-papers that he lived near Mrs Maybrick and knew her very well. It was agreed by the chemist who sold the second lot of fly-papers that Mrs Maybrick had an account running at his shop. It was agreed by this same gentleman that arsenic is used in many cosmetic preparations. It was agreed by Edwin Maybrick, another of James's brothers, that on April 30th he took Mrs Maybrick to a ball. (This statement, seemingly so trivial, was to grow in importance as the case developed.)

When Russell left the court at the end of the first day, he could look with satisfaction on the progress so far made. He had proved out of the mouths of prosecution witnesses that suspicion had been planted and Mrs Maybrick's guilt assumed; that the purchase of the fly-papers was frank and above board; that arsenic was a common constituent of cosmetics; and that Maybrick was accustomed to eat arsenic himself.

An effective defence had started to take shape.

8

The most sensational event in the second day's hearing was Russell's cross-examination of the nursemaid Alice Yapp.

In one sense, Russell was on very sure ground. Yapp's story as it stood did her the minimum of credit. She sought to justify her act in opening the letter by a tale which would strain the belief of the most credulous. Without colourable excuse she had read the letter's contents—a mean form of prying that invited strong contempt. By any standard, her behaviour was despicable. She may have felt sorry for it by the time Russell had done.

Before coming to the letter, he questioned Yapp about the soaking of the fly-papers.

'Did the housemaid tell you she had seen them in the morning?'

'Yes.'

'And you went into the room after dinner was over?'

'It was about two hours after when I went into the room.'

'Out of curiosity?'

'Yes.'

'You had no business in the room?'

'No.'

'You found them still there as the housemaid had described them?'

'Yes.'

'Where were they?'

'On the wash-stand.'

'In the principal bedroom?'

'Yes.'

'In the bedroom which is directly approached from the landing?'

'Yes.'

'Could you see this wash-stand on entering the door?'

'Yes.'

'These fly-papers were reported to you as having been there early in the morning, and you have no reason to suppose that they didn't continue there the whole day until you saw them?'

'No.'

So the soaking of the fly-papers was as open as their purchase. No need to stress it further. Having elicited from Yapp one more important fact—that Maybrick had got wet on the day he first took ill—Russell switched to the vulnerable flank.

'Now,' he said slowly, 'with regard to this letter.'

Alice Yapp must have been waiting for this moment; waiting with dread for the impending storm to break. She had doubtless heard a great deal about Charles Russell and his tearing asunder of shufflers and knaves. Not that she, Alice Yapp, was to be bracketed with these, but still . . . a clever lawyer might present her in that light. Small wonder if her heart quailed as she gazed on the spectacle : the judge aloft in scarlet, the rows of enthralled onlookers, the terrifying Russell standing there below.

He lost no time in striking at the heart.

'With regard to this letter. Why did you open it?'

Alice Yapp hesitated.

'Because Mrs Maybrick wished that it should go by that post.'

'Why did you open it?'

Alice Yapp had made one nebulous reply. Now she stood tongue-tied and made no reply at all.

The judge intervened.

'Did anything happen to the letter?'

'Yes,' said Alice Yapp, 'it fell in the dirt.'

'Why did you open it?' Russell thundered.

'To put it in a clean envelope.'

'Why didn't you put it in a clean envelope without opening it?'

This was a poser. Alice Yapp said nothing.

'Was it a wet day?'

'It was showery.'

'Are you sure of that?'

'Yes.'

'Will you undertake to say that?' It was like a warning bell. 'I ask you to consider. Was it a wet day?'

Again Alice Yapp said nothing.

'Aye or no?'

Silence.

'Was it a wet or a dry day?'

Silence.

'Will you swear that it was showery?'

'I cannot say positively.'

It was now apparent that Yapp could not remember and was unwilling to commit herself. And it was equally apparent that if the ground was dry there could not have been much dirt for the letter to be dropped in.

'Let me see the letter,' Russell said. He turned it over, examining it closely. 'Where was it dropped?'

'By the post-office.'

'Then you picked it up?'

'Yes.'

'And saw this mark on it, did you?'

Yes.'

'Usher; give the letter to the witness.' The envelope, with its pathetic inscription, was passed across the court. 'Just take it in your hand. Is the direction clear enough?'

Alice Yapp reflected.

'It was very much dirtier at the time.'

'It has not obscured the direction?'

'No.'

'You didn't rub the mud off?'

'No.'

'What did you do?'

'I went into the post-office and asked for a clean envelope to re-address it. I opened it as I was going in.'

'There is no running of the ink?'

'No.'

Russell glared at her, his underlip thrust forward.

'Can you suggest how there can be any damp or wet without causing some running of the ink?'

'I cannot.'

'On your oath, girl, did you not manufacture that stain as an excuse for opening your mistress's letter?'

'I did not.'

'Have you any explanation to offer about the running of the ink?'

'I have not.'

Russell sat down and Alice Yapp thankfully vanished from the scene. Her public humiliation was thorough and deserved.

But where exactly did this cross-examination lead? Alice Yapp had been demolished; the letter remained with its detrimental phrases. 'He is sick unto death.' 'All depends on how long his strength can hold out.'

Later Russell pleaded that the servants and the nurses, together with certain visiting friends, had formed a gloomier view of Maybrick's illness than the doctors and that Mrs Maybrick was influenced by them. 'That letter—take it, read it, scan it as you will—is it the letter of a guilty woman who is planning the murder of her husband?'

Maybe, maybe not. But the letter was the one item in the Crown's evidence that retained its early force unimpaired right till the end.

9

Thus far the trial had proceeded on the footing that there was only one question for the jury to decide : did Mrs Maybrick wilfully administer the quantities of arsenic that caused her husband's death? 'There is no reason to doubt,' Addison had said, 'what the doctors will swear—that Maybrick died by arsenic.'

But now Russell was to challenge this assumption. He was to bring into discussion a second vital question : did Maybrick die by arsenic at all?

This new factor was impressively introduced just before the court rose on the second afternoon. The three other servants had followed Alice Yapp, and now Dr Humphreys occupied the box. He was the first Crown witness—there were several more to come—who supported Addison's statement on the cause of Maybrick's death. 'He died', said Humphreys, 'from arsenical poisoning.'

The interrogation by prosecuting counsel had concluded, and Humphreys turned a little to face Russell. It was getting very late. There was only just sufficient time to start the cross-examination—a state of affairs which every advocate dislikes. Too often the choice lies between a premature disclosure of one's hand and the undignified expedient of 'playing out time'.

Russell did neither. With consummate skill he turned the situation to his favour. Altogether that evening he put about a dozen questions. The last five (and the replies they drew) were these.

'Had you ever before assisted at a post-mortem examination of any persons supposed to have died from arsenical poisoning?'

'No.'

'Had you ever before assisted at a post-mortem where it was alleged that death was due to irritant poisoning?'

'No.'

'Up to the time that the communication was made to you which suggested that there might be foul play, did it in any way occur to you that there were symptoms present of arsenical poisoning?'

'No.'

'When was it that the idea was first suggested to you?'

'On Thursday or Wednesday night.'

'By Mr Michael Maybrick?'

'Yes.'

The court adjourned in excitement. That last few minutes had achieved a transformation. An astonishing possibility now loomed on the horizon—that the doctors would never have bethought themselves of poisoning if Michael Maybrick hadn't put the idea into their heads.

That night the jurymen had something to think over.

Next day—the third of Mrs Maybrick's trial—Russell resumed his questioning of Humphreys with the satisfying certainty that he held the initiative. The doctor was placed on the defensive from the start and, despite his struggles, beat retreat after retreat.

Over Reinsch's test he had a specially rough passage. This test is designed to detect metallic irritants; a sample of excreta is boiled under specified conditions, and if the irritant is present it should show as a deposit.

Dr Humphreys had carried out this test on Maybrick forty-eight hours before the latter died. There had been no deposit, as he honestly confessed. He tried very hard, but not very successfully, to reconcile this illuminating fact with the theory of poisoning to which he now subscribed.

The exchanges on this matter are worth reporting fully. They show what can happen when a witness seeks to temporise under the guns of a first-class cross-examiner.

'So the test was negative?' said Russell, after Humphreys had described it.

'No,' Humphreys said. 'Not of necessity.'

'Why not?'

Doctor Humphreys made a most ingenuous reply.

'Because the quantity I used was so small, and the time I boiled it so short that there might not have been time for any deposit to take place. Further I am not skilled in the details of testing and my test might have been inefficient.'

'That is candid, doctor.' No doubt Russell's acknowledgment was genuine but he knew that Humphreys had played into his hands. 'That is candid. Then you mean to say that although you tried this experiment, you were not able to conduct it successfully?'

A nasty question for a medical man. But Humphreys resolutely spurned the bait.

'I do not pretend to have any skill in these matters.'

'It is not a difficult test?'

'No.'

'And if there is arsenic it is supposed to make a deposit?'

'Yes, if it is boiled long enough.'

'How long did you boil it?'

'About two minutes.'

'What quantity did you take?'

'About an ounce.'

'Was this quantity sufficient?'

'Quite sufficient.'

'So I should have thought. Did you not at that time think your experiment was properly conducted?'

Humphreys floundered.

'I really couldn't tell.'

'Dr Humphreys, you were making the experiment with some object?'

'Yes.'

'Were you satisfied at the time that it was properly conducted?'

'At the time I had no books to refer to.'

'When you came to refresh your memory from books were you satisfied there was nothing you omitted?'

'Yes.' Whichever way he turned the doctor found escape shut off. He made another desperate bid. 'I don't know whether the instruments were absolutely pure.'

'But see, Dr. Humphreys, if they were not pure, would you not get a greater amount of deposit?'

'It depends on what the impurity was.'

'What impurity do you suggest may have existed?'

'Arsenic.'

'If there was arsenic, would it not make it more certain you would get a deposit?'

'Yes.'

'Did you find any?'

'I found none.'

After that, Russell moved in to the kill.

'Had it not been for the suggestion of arsenic by Michael Maybrick, were you prepared to give a death certificate if James had died on Wednesday?'

'Yes.'

'With what cause of death?'

'Gastro-enteritis.'

It was a tremendous, breath-taking admission. The judge wanted to make absolutely sure.

'If nothing about poisoning had been suggested to you, you would have certified that he died of gastro-enteritis?'

'Yes, my lord.'

The judge wrote solemnly in his book. There was not much left of Dr Humphreys now, but Russell fired one final telling shot.

'Can you mention any post-mortem symptom which is distinctive of arsenical poisoning and not also distinctive of gastro-enteritis?'

The witness thought.

'No,' he said, 'I can't give you any.'

This triumphant climax shook the whole fabric of the prosecution's case. All that day and half the next they tried to shore it up while Russell tenaciously clung to his advantage. In vain for Dr Carter, who had been called in for consultations, to add *his* opinion that death was due to arsenical poisoning; he had to admit that the symptoms caused by arsenic might equally be caused by impure food. In vain for Dr Stevenson, the Home Office toxicologist, to throw his reputation and prestige into the scale; exceptional experience made him a subtler duellist, but he also gave ground to Russell in the end.

'Will you indicate any one symptom,' Russell asked him, 'which you say is distinctly an arsenical poisoning symptom and which is not to be found in cases of gastro-enteritis?'

'I would form no opinion from one single symptom.'

'What do you mean by that answer? That you cannot point to any distinct symptom of arsenical poisoning differentiating it from gastro-enteritis?'

Dr Stevenson had to face it.

'There is no distinctive diagnostic symptom of arsenical

poisoning,' he said. '*The diagnostic thing is finding the arsenic.*'

Which, of course, was precisely Russell's point. They found some arsenic, so they called it arsenic poisoning. If they had not found arsenic, they would have called it something else. And Russell had shown how the arsenic might have come there : in a series of self-administered, non-fatal doses, unconnected with the ailment from which Maybrick really died.

There was in fact *no murder at all*; the chronic arsenic-eater had met his death from natural causes. That, in a nutshell, was the case for the defence.

10

When the Crown case closed at the end of the fourth morning, the defence held a position of considerable strength. Measures were now taken to render it still stronger. Russell in his turn called three distinguished doctors; each affirmed that the cause of death was gastro-enteritis. A whole series of witnesses, from England and abroad, cast further light on Maybrick's arsenic addiction. One, Sir James Poole, a former Mayor of the city, said that Maybrick once had 'blurted out' his taste for poisonous medicines. Sir James had been horrified and given him a lecture. ('The more you take, the more you will require; you will go on till they carry you off.')

The Crown, it should be noted, did not dispute this evidence.

Viewed broadly then, the prisoner's case was powerful and imposing. But two important points remained that needed clearing up.

Still those fly-papers—why had Mrs Maybrick soaked the fly-papers? The ground had been admirably prepared for an answer, but the answer itself had not yet been forthcoming. Still that meat-juice—what on earth had happened to that meat-juice? Here was a wide gap in the walls of the defence.

These matters still urgently called for explanation, and the fact was that only Mrs Maybrick could explain them. Only she could account for her own conduct. Only she could relate what she had done.

Had Mrs Maybrick's trial been taking place today, as a matter of course she would have gone into the box. But sixty years ago, before the Criminal Evidence Act, no prisoner could testify on his own behalf. By leave, an unsworn statement might be delivered from the dock.

Such statements laboured under heavy handicap. They lacked the sanction which attaches to the oath. They lacked the logical development imposed by guiding questions. They could not be made the subject of cross-examination, but even this rule had a double-edged effect.

Should Mrs Maybrick make such a statement? She herself was willing but on Russell lay the burden of decision. The problem must have exercised him greatly. The risks would be acute, the strain almost intolerable but—how else to close that catastrophic gap . . . ?

As the last of his witnesses departed from the box, Russell turned to his client, sitting in the dock behind him. They spoke briefly in undertones; then Russell faced the judge.

'My lord,' he said, 'I wish to tell you what has taken place. I asked Mrs Maybrick if it was her wish to make a statement. She said yes. I asked her if it was written. She said no.'

11

She stood up in the dock, hands trembling but head erect. It was the worst moment of all. Agony enough to sit silent hour by hour while the crowds in court eyed you and whispered. Worse agony by far to lose the shield of counsel, and yourself speak the words on which the verdict might depend. This was the ordeal of young Mrs Maybrick on the fifth successive day of the trial for her life.

At first she faltered, and the sentences came stumbling. 'My lord, I wish to make a statement, as well as I can, to you—a few facts in connection with this dreadfully crushing charge.' But her voice soon steadied, she kept her nerves under control and, whatever its faults, her statement was relevant and apt.

She explained first how the fly-papers were bought for a cosmetic. She had lost, she said, an American prescription containing arsenic and, having a slight skin eruption, tried to concoct a substitute. She was particularly concerned to get rid of this eruption before April 30th when she was going to a ball.

There had been numerous signposts to this part of her story. On the subject of the meat-juice she sprang more of a surprise.

Maybrick, she said, had complained of being depressed; he had pointed out a powder which he referred to as harmless and implored Mrs Maybrick to put it in his food. 'I was over-wrought, terribly anxious, miserably unhappy, and his evident distress entirely unnerved me. I consented. My lord, I had not one true or honest friend in that house; I had no one to consult and no one to advise me.'

The statement lasted five torturing minutes—torturing to speaker and to listeners alike. At last it was over and she sank back in her chair.

Russell, pulling his gown about him, gathered himself for his big speech to the jury.

12

Russell was not a rhetorician; no purple patches ornamented his address. It was like the man himself; forceful, incisive, firmly based on fact.

He reminded the jury that there were two distinct questions for them to consider. Was it a death by arsenical poisoning? If they were not satisfied of that, there was an end to the case. If, however, they found that arsenic was indeed the cause of death, was such arsenic administered by the prisoner? If they were not satisfied of that, there was an end to the case also.

Russell then reviewed the medical evidence in detail. He recalled the opinions categorically expressed by the three eminent experts brought by the defence. He recalled the failure by the experts for the Crown to name a single symptom that was not shared in common by arsenical poisoning and gastro-enteritis. He recalled the long history of Maybrick's dyspepsia and the equally long history of his arsenic addiction. He recalled, in this context, the results of the analysis which disclosed only a small amount of arsenic in the corpse. He wound up this part of his speech, with a powerful plea deriving from long acquaintance with the psychology of juries.

'It would only be natural,' Russell said, 'that the thought should arise in your minds : if not arsenical poisoning, we should like to have some suggestion what it was. Now I am not called upon to advance any theory. Counsel representing the prisoner is entitled to stand upon a defence and to say "You have not proved the case which you alleged." But passing that by, is there no reasonable hypothesis? Is it improbable that a man who had been dosing himself, admittedly taking poisonous medicines—is it remarkable that this man's

36

constitution had suffered so that he should always be com-
plaining of derangement of the stomach? Is it or is it not
reasonable to say that a man who had been pursuing such a
course would have his constitution liable to attack from
causes which in a healthy man would be of no effect?' And
thus to the submission : 'There is no safe resting-place on
which you can justify to yourselves a finding that this was a
death of arsenical poisoning.'

This had become the strongest plank in the defence—so
strong indeed that it would not have been surprising if the
jury had acquitted without hearing any more. Russell himself seems to have half expected this. 'I must ask you', he had
said, *even at the outset* whether it is possible for you to find
the prisoner guilty.' That was a broad hint that they could
stop it if they wished.

But the jury did not stop it, and Russell, rightly declining
any vestige of a gamble, went on to discuss the second question he had posed.

Had Mrs Maybrick administered arsenic (barring always
the isolated instance of the meat-juice)? He summarised his
previous points and added a few fresh ones. Mrs Maybrick,
he emphasised, knew she was a suspect from May 8th. The
searching of the house, with its abundant haul of arsenic,
did not take place until the 11th or the 12th. Why, if she was
guilty, did not Mrs Maybrick cover up the traces of her
crime? 'If a woman had the nerve and fibre to plan such a
murder, cold and deliberate, would she have not also had
the instinct of self-preservation?' Neatly, he made the large
amount of arsenic found seem to operate in Mrs Maybrick's
favour. 'If, as is clear, there was in that house a quantity of
poison capable of being fatally applied; if there was one
packet of arsenic with which admittedly fly-papers had
nothing to do; if there was a bottle in which grains of arsenic

were found with which admittedly fly-papers had nothing to do; I ask why, with these means at her command, should she have resorted to the clumsy, the stupid contrivance of trying to steep fly-papers in water?'

There was no peroration in the accepted sense; no rolling periods, no high-flown similes. But who could fail to be impressed by the awful gravity with which he summoned the jurors to the climax of their task? 'You are in number large enough to prevent the individual views and prejudices and prepossessions of one from affecting all, but in numbers small enough to preserve to each one of you the undivided sense of individual responsibility. The verdict is to be the verdict of each one of you and the verdict of you all. I make no appeal for mercy; let that be clearly understood. You are administering a law which is merciful; you are administering a law which forbids you to pronounce a verdict of guilty unless all reasonable hypotheses of innocence have been excluded. I end as I began by asking you, in the perplexities, in the doubts, in the difficulties which surround this case, can you with safe conscience say that this woman is guilty? If your duty compels you to do it you will do it, you must do it; but you will not, you must not, unless the whole burden and facts and weight of the case drive you irresistibly to that conclusion.'

13

Addison's reply was vigorous and barbed. His assertions about Maybrick seemed to verge on the extravagant: he was not an arsenic-eater; he was a healthy, careful man; in April he was sick for the first time in his life. Addison bitterly criticised Mrs Maybrick's statement—'carefully thought out and ably delivered'. He made a shrewd thrust at the suggestion that Maybrick took arsenic shortly before his death; 'he, who knew medicines so well and was so fond of talking about them, never suggested to a soul that the symptoms might be due to that'. Without mercy he dissected the famous note to Brierley: 'I protest against the notion of any tenderness for a husband in a woman who wrote that letter.' And finally: 'If she be guilty, we have brought to light a very terrible deed of darkness, and proved a murder founded upon profligacy and adultery, and carried out with a hypocrisy and cunning which have been rarely equalled in the annals of crime.'

It was the evening of the fifth day and the court rose. Next morning the judge began his long, painstaking, intermittently intelligible summing-up.

14

A word about the judge into whose hands the directing reins now passed.

Mr Justice Fitzjames Stephen was a man of high attainments. Littérateur of taste, essayist of note, close friend of Froude and of Carlyle, he embraced and enjoyed a wider range of interests than is customary among members of the legal profession. As a judge, he adhered to broad principles and disliked mere technicalities; his mind, hard and clear rather than subtle, was adept in the marshalling of facts. He was scrupulously fair, conscientiously humane, and a recognised authority on the rules of criminal evidence. Few men would have been better fitted to try the Maybrick case than Mr Justice Stephen in his prime.

But it is the undeniable and tragic fact that by the late summer of 1889 this able and distinguished mind was on the wane.

Four years earlier Stephen had had a stroke which caused

him temporarily to give up work. Soon after he resumed a slow decline set in; gradually, over a period of years, his mental powers diminished. At last, prompted by reports of public uneasiness, the anxious judge consulted his physician. An insidious disease was diagnosed, and he instantly resigned.

How long this disease had flourished undetected cannot be asserted with precision, but everything suggests it was already stirring at the time of the Maybrick trial, twenty months before. The summing-up, so thorough in conception —it took the best part of two days to deliver—was in execution rambling and blurred. From first to last the judge seemed all at sea. He told the jury that the fly-papers had been purchased in March and was somewhat testy when corrected. He attributed the opinions of one doctor to another. He read out a letter which had not been put in evidence. He said things which were dangerously misleading ('If you can show a sufficient quantity of arsenic to cause death, why then, you need go no further'). He said things which were highly prejudicial in effect ('On that day began the symptoms of *what may be called the fatal dose*'). He said things which were free from any meaning whatsoever ('You are apt to assume a connection between the thing which is a proof in the result at which you are to arrive—because it is put before you—and in that way you may be led to do a greater or less degree of injustice according to the state of the case').

The complaint that lies against the judge is not one of undue bias. He did his best, no doubt, to hold the balance. His shortcoming was this: that he failed to clarify the issues, to state accurately the facts, and to group the evidence in appropriate perspective. Thus, at the end of a momentous and complicated case, the jury received no adequate direction.

Whether this particular jury would have profited by such is an entirely different matter.

15

At twenty past three on the seventh afternoon, the jury retired to deliberate in private.

If they had made up their minds in favour of acquittal, it might be assumed that they would not be absent long. If not, the field of discussion was so vast and the matters to be weighed so debatable and intricate, that an interval of hours could occasion no surprise.

They were back at five to four. Ten minutes later their verdict had been given and Mrs Maybrick had been sentenced to be hanged.

16

Whatever the immediate Liverpool reaction, the country as a whole was deeply shocked by this result. *The Times* condemned it editorially; leading lawyers and doctors set on record their disquiet; meetings were held to voice protest and dissent; petitions for reprieve were signed by tens of thousands. Nor were official circles lacking in activity. The Home Secretary, Henry Matthews, held a series of long conferences: with the judge, with the Lord Chancellor, with certain witnesses, with the judge again, with the judge and Mr Addison. These indications of misgiving in high places corresponded with the raging tide of public disapproval.

Meanwhile the days slipped by and the condemned woman lay in Walton Gaol, where the tedium of solitary confinement was relieved by the hammering of the workmen setting up her scaffold.

On August 22nd, with only one more Sunday between her and the rope, Mrs Maybrick was reprieved. The death sentence was rescinded and replaced by one of penal servitude for life.

At that time reprieves were not come by two a penny, nor was there much squeamishness at the thought of hanging women. Mrs Maybrick's neck was saved for the most logical of reasons : because the case against her fell short of legal proof. 'Although', said the Home Secretary, 'the evidence leads clearly to the conclusion that the prisoner administered, and attempted to administer, arsenic to her husband with intent to murder, yet it does not wholly exclude a reasonable doubt whether his death was in fact caused by the administration of arsenic.'

If there was 'reasonable doubt', she was not guilty of murder. That was the only indictment upon which she had been tried. The life sentence was administratively imposed for an attempt to murder with which she had not been charged.

Russell, first as counsel, then as head of the judiciary, never ceased to press for Mrs Maybrick's release. He met with no success. He himself died in 1900; Mrs Maybrick was not freed till 1904. She had lost her youth, her spirit, and fifteen years out of her life.

17

Did Mrs Maybrick do it? That is not the problem. Was her guilt proved? Unquestionably no.

In later years a verdict so perverse would have been quashed by the Court of Criminal Appeal. In 1889 that Court did not exist. All that could be done was done, but this was not enough, and the verdict of that jury unhappily remains to mock at and discredit the fair name of British justice.

STEINIE MORRISON

1

WHAT should defending counsel do when he believes his client is guilty?

Of all the problems that arise to plague a barrister, this one is surely the most familiar. It is constantly debated by all kinds of people, just as if Johnson hadn't settled it two centuries ago.

'What do you think', Boswell had asked him, 'of supporting a cause you know to be bad?'

'Sir,' Johnson answered, 'you do not know it is good or bad till the judge determines it. It is his business to judge; and you are not to be confident in your opinion that a cause is bad, but to say all you can for your client and then hear the judge's opinion.'

Read 'jury' for 'judge' in this admirable analysis and it can usefully be extended to cover criminal trials. Let the advocate follow Johnson's wise advice and the famous question is rapidly disposed of.

There is another problem, though, much knottier than this, which is far less often made the subject of discussion. Suppose defending counsel is convinced of his client's *innocence*. Suppose that, none the less, he sees great risk of being found guilty. What should he do *then*?

The temptation is apparent: to depart from the beaten track of advocacy in frantic endeavour to procure means of escape. Such departures are conceived in a spirit of self-sacrifice and counsel often suffer for them grievously. Dr Kenealy was formally disbarred for his fanatical defence of the

43

Tichborne Claimant. Marshall Hall's practice was seriously damaged by the bluntness of his language when he thought a judge unfair. And Edward Abinger, a lesser man than these but able and sincere, raised up against himself a whirlwind of criticism by his unorthodox defence of Steinie Morrison.

2

Steinie Morrison was brought up at the Old Bailey in March, 1911, and there charged with murdering Leon Beron, whose body, stripped of money and valuables, had been found on Clapham Common early on New Year's Day. He had been killed by a series of blows upon the head, and after death had been stabbed and cut about the face. A doctor who saw his body at nine o'clock that morning formed the view that Beron had then been dead six hours.

Legend soon grows around a classic crime, and Beron has been spoken of as rich and old. He was not old; he was forty-eight. He was not rich; his yearly income was but five and twenty pounds, derived from some small property. But notwithstanding this he always carried money on him; often there would be thirty sovereigns in his purse. He also sported a massive watch and chain which it was one of his foibles to show off to acquaintances.

Neither chain nor watch nor money was found upon his corpse.

Beron did not live near Clapham Common nor has it ever been discovered what induced him to go out there. He lodged with his brother near the Mile End Road and spent most of his time in a cheap Whitechapel eating-house. This place, the Warsaw Restaurant, forms an exceptionally outlandish patch in the fantastic background to the crime.

The Warsaw Restaurant served as a kind of club for the

curious foreign colony to which Beron belonged. They came there early and they stayed there late; they ate, talked, sat about, dozed, meditated, quarrelled and then ate again. They may have gone to bed elsewhere, but for many of them the Warsaw Restaurant was home. Beron not least; for years it had been his habit to settle there each day at two o'clock and remain till about twelve.

In the last few weeks of 1910 one Steinie Morrison joined the corps of 'regulars'; that is, he would call at the Warsaw nearly every day, though he limited his visits to more rational proportions. This Steinie was a striking, even fascinating figure; well-spoken, handsome and magnificently built. He must have looked out of his element in that bizarre assembly, as if Apollo at a fairground had strayed among the freaks.

What could there be in common between this dashing newcomer and the short, stumpy, eccentric little Beron? Perhaps opposites attracted or secret interests coalesced. At any rate the couple spent a lot of time together and they were often observed deep in private conversation during the last days of the dying year.

Beron, faithful to his custom, sat on at the Warsaw right through New Year's Eve. He left only a few minutes before the bells rang in a year which was to grant him so short a breathing space.

He left, it was alleged, with Steinie Morrison. Some three hours later he was cruelly clubbed to death.

The results achieved by following this pointer provided the quintessence of the prosecution's charge.

3

Steinie's case sprang into instant notoriety as the 'Riddle of the Scarlet S'. This tag owed its origin to two of the slashes on the dead man's face which were spoken of as 'S-shaped' by a doctor at the inquest. Many people took this rough description literally and indulged in the most wild and fanciful conjectures. Some thought they were the symbol of an anarchist society; some thought they stood for 'spic', the Russian word for spy; some—and these were the most gullible of all—believed that the assassin had recorded his initial.

None of these theories was shared by Scotland Yard, nor did they cut much ice at the Old Bailey. 'Anyone', said the presiding judge, 'who sees the letter S in either of these scratches has either better eyes than I, or a more vivid imagination.'

But there was no need of a scarlet S to make Steinie's trial dramatic. No case in the whole history of crime has worked up more feverish, uncontrolled excitement. Outside the court, in London's foreign quarter, witnesses were coaxed, threatened, drilled and even beaten by partisan groups owing warped allegiance either to Beron's family or the prisoner. At the Old Bailey itself, as day succeeded day, angry scene succeeded angry scene—between counsel and witness, between counsel and judge, between counsel and counsel. The tension, beginning at a morbid pitch, contrived uncannily to rise with every hour until at the end it grew almost beyond bearing. Wholly beyond bearing for one interested party. During Abinger's impassioned closing speech, Leon Beron's brother went clean out of his mind. Raving and gibbering, he hurled himself at counsel; he was dragged off, pinioned and taken from the court to permanent lodgment in a madhouse cell.

Such a shocking and sensational occurrence would have completely overshadowed any other case. In the trial of Steinie Morrison it was a passing incident.

4

On Monday, March 6th, the trial began. Mr Justice Darling took his seat upon the bench; Steinie was put up in the dock. When asked to plead, he said, 'My lord, if I were standing before the Almighty, I could give but one answer. I am not guilty.'

The theatrical note was struck at once, and the curtain forthwith rose on a tumultuous drama that was to play to crowded houses for nine eventful days.

The two chief forensic actors were Abinger himself and Richard Muir. They fitted the popular conception of their rôles. Abinger, defending, was impulsive and emotional; Muir, for the Crown, was long-headed and case-hardened. A tough rock of a man who never spared himself or others, he had powers of endurance that seemed almost inexhaustible. He did not greatly care for kid-glove methods, and the case against Morrison was mercilessly pressed to the uttermost limits permitted by the law.

Muir's opening speech was characteristically thorough. It consisted in the main of solid narrative, occasionally seasoned with a comment strictly practical. He told how Steinie had become a friend of Beron's; how he had been seen examining Beron's watch; how on New Year's Eve he had turned up at the Warsaw with a long paper parcel which he said contained a flute; how a waiter who handled it thought it felt like an iron bar; how Steinie was familiar with the Clapham Common district; how straight after the murder he had deserted his old haunts; how he never again set foot inside the Warsaw; how he forsook his lodging in Newark Street, nearby, and went to share the room of a prostitute in Lambeth; how till the moment of the murder he had been hard up; how henceforward he was flush; how at a station cloakroom on New Year's morning he deposited a package containing a revolver ('anticipating arrest?' Muir slyly enquired); how exactly a week later, when Steinie *was* arrested, slight human bloodstains were detected on his shirt.

Thus was woven a fine web of suspicion. But all was subsidiary to Muir's main contention—that from midnight Steinie had been Beron's sole companion and was with him at Clapham Common shortly before three. The prosecutor was emphatic here; slowly and impressively he dealt his strongest cards. It would be proved, he said, that from midnight onwards the pair had walked together in the streets of the East End. It would be proved that at two o'clock they took a cab to Clapham, alighting by the Common about twenty to three. It would be proved that at three fifteen a cab was hailed at Clapham by a man who gave the driver the vague direction 'Kennington'. That man, Muir said, was Steinie, and he was alone.

This time-table was the real crux of the case. It depended on two separate groups of witnesses. The first consisted of Whitechapel inhabitants who had previously known Beron, or Morrison, or both. The second consisted of the cab drivers concerned, whose fares were naturally unknown to them at the time, but who claimed to have subsequently identified Steinie when given the opportunity at a police station parade.

These witnesses were bound to be of paramount importance. If their evidence in the box lived up to Muir's opening, Steinie's chances would look very slim indeed.

5

The formal and semi-formal witnesses had departed; the plans had been produced and the photographs received; now the Crown called for Solomon Beron and the temperature embarked on its uninterrupted rise.

The dead man's brother typified those unassimilated aliens for whom the Warsaw Restaurant was the centre of the world. He might almost have been peering out from that esoteric spot; puzzled, hostile, infinitely suspicious. He didn't like the methods of this damfool country; they let Steinie kill his brother and then allowed him a defence.

Solomon's mental instability was immediately apparent. Prosecuting counsel found him difficult to manage while he gave some simple evidence about his brother's habits. When Abinger got up to cross-examine, the witness did not trouble to conceal his rage.

'Did you describe yourself', he was asked, 'as an independent gentleman?'

'Yes.'

'Are you living in a Rowton House at sevenpence a night?'

Beron went up in smoke.

'What has that to do with the case?' Anger made his foreign accent even more pronounced. 'What has that to do with the crime? If you ask me impudent questions I will not answer you.'

'Did anybody help the deceased man with his rent?'

'You go and ask him. I cannot tell you. If you ask me silly questions I will give you no answer.'

Abinger ran his eye over the independent gentleman who lived at Rowton House. Solomon Beron was tidy, almost smart, in a big dark overcoat with a velvet collar.

'You look very nicely dressed. Where did those clothes come from?'

In studying these questions, it is not easy to perceive what useful object Abinger had in view. Solomon Beron's evidence did not implicate the prisoner and there was little to be gained by an attack upon his credit.

If it was meant merely to goad him, it succeeded. The witness was now almost beside himself with fury.

'Very well,' he shouted. 'You want to know where these clothes came from? I am not going to tell you.' Then as Mr Justice Darling stirred slightly, he added, 'If the judge asks me I will tell you.'

'You must answer the question,' said the judge quietly.

Beron bowed to this ruling, but he would not deal with Abinger. He addressed himself directly to the judge.

'If I must answer the question you may tell him that I have brought over to London about one hundred pounds that I have saved in Paris from my business.'

Mr Justice Darling preserved impassive silence. Abinger continued. He had one important point that it was necessary to put—and which might, with profit, have been put earlier. It was to be part of the defence that the witnesses from the Warsaw, prompted by a kind of tribal loyalty to Beron, had in concert shaped their evidence to ensure he was avenged.

This suggestion received the usual warm reception.

'I do not take any interest in it,' Solomon Beron stormed. 'It has nothing to do with this case. Do not put me so many questions or I will go out from here.'

But Abinger persisted.

'How many hours each day do you pass at the Warsaw?'

'All the time I got.'

'What time do you get there?'

'About one o'clock. I do not spend all the time.'

'Where else do you spend your time?'

'I go nowhere else.'

'Nowhere else?'

'Only to my business.'

'What business?'

This pressure upon his rocking mind was more than Solomon Beron could endure.

'I go to my solicitors,' he yelled. 'What are you laughing at? I cannot see the joke. What are you laughing at?'

The veins bulged from his forehead; frenzy was consuming him like fire. When presently he stumbled from the box, the temper of the trial had been irrevocably set.

6

Let us pause a moment and take stock of the position as the defence would see it at the end of the first day.

In a long trial—as Steinie's was clearly bound to be—this is often the crucial moment for planning defence strategy. The Crown case has been revealed. Its strength and weakness can be approximately assessed. With tolerable certitude, the prisoner's advocate can chart his future course.

Abinger had thrown himself into the fight for Steinie with all the ardour of his generous nature. That first evening, one may be absolutely sure, he spent many hours in hard and anxious thought.

His main task stood out. If he was to have any chance of gaining an acquittal, he must smash the Crown's story of Steinie's New Year's night. He must break that chain of evidence which linked his client so damningly with the time, the place and the victim of the murder. In other words, he must satisfy the jury that some or all those witnesses ought not to be believed.

Under the strict but beneficent rules of British legal practice there is more than one method of inducing disbelief. You may seek to show mistake; this was the obvious way of handling the cab drivers who claimed to recognise a

stranger they had only once set eyes on, and that in the doubtful darkness of the night. You may seek to show lying; something of that kind had already been foreshadowed in the
questions put by Abinger to Beron. And you may seek to
establish the witness's bad character; to show that he is a
person of such dubious morality that his sworn statement is
unworthy of belief. Any jury will think again and yet again
before convicting on the word of a blackmailer or thief.

The attack upon character, appropriately used, gives the
defender an invaluable weapon. But it is a weapon capable of
boomerang effect. If it is used by the defence against a witness for the Crown, it may be used by the Crown against the
prisoner himself. The latter thus forfeits his right to be protected against any mention of his 'record' or his 'past'.

Of course, if you have neither a 'record' nor a 'past', this
is of no consequence; you may make attacks on character
with comparative impunity. But Abinger's client was not in
that happy position.

The handsome Steinie, impressing all beholders by his
dignity of bearing, was a convict by status and a burglar by
trade.

7

To attack or not?

Here was a grave decision, perhaps the gravest in the case,
and it must be made that night. For Abinger had reason to
suppose that the Crown was not invulnerable on the score of
character, and that the chance of proving this would be
offered him next day. But if he took that chance, if he made
character an issue, he would make Steinie liable to similar
attack.

It is easy to criticise in subsequent detachment, far from
the arena's dust and heat. None the less, one cannot help ex-

pressing the opinion that in Steinie's case it was unwise to take the risk.

Abinger thought differently. He had already discussed the matter with his client, who had approved, maybe even instigated, the adoption of bold tactics. But counsel of experience advise their clients; they are not advised by them. Abinger would have been the last to deny that in the ultimate resort the decision was his own.

He decided to attack.

8

Next morning the first witness was Joe Mintz. He was the waiter from the Warsaw Restaurant who had thought Steinie's parcel much too heavy for a flute.

'Have you ever tried to hang yourself?' Abinger asked him.

'That has nothing to do with the case,' the witness snapped. (Frequenters of the Warsaw seemed curiously prone to *ex cathedra* pronouncements upon relevance.)

'But is it true?'

'It is true, but it has got nothing to do with the case.'

'And did you afterwards go to Colney Hatch Asylum?'

'Yes, I have been there.'

At this point Mr Justice Darling intervened.

'I suppose you realise, Mr Abinger, that suicide is a felony and that you are asking this man whether he attempted a felony?'

'If your lordship thinks I should not pursue this——' Abinger began.

The judge was quick with a correction.

'I am not saying you should not pursue it, Mr Abinger. I did not quite know whether you knew what it might lead to.'

Darling was in fact making absolutely sure that Abinger did not expose his client to unnecessary danger through mere forgetfulness or misreading of the rules. In effect, the judge was offering a reminder : if you attack character, you in turn will be attacked.

Whether these questions to Mintz really constituted an attack on character in the strictly legal sense is a question that will always be open to debate. The judge apparently considered that they did. But Abinger maintained, with some plausibility, that he was not seeking to impute an offence but to establish that Mintz was mentally deranged.

The point, to say the least of it, was arguable. Before the end of the day, though, it had become academic. An attack by Abinger upon one Mrs Deitch put the Mintz affair completely in the shade.

Mrs Deitch's evidence was awkward for the prisoner. She swore she had seen him in Whitechapel with Beron on New Year's morning between one and two o'clock. That came uncomfortably close to the time when they were supposed to have set off for Clapham in a cab.

Mrs Deitch had had a rough passage at the police court. Rightly anticipating a similar ordeal, she had worked herself up into a fine state of resentment. If Abinger was lying in wait for her, Mrs Deitch was equally lying in wait for him.

There were no preliminaries; no smooth approaches, no subtle skirting round. Both parties got to grips at once like a pair of fighting cocks.

'What is your husband?' was Abinger's first question.

'He is a gas-fitter.'

'And what are you?'

The path to insolence lay wide open. Mrs Deitch was in no mood to reject it.

'What am I? I am a woman of course.'

'I can see that,' said Abinger, 'But what is your occupation?'

'That is a fine question to ask me,' Mrs Deitch exclaimed, with what must have seemed, at that moment, excessive sensitivity. 'I am at home in the house, looking after my children.'

'Do you know a woman named Lizzie Holmes?'

'No.'

'You pledge your oath she did not live in your house?'

'I have never had any girls living in my house.'

'Didn't Lizzie Holmes have a room with you for which she paid you three shillings a week?'

'No.'

Then they came—the questions intended to encompass the rout of Mrs Deitch, but which carried in their train the destruction of another.

'Used she to take men in?'

'No such thing.'

'Did they not sleep with her, or stay a short time?'

'Never.'

'Did she not pay you three shillings for every man that stopped all night?'

'That is an untruth.'

'And a shilling for every man that stopped a short time?'

'I never heard of such a thing.'

'Where did you get that fur from?'

'That is my business.'

'Tell us, please.'

Mrs Deitch now gave way to that uninhibited rage which was the sign manual of actors in this extraordinary trial.

'Why should I tell you?' She spat the words at Abinger. 'You insulted me last time, but you will not insult me today. You asked me last time where I got my fur from. My husband bought it, what he worked for. I do not ask you where your wife got her fur from.'

Abinger prudently ignored this impudent ripost. He continued, however, to press for information about this Lizzie Holmes. Hadn't she followed Mrs Deitch from one house to another? Hadn't Mrs Deitch sent for her? Wasn't there a specific occasion in March of last year when Lizzie had 'gone with a man' and Mrs Deitch had got ten shillings? All of which gave rise to further vehement denials.

When the string of questions at last came to an end, the judge enquired if Lizzie Holmes was present. She was not.

'I expect her here tomorrow,' said Mr Justice Darling, 'and this witness shall be here also.'

Abinger did better than had been desired. When the court resumed next day, not only Lizzie Holmes but four other harlots lined up before the box. Each in turn confronted Mrs Deitch; each in turn was flatly disavowed. The girls shouted 'Liar', Mrs Deitch shouted back, and the episode was suspended on this inconclusive note.

So far the comic element was uppermost. But the seeds of tragedy had been already sowed.

9

The jury's view of Mrs Deitch can only be conjectured. They may have thought she was a back-street procuress; they may have thought she was a lady wickedly traduced. But from Steinie's standpoint, the sole test was this : were they now any less likely to believe that she had seen him with Beron where and when she said? It was the breaking of the Crown's time-table that mattered, not whether people kept a stew or tried to hang themselves.

Unhappily the uproar raised over the latter tended to obscure Abinger's march towards the former. In between the angry scenes, all through the second day, he had been quietly displacing various props of Muir's case.

Mrs Deitch herself had conceded a point which, unlike her morals, was of primary concern. She still insisted she had seen Leon Beron with the prisoner, but, under Abinger's cross-examination, was driven to declare she had been mistaken in the time. She fixed it now at two fifteen; a quarter of an hour after—on the prosecution's showing—Steinie and Beron left for Clapham in the cab.

This was a very valuable advance and gained without running any countervailing risk.

Then there was Weissberg, who swore he had seen Steinie walking with Beron at about twelve forty-five. Abinger ascertained that this witness had had supper at the Warsaw, that he had left there shortly after eight in company with one Zaltsman, and that they were still together shortly before one. Asked to recount their movements in the interval, Weissberg could only say that they had 'walked about'.

'You must have been getting rather weary,' Abinger suggested.

'I met a girl friend,' replied Weissberg, as though this had kept him going, 'and I had a conversation with her.'

'So the three of you walked about—you and Zaltsman and the girl?'

'The girl left us about eleven.'

'Then did you and Zaltsman go on walking until a quarter to one?'

'Yes.'

'Where?'

'Backwards and forwards, from Aldgate to Mile End.'

'How many times?'

'Five or six or more.'

'You would then be getting *very* tired,' remarked Abinger with sarcasm.

'Yes, we got very tired,' said the witness innocently.

Weissberg's story now sounded ludicrous. But Abinger's full triumph was only consummated when Zaltsman followed his friend into the box. As witnesses were kept out of court until they gave their testimony, Zaltsman of course knew nothing of what had just transpired.

He repeated the tale of the protracted, pointless walk, and then once again it was Abinger's turn.

'Did you meet anybody?' he asked, 'besides Morrison and Beron?'

'No.'

'Think carefully whether you did not meet someone else and walk with someone else.'

Did the witness then half guess and did he try a sporting shot? At any rate he permitted his memory to be jogged.

'Oh, yes, someone else walked with us, but I do not know *him* by name.'

Abinger was expressionless.

'Anybody else besides that *man*?'

'Nobody else spoke to us besides that man.'

Abinger sat down. When Muir, re-examining, put a leading question ('Did you have any conversation with a *woman*?') Abinger objected, and the judge rightly forbade this attempt to reconstitute a broken-down position. Messrs Weissberg and Zaltsman had been settled for good by the invisible girl friend and the five-hour promenade.

The first part of the time-table was looking somewhat shaky. It had seemed far more convincing on the lips of Mr Muir.

10

If this had been a normal case, conventionally conducted, the deciding factor would have been the evidence of the cabmen. Even amid the shoals of red herrings and the hysterical spasms that marked Steinie's trial, it was obvious that a great deal must depend on Abinger's handling of these key witnesses.

In a sense, of course, their evidence was only indirect. But indirect evidence can be powerfully persuasive. If the jury took these men at their face value; if they thought them neither dishonest nor mistaken; if they believed in the drives to and from Clapham and that Beron and Steinie were the passengers concerned—then one would surely plead with them in vain to look upon it all as pure coincidence. Juries are seldom scholastic logicians; they deal in probabilities, not absolutes.

In one respect, the cabmen lay wide open to attack. Recognising someone at the time is one thing; *identifying* someone subsequently is another, especially when a substantial period has elapsed. If you say 'I saw so-and-so whom I *know*', the room for error there is infinitesimally small. If you say, 'This is a stranger whom I saw on one occasion', the room for error there is almost without limit. And this was what, in sum, the cab drivers were saying when they picked out Steinie at the police station parade.

The whole technique of parades has been justly criticised, though it is hard to see what method could be adopted in its stead. It certainly offers opportunities for abuse; the long halt, the lifted eyebrow, the hand-picked crowd from which the wretched suspect unwillingly stands out. But deliberate rigging is exceptional; as a rule, no doubt, every effort is made to be fair. There are, however, certain defects which are inherent in the system. The more distinguished-looking your suspect, the less easy to place him with men reasonably like. The less contrasted your full line-up, the more encouragement to guess-work. And—worst of all—if a case has already had considerable publicity, the witness may no longer be identifying a *person*; he may merely identify the source of a description or the original of a photograph.

Abinger seized upon this latter point when he came to cross-examine Hayman. Hayman was the first of the Crown's cab drivers and, in lawyers' jargon, he came right up to proof. On New Year's night he had been in Mile End with his hansom; he had been hailed and engaged by two men; he had set them down, on their request, at Clapham; one of the men was short—not more than five foot five; the other he had since picked out as the accused.

'And when did you first go to the police?' Abinger asked.

'About a week afterwards—either the 9th or 10th.'

'Before you went to the police, did you see the *Evening News* of the 9th, with a description of Morrison?'

'No.'

'If you didn't see it, why had you not been to the police on the 2nd, 3rd, 4th, 5th, 6th, 7th or 8th?'

'Well, I went to the station as soon as I could.'

'Why did you not go before the 9th?'

'I don't know.'

Abinger held up a police notice.

'This is dated the 6th January. Did you see it?'

'It was down in the cab yard.'

'Then if you saw this police notice, offering a reward to cabmen, why did you not go to the station till the 9th or 10th?'

'I went when I thought proper.'

'Why did you not go before?'

Hayman was now at the end of his excuses.

'I can't give you a reason,' he said.

'When were you taken to identify the man?'

'On the 17th.'

'Had you seen portraits of the accused in the newspapers before you went to identify him?'

'Yes.'

This was an unqualified success for the defence. It seemed possible, if not probable, that Hayman had relied less on a genuine recollection of his fare than on what he had seen in the press and on posters.

The second cabman, Stephens, made a similar admission; he had seen a portrait before going to the police. But this fact was overshadowed by a further, new development, which Abinger exploited with admirable skill.

11

For the Crown to gain its purpose, the cabmen's times must dovetail, as they had done so perfectly in Muir's opening speech. Hayman in the witness box had spoken, as forecast, of leaving Mile End at two and reaching Clapham at two forty. Stephens now took up the tale : he had been with his cab at Clapham Cross, where he was hired by the supposed Steinie at twelve minutes past three. This conveniently earmarked half an hour for carrying out the murder and any accessories thereto.

Abinger had a document passed up to this witness. Stephens looked at it without enthusiasm.

'Is that the statement you made to the police on January 10th?'

'Yes.'

'I am going to read it.'

The first few sentences were merely introductory; Abinger

slower, glancing up at times, giving each word due emphasis and weight.

' "I remained on the rank until just before *half past two*, when a man alone came from the direction of the Old Town, Clapham. He said 'Kennington' and then got in the cab. I have seen a photograph of Steinie Morrison and identify him as being that man." '

Abinger laid the paper down deliberately.

'So you told the police that you picked this man up at half past two?'

'I told the police I was not sure of the time, but it was about one hour after the last tram. The police asked me the time of the last tram and I said it was about half past one.'

'You know, don't you, that if your statement is true, that you picked up the man at half past two, Hayman's evidence cannot be true, because according to that he would be in Hayman's cab at that time?'

The form of this question left out of account the possibility that they had carried two entirely different men. But here Abinger was tactically justified; in dealing with juries, one point at a time.

'According to Hayman, at half past two the man would be in Hayman's cab, wouldn't he?'

'I don't know.'

Certainly a strange picture was evolving—a picture of Steinie, in one case accompanied, in the other case alone, travelling simultaneously in opposite directions.

Abinger now had Stephens with his back to the wall. The final blows were swiftly delivered.

'Do you tell the jury that you do not know that Hayman has sworn that Morrison was in his cab at half past two?'

'I do not know.'

'Have you spoken to Hayman?'

'Yes.'

'I suggest that you altered your time to twelve minutes past three because that fits in with Hayman's time?'

'If it had been true,' said Stephens, 'I should have stuck to my time. I went to the tramway company and made enquiries about the last tram and on their statement I went to the police and altered the time.'

What prompted Stephens to make these enquiries never came to light. He was suffered to withdraw, greatly the worse for wear. His story was not disproved, but, in the strictest sense, discredited. People often try to fix times by events and afterwards discover themselves wrong. But in Stephens's case the adjustment was a shade too providential for a jury to rely on when a man's life was at stake.

By theatrical canons, here should end the chronicle of the cabmen. But for the record, one must perforce make mention of a third, who thought he had picked Steinie up at half past three in Kennington, and driven him with another man to Seven Sisters Road. He was examined and cross-examined with as much care and solemnity as if nothing had gone wrong with this integrated sequence.

The courts, which so often produce orgasms of drama, are not concerned to avoid an occasional anti-climax.

12

The feeling of deflation, however, was short-lived. Battle was joined again on a harmless-looking matter : the evidence of the prisoner's capture and arrest.

Steinie was arrested by Inspector Frederick Wensley, who was destined to scale the topmost peak of his profession and become the first Chief Constable of Britain's C.I.D. He was a square, stern man with a burning sense of mission; as a Templar fought the Saracens so he fought the world of crime. He had fallen upon Steinie on January 8th at a coffee-house in Fieldgate Street as the latter sat at breakfast. 'I said: "I want you, Steinie," ' Wensley told the court. 'I told him he would be detained, but I did not charge him with murder. I did not mention Beron or the murder in his hearing.' Needless to say, the Inspector was corroborated *in toto* by every officer who had been personally involved. Nor, it was affirmed, either *en route* or at the station, had any other person enlightened the accused. He was apparently left to infer, if he so chose, that he was being taken in as a convict upon licence who had failed to notify a change in his address.

The significance of this presently unfolded. Shortly after Steinie had been shut up in his cell, he asked to see Wensley so that he might make a statement. 'You have accused me of murder——' Steinie began. 'No,' Wensley interrupted, 'I have done nothing of the kind.'

Muir attached great importance to this matter as tending to reveal the prisoner's guilty knowledge. When Wensley himself came into the box, Abinger challenged his account of the arrest, suggesting that he had really said, 'I want you *for murder*.' Wensley insisted that his version was correct.

A lively exchange followed.

'Do you pledge your oath that you did not arrest him on suspicion of having committed murder?'

'Certainly.'

'On the date of Morrison's arrest had the police received no statement or information connecting him with this murder?'

'No.'

'When did Mrs Deitch make her statement?'

'I think it was on January 2nd.'

'Do you say that Mrs Deitch's statement does not connect Morrison with this murder?'

'Not beyond the description.'

'When did Castlin [the third cab driver] make his statement?'

'On January 4th.'

'After Castlin's statement did you not connect Morrison with this murder?'

'I did not connect him with the murder till he was identified.'

'Let me show you a copy of the *Daily Graphic* of January 9th. Do you see a photograph of the restaurant where Morrison was arrested?'

'I do.'

'If you did not mention at that restaurant that you were arresting Morrison for murder, how could that photograph have got into the paper the next day?'

It was a very, very awkward question. Wensley had no decisive answer.

'I don't know,' he said. 'It might have got there by many means.'

This passage shows Abinger at his best: acute, tenacious, rigorously germane, equally in command of the situation and himself. Nobody hearing it could possibly feel confident that, somehow or somewhere, the word 'murder' wasn't used.

At this stage neither side could carry the point further. It was to flare up again several days later in the shape of an unlooked for and last-minute sensation.

13

Halfway through the fourth day the Crown case was closed and Abinger opened Steinie Morrison's defence.

The official halfway mark and turning point is sometimes followed by a change in atmosphere that puzzles and disturbs the lay observer. So far, he argues, we have heard what can be said *against* this man; now we are going to hear what can be said *for* him. So any change henceforth should operate, not to the prisoner's hurt, but in his favour.

This reasoning ignores two cognate factors : the power disposed by cross-examination and the pattern traced by every English trial. The Crown evidence offers defence counsel an Aunt Sally, and rare is the case where he does not in some degree diminish the effect of the prosecutor's opening. During this phase, indeed, it is the defender who attacks and the prosecutor who defends.

But with the transfer of the bidding, the position is reversed. It is the defence's evidence that offers an Aunt Sally. It is the prisoner and his witnesses who come under raking fire. It is the prosecutor who gets the opportunity to whittle away the fabric set up by his opponent.

The more substantive and positive the defence's case, the greater the risk of undoing and disaster.

14

No defence could be more substantive than an alibi. It was in part upon an alibi that Abinger relied. Departing from the usual order of events, he called the witnesses on this issue before Morrison himself.

The first two were a Mr and Mrs Zimmerman, with whom Steinie had been lodging in Newark Street, Mile End. Both swore that on New Year's Eve he had come home about midnight, taken the key of his own room and then retired to bed. Both swore that he was in the house when they got up next morning and the woman said his bed appeared to have been slept in. Both swore that the street door had been bolted for the night, that the bolt was stiff and exceptionally noisy, that they slept lightly and would have heard if the bolt had been withdrawn.

The Zimmermans were not without material support: a reputable surveyor said the bolt 'shrieked terrifically', and a next door neighbour spoke of seeing Steinie arrive home.

Muir questioned these people without notable success. The surveyor's evidence was virtually unchallengeable, and there seemed no ground for disbelieving the assertions of the others that they had seen Steinie Morrison as and when they said. But the inference that he stayed home all night depended on two assumptions: (1) that otherwise he must have opened the street door, (2) that the bolt was an infallible alarm. Perhaps Steinie (who had a ground floor room) made a doorway of his window. Perhaps Mr and Mrs Zimmerman slept sounder than they knew.

What may conveniently be called the Zimmerman evidence was not, therefore, conclusive. So far as it went, though, it assisted Steinie's case; nothing was lost by calling it and perhaps a little gained. The same cannot be said of the evidence of the Brodskys.

One wonders why Abinger ever called these two young sisters. They had nothing to say that was really to the point. They claimed to have gone on New Year's Eve to a show at the Shoreditch Empire, where they saw Steinie Morrison sitting near them in the stalls. They did not speak to him, as at that time they only just knew him by sight.

Supposing they were believed, what then? Would Steinie's cause be in any way advanced? They would have fixed his whereabouts from nine until eleven—four hours before the murder was committed. They would have made liars of the habitués from the Warsaw who said that Steinie spent the evening in their midst. They would have confirmed a part—an inessential part—of the story that Steinie was presently to tell. But what bearing could the Shoreditch Empire have upon the vital hours after twelve?

If, on the other hand, the girls were *not* believed, better by far that they had never come to court. A false witness—who is for this purpose one so deemed by the jury—blackens the prisoner on whose behalf he speaks.

Even a genuine alibi is difficult to prove, and often provides a field day for a clever cross-examiner. Muir had had an unexpected rebuff with the Zimmermans, but he was soon making headway with the Misses Brodsky.

A single devastating question and reply wiped the elder sister completely off the map.

'Can you tell me,' Muir enquired, 'any single item in the programme which you saw?'

'No,' Miss Brodsky said.

But Muir's real duel was with the younger sister, Jane. She was only sixteen, but mature for her years and she stood up for herself with energy and spirit. She expressed her 'certainty' that Steinie was the man who had sat in the same row at the show on New Year's Eve. She did something to repair her sister's swift collapse by recalling in detail at least one turn on the bill ('Harry Champion; he was the favourite; he comes on with a ginger wig and sings "Ginger, you're barmy" '). She spoke with indignation of the attentions of the police ('They fetched me to the station four or five times; I've signed three different statements on three different occasions').

When Muir began to cross-examine Jane, he used this as the basis for a neat counter-attack.

'Did you ever at any of these interviews,' he asked, 'tell

the police you had seen Morrison in the Shoreditch Empire on New Year's Eve?'

'No.'

'Why not?'

'Because I was angry at the time and would not answer any questions.'

'What were you angry about?'

'The people in the street were talking of policemen coming to my door. I asked them several times not to, but they went on doing it.'

'You told the police that you had seen Morrison on January 2nd.'

'Yes.'

'Also at the Shoreditch Empire?'

'Yes.'

'Why did you keep back from them that you had seen him sitting in the same row of stalls on New Year's Eve?'

'They did not ask me the question, and I did not answer them.'

Jane was hitting back, but she was now on the defensive. Muir, moreover, had reserves of ammunition. Piece by piece he used it to draw damaging admissions—that Jane had lately become closely linked with Steinie, that she had frequently visited him in Brixton Prison, that he had asked her to marry him, that she had told him she 'would see'. It could hardly be maintained in face of this that Jane was altogether free from partiality.

To deliver his *coup de grâce*, Muir had both the girls recalled for questioning 'on a point on which I have just received information'.

They had sworn that they had paid a shilling each for seats. They swore it again and would not be dissuaded.

'I suggest', Muir said to Jane, 'that on New Year's Eve

the price for stalls was raised to one and six.'

'I do not know that.'

'And that well before nine o'clock, when you say that you arrived, there were people standing and there were no seats in the house?'

'People may have been standing,' Jane responded doughtily, 'but I got two vacant seats.'

In due course Muir produced the theatre manager, who confirmed upon oath that his suggestions were well founded.

The Brodskys, it may be taken, did not impress the jury. It is absolutely certain that they did not impress the judge. After counsel had finished, Mr Justice Darling questioned Jane, and he made a scathing reference to them in his summing-up. 'You may come to the conclusion that this is a fabricated alibi, sworn to falsely by the Brodskys.' He added, though, this caution. 'The fact that a man calls a false alibi does not by a long way prove that he is guilty. Is it not very common among people of certain classes and certain nationalities if they have got a good case not to rest on that good case? If you have ever talked to anybody who has administered justice in India, you will know that. If you come to the conclusion that this alibi is false, you should not judge it as strictly against the prisoner as if it had been produced by an Englishman.'

Despite the overtones of sententious insularity, the warning was a wise and fair one. It is questionable, though, whether the jury paid regard once they had heard the words 'fabricated alibi'.

If the Shoreditch Empire alibi had been successfully established, its effect upon the case would have been comparatively small. Since it had ignominiously broken down, its effect on the case was likely to be great.

This kind of paradox is familiar in the courts.

15

In the late afternoon of the fifth day of his trial, Steinie Morrison went into the box. He remained there the rest of that day, the whole of the day after, and most of the morning of the day after that. For more than half of this time he was being cross-examined with a severity rare among twentieth-century prosecutors.

First, however, Steinie placed on record his own story. During December, he said, he had been travelling in jewellery, mostly around the Jewish area of Whitechapel. He made a number of sales which brought him a small return, and during the same period had profited by two windfalls: £20 from his mother in Russia, and £35 from a lucky faro game. So far as he was 'flush' at all, here was the reason why—and the flush condition dated back some weeks before New Year.

As to the 31st December, that was simple. He had called in at the Warsaw about eight o'clock that night and left a flute that he had bought during the day. From the Warsaw he went on to the Shoreditch Empire, where he sat—just as the Brodskys said—in the stalls, alone. After the performance he returned to the Warsaw, where he collected his flute and had some refreshment. He left there before twelve, and on his way home saw Beron standing with a tall man in the street. Beron had called out to him in greeting: Steinie had responded. Then he had made tracks for his lodging and his bed.

Next day? Oh yes—why should he deny it?—Steinie had suddenly uprooted his home. It was an *affaire de cœur,* if you care to call it so; more crudely, an arrangement with a woman of the town. It was to go to her he left the sympathetic Zimmermans. It was to spare her feelings he got rid of the revolver. (The woman herself had already been called to substantiate at least the first of these assertions.)

And the days following? Steinie strongly contested the charge that he had flown. He had gone about his business every day in the East End; he had eaten at restaurants in his usual neighbourhood; why, Wensley had arrested him a stone's throw from the Warsaw. True, he had given the latter place the go-by, but that was because on New Year's Eve he had had words with Joe Mintz. ('Are you trying to hang yourself again?' Steinie had shouted, and Mintz had darkly threatened 'to get it out of him'. 'I believe', Steinie said, 'he is getting it out of me now.')

In Steinie's story, certain things were hard to swallow. The flute (even though one was produced in court); the money (even though there was some play with receipts); the revolver (even though his tenderness with women was established). It all *might* have been true, but it had an unreal air—like Stephens' excuse for altering the time.

16

A tradition has gradually grown up in England—where persons are held innocent until guilt is proved—that a prisoner, especially on a capital charge, should not be browbeaten or harried in the box. This need not make his cross-examination ineffective. Sir Patrick Hastings, in his questioning of Vaquier, showed how a great advocate can be a deadly prosecutor without aping the methods of a petty sessions despot.

No one should underrate Muir's array of gifts : his shrewdness, his integrity, his mastery of detail. But he belonged, by legal upbringing and nature, to what is now affectionately termed 'the old school'. Defending or prosecuting, it made no difference to Muir; he went all out for the triumph of his side. Steinie's case, with its partisan setting and its personal antagonisms, can only have served to accentuate this tendency.

When they faced each other in the crowded court, the burglar with the clean-cut profile and the lawyer with the granite face and heavy jowls, there was no hint of quarter being given or received. It was to be, in the dreadful literal sense, a battle to the death.

Muir did not play at once the ace that Abinger had thrust into his hand. He began instead with an enquiry, grim, harsh and undisguisedly hostile, into the sources from which Steinie's money came. What date was the game of faro? December 1st. Had Steinie ever been to that gaming-house before? Yes, once. Had he any witness who would say he won that money? Yes, the croupier. Had he any witness?

'I can give you the name of the croupier,' Steinie said.

'Have you any witness?'

This was the third time of asking, as the tone implied.

'I tell you,' Steinie repeated, 'I can give you the name of the croupier.'

'Answer my question,' Muir rapped out sharply.

'He is trying to answer it,' Mr Justice Darling said. 'He says he can give you the name of the croupier.'

It is happily seldom that judges have to protect a prisoner in this fashion.

Muir went on with his research into Morrison's finances. Had he the letter that accompanied the money from his mother? It had been destroyed. How much had he made each week selling jewellery? £2 or £2 10s. Might Muir call his attention to the large sum he had spent on personal purchases on one particular day?

The implications were still half veiled, but growing clearer every moment. The crisis was at hand.

Abinger stood up.

'May I ask my friend to what issue this cross-examination is directed?'

'Yes,' said Muir, 'to the issue whether he was, on January 1st, in possession of the proceeds of the robbery of Beron.'

'Ah!' Abinger exclaimed. 'Then that is directed to the credit of the witness and I object to it.'

The judge was patently—and understandably—surprised.

'You object, Mr Abinger? On what ground?'

'On the ground that such questions can only be put to a prisoner if the prisoner or his advocate have brought themselves within the provisions of Section One of the Criminal Evidence Act 1898. May I remind your lordship of those provisions?'

'I know them quite well,' Mr Justice Darling said. 'Have you forgotten your cross-examination of Mrs Deitch?'

'I have forgotten nothing,' said Abinger stubbornly.

'But did you not impute to Mrs Deitch that she kept a brothel?'

'Will your lordship allow me to deal with this in order? It is a most serious matter. I respectfully call your lordship's attention to the language of the Section.' Abinger began to read it while the judge waited with what patience he could muster. ' "The prisoner shall not be asked any questions tending to show that he has committed any offence other than that wherewith he is charged or that he has a bad character *unless* the conduct of the defence is such as to involve imputations on the character of witnesses for the prosecution." '

'Well?' Mr Justice Darling said.

Abinger now developed an extraordinary argument. At the police court two persons who had given evidence for the Crown later withdrew their statements and said they were untrue. Neither was called by Muir at the Old Bailey. This was a proper and fruitful theme for comment, but Abinger went further; he tried to make it the basis for a justification of his attack on Mrs Deitch. 'When a man is being tried for his life,' he said, 'and it has been established that two witnesses who have given deadly evidence against him have stated that which is untrue, is his counsel to stand mute when a woman who may be of immoral character gives evidence against him?'

'No, he is not bound to stand mute,' Mr Justice Darling said, 'but if he puts questions that come within the Criminal Evidence Act, he takes the consequences.'

Abinger was labouring under considerable stress. The all-important battle was being lost; gathering round Steinie were the lowering shades of doom. 'It would be barbaric cruelty,' Abinger cried, 'if a man on trial for his life is to have to stand mute by his counsel while a person of the most infamous character gives evidence against him, and if his counsel dares——'

The judge cut into this outburst.

'Please do not address me, Mr Abinger, in such rhetorical terms. I am bound by the Act of Parliament, and I am not to consider whether it is barbaric or otherwise. If it is within the Act, I shall allow the cross-examination. If it is outside the Act, I shall reject it.'

This logic was unanswerable. Abinger struggled on a little longer. He urged the judge to 'exercise a discretion' (for which the Act does not provide) and talked vaguely about the prisoner 'having his whole life ransacked'. Then, in some distress, he resumed his seat.

The judge did not call on Muir to argue. He briefly summarised the law, and said that there could be no graver imputation on a woman than that which Abinger had made on

Mrs Deitch. 'Therefore it seems to me that the conduct of the defence has been such as to involve imputations on the character, certainly of Mrs Deitch, and I think also of Mintz —but I give the go-by to that : I found my decision on the imputation on the character of Mrs Deitch. The consequence is that the prisoner may be cross-examined like any other witness. His privileged position has been lost; the matter is now at large.'

17

The floodgates were opened; the questions poured through.

'Were you first convicted for felony in December 1898?'

'That may be so.'

'Was it for stealing?'

'I was charged with that.'

'Did you get a month's hard labour?'

'I did.'

'Were you sentenced to six months' hard labour for burglary in August 1899?'

'Yes.'

'Were you arrested in April 1900 for being in possession of the proceeds of a burglary?'

'Yes, and I got fifteen months' imprisonment for a crime I had nothing to do with.'

'Were you sentenced to five years' penal servitude for burglary in September 1901?'

'Yes.'

'Did you plead guilty?'

'I believe I did.'

'In August 1905 were you released on licence?'

'Yes.'

'In January 1906 were you arrested on the charge of being a suspected person?'

'Yes.'

'When you were arrested had you a brace and bit in your possession?'

'Yes.'

'And the proceeds of three burglaries?'

'Yes.'

There was much else besides, but this was what really mattered. Steinie, who had left the dock an ordinary citizen, returned a desperado with a dossier of crime.

18

In theory, disclosure of a prisoner's bad character should have no influence on the outcome of his trial. In practice, it almost invariably has. Why otherwise, as Abinger pertinently asked, did Muir insist on raking up the past of Steinie?

The effect made on the jury was probably twofold. First, as the judge observed when he addressed them later, they were now liable to misinterpret all the prisoner's acts. 'It is almost impossible', said Mr Justice Darling, 'to put as good a construction upon the most innocent thing that man may have done as it was when you believed him to be unconvicted.'

Second, the jury might be betrayed into assuming a special relationship between the prisoner and society. Here was a burglar, a worthless individual, a man who if set free would be a constant malefactor. Why then split legal hairs and balance fine distinctions if we *feel* that he is guilty—feel it in our bones . . . ?

This was the result of introducing 'character'. This was the price paid for asking Mrs Deitch whether her house was a resorting place of drabs.

19

The strain imposed on defending counsel by a long trial for murder has few, if any, parallels. One can think only of the surgeon who, in the operating theatre, holds the life of his charge in the skill of his two hands. But the surgeon's burden lasts only hours; the barrister's lasts for days, sometimes for weeks, during which the trial absorbs his every waking moment. It does not admit of limited endeavour; it cannot be put aside at a fixed time. An idea conceived in the solitude of chambers may be the precious instrument of acquittal, just as an indiscreet utterance in court may set the seal upon an adverse verdict.

Such continuous and anxious concentration tests the nervous stamina of the strongest. This test is twenty times as great when things are going badly, when counsel senses that the tide of events is running inexorably against his client.

Abinger had been conscious from the start that his was an uphill and ungrateful task. He had tried to compensate for this by daring tactics and sheer force of will, but these, so far from rendering him aid, had merely served to make his prospects worse. Steinie's chance of freedom dwindled daily, and with it Abinger's poise and self-control. As the trial wore on his touchiness increased, involving him in scenes that grew more frequent and more violent. In particular it brought him into conflict with the judge.

Judges are not always right, nor always patient; the blame may rest with either side when Bench falls out with Bar. But here there can be little doubt where provocation lay. It was Abinger, by his curious conduct of the case, who often forced the judge against his will to intervene. It was Abinger who, by the warmth of his reaction, made these interventions so bitter and prolonged. It was Abinger who tried to make the jury act as arbitrators, and who transformed arguments on cold points of law into passionate tirades and emotional appeals.

The friction that resulted reached its unwelcome zenith in the last phase of the trial.

Abinger began his final speech late on the seventh day and did not finish until the next mid-afternoon. He had many points to make and made them forcibly, but ever and anon returned to one—the issue of character and his grounds for introducing it. He said he was glad that the jury now knew Steinie's history (a statement hard to reconcile with his fight to keep it from them). He reiterated his views about Joe Mintz and Mrs Deitch. He spoke at great length of Eva Flitterman and Rosen, the witnesses from the police court whom Muir had failed to call. 'There is a woman', he declared, referring to the former, 'who can be found to come to court and invoke the name of the Almighty and swear a lie—and in a murder trial! It is appalling! You have consciences; we have consciences; has that woman?'

The vigour of this was more apparent than its point. The judge, one thinks, was genuinely perplexed.

'Mr Abinger, what *do* you want? Do you want the prosecution to call Flitterman or not?'

'No, my lord, it would be a terrible spectacle. May I respectfully tell your lordship *what* I want?'

'Do, certainly,' said Darling, who doubtless longed to know.

'I want that woman to be brought into court so that the jury may see the class of woman that she is.'

The judge responded temperately to this singular request.

'But you have got it established that what she says is not true. What is the use of looking at one liar more or less?'

Deliberately Abinger swung round to face the jury.

'Gentlemen, I pass from that,' he said, ignoring the judge as though he were some petty official. 'I pass from that. But you won't. What my lord meant by saying one liar more or less is easy enough to guess. My lord must have been thinking of Rosen.'

'I was not thinking of Rosen,' said Mr Justice Darling quietly. 'I was thinking of King David.'

This scriptural allusion excited Abinger's scorn.

'Gentlemen,' he cried. 'I wish I had the remarkable abilities of my lord, who is able to allow his mind the luxury of dwelling upon King David when we are discussing this sordid case.'

A more offensive observation can seldom have been made in open court by counsel about judge. It speaks volumes for Mr Justice Darling's magnanimity that Abinger was permitted to proceed without rebuke.

20

Without rebuke, but not without much further interruption, for which the fiery advocate had himself to thank. The judge would not descend to *quarrel*, but neither would he tolerate distortions of the evidence or transgressions of the rules. As Abinger's speech pursued its turbulent course; as far-fetched theories were outlined, Cabinet Ministers criticised, and alternative murderers suggested *ex hypothesi*, so Darling insisted, in cool, firm tones, on conformity with the normal practice of the courts. Abinger contested each objection to the last, and long before the end his speech had ceased to be a solo; it was more like a duet between barrister and judge.

When Muir followed Abinger, the duet became a trio. Muir spoke; Abinger protested; Darling mediated—and occasionally the trio turned into a quartet when Steinie interjected something from the dock.

Heat always begets heat. Excitement breeds excitement. Hysteria's harvest was now being fully reaped.

21

The whole of the eighth day had been spent on speeches. In the evening, when the court adjourned, Muir, Abinger, Darling and Steinie were about halfway through Muir's.

The end of the trial was now in sight. The moment of decision could not be long delayed. But, in an assembly almost jaded with sensations, one last surprise had yet to come.

Next morning, when Mr Justice Darling sat, it was Abinger, not Muir, who stood up in his place. Looking tired and drawn (he had been busy half the night), he applied for leave to call some further evidence. The judge gave his assent and, amidst a rustling of whispered speculations, Police Constable Greaves made his way towards the box.

Who was he? Where did he come from? What had he got to say?

The mystery was soon solved. Greaves had been on duty in the charge room at the station when the detectives brought the prisoner in. He had heard Steinie ask 'What am I brought here for?' and he had also heard one of the officers reply: 'I told you before; you are on suspicion of *murder*.' Immediately after, they took Steinie to the cells.

At the time Greaves attached no importance to this incident. He only felt himself compelled to take action when he read in the paper an account of Steinie's trial. He then wrote a letter direct to Mr Abinger, stating what he knew, expressing reluctance to give evidence, but affirming his concern for 'the interests of justice'. As a result, last night he was summoned from his duty to the station, where he was interviewed by Abinger and the head of the C.I.D.

If Greaves was telling the truth about the charge-room conversation—or, to be crudely practical, if the jury thought he was—here finally collapsed one of Muir's most cherished points. No matter now whether Wensley mentioned 'murder' on arrest. Steinie, said Greaves, had heard the word before going to the cells, and it was only in the cells that he had mentioned it himself.

Muir swooped down on this supernumerary witness with the relish of a gourmand for an unexpected meal. A policeman, too, was he? A traitor to his side. This made the proffered feast the sweeter.

'When did you first speak of this conversation?' Muir asked.

'Two or three days ago.'

'To whom?'

'Some officers.'

'Who are they?'

'I can't say with certainty,' Graves answered, 'but I think one of them was 299H—Police Constable Heiler.'

'Let Heiler be telephoned for,' said Mr Justice Darling, 'and not be informed by anyone what this witness is saying.'

While Heiler was sought out and fetched, Muir went on cross-examining in the fashion that had become part and parcel of the case. Had Greaves frequently been transferred from Division to Division? Yes. Had he corresponded with an ex-Inspector Syme? Yes. Had Syme accused the police of perjury and corruption? Yes. Had Greaves on one occasion been suspended from the Force? Yes. Was that for making a false accusation against a superior officer? Well, not exactly. He was suspended for making accusations he was not able to prove.

Meanwhile Heiler had arrived at the Old Bailey and an element of lottery crept into the proceedings. Not even counsel knew what he was going to say. Abinger put him in the box, asked his name and rank, then cannily sat down again and left the rest to Muir.

Muir must have found the sequel irritating. All Heiler's answers favoured the defence. So far as it lay with him he confirmed Greaves absolutely. They had met on the beat, he said, a couple of nights ago, and Greaves had described what took place in the charge room. His story, as repeated by Heiler upon oath, corresponded with the story that Greaves had told in court.

Heiler's record was exemplary; Muir could do nothing with him. He passed from the box unshaken and unsullied —a rare event in this pageant of detraction.

Little now remained of Muir's hard-run theory that the murder charge was conjured up in Steinie's guilty mind. But it was the judge's lance that despatched the dying monster. 'This point,' he said, 'which has been represented to you as though it were the critical and crucial point of the whole case, is to my mind one of the smallest points in it. It would not seem to me at all unnatural that a man arrested where he was, within a few days of the notorious Clapham Common murder, should assume, even with nothing said, that he was arrested for murder.'

Envious, perhaps, of the universal loquacity, the foreman of the jury attempted to reply.

'May I say——' he began.

'No, no.' Mr Justice Darling stopped him instantly. 'Don't you say a word. Juries should never express any opinion, except by their verdict.'

22

Nothing now stood between the prisoner and that verdict
save only Mr Justice Darling's summing-up.

This was not the kind of case in which his lordship felt at
home. Some judges—not so many—would have taken it in
their stride: Avory, for instance, with his impersonal logic,
and Travers Humphreys, with his hardy worldliness. But
Darling—Darling was the exquisite of the Bench; the wit,
the beau, the laughing cavalier. His delight was to preside
over a Special Jury suit, in which the stake was merely
money which both parties could afford, and wherein he was
frequently presented with the chance of bandying epigrams
with fashionable counsel. The raw inelegance of Steinie's
trial can only have induced in him a nausea of distaste.

None the less, within the limits of his personality and
reputation, Darling tried the Morrison case well. If he could
not prevent others losing their equanimity, at least he carefully preserved his own. If he could not exclude scenes tinged
with macabre humour, he refrained from embellishing them
with ironic jest. If he could not stop a reference to ' my lord's
literary talents', he did nothing to earn the mockery with
which Abinger invested it. If there were moments in the trial
when everyone, judge included, seemed to be bobbing about
like corks on an unpredictable sea, in perspective it is plain
that Darling kept a clear sense of direction and strove gallantly to impress it on the rest.

The summing-up fittingly crowned his long effort. Into a
court still rocking with the clash of factions and echoing
with the sound of voices raised in anger, the judge's even
accents flowed like a solvent. Whatever could be done to lay
the dust, he did.

It was a closely-knit review, analytical and balanced, which deftly disentangled the true issues from the false. Essentials were exhibited and stressed; irrelevancies were branded and dismissed. The case against the prisoner was put afresh, shorn of vindictiveness and rancour. The case in his favour was equally examined and cleansed of prejudice, implanted or ingrained.

Above all, Darling placed the facts in due proportion. No one could tell—no one can tell now—what had influenced the jury most in those nine days of frenzy. But despite the mass of detail which distracted and confused, Darling tried to keep their minds fixed on the point that mattered. 'Are you satisfied', he asked them, 'beyond reasonable doubt that that is the man who was in Hayman's cab, in Stephens's cab, in Castlin's cab that night? . . . Think for yourselves. With what certainty could you swear to a man whom you saw on a night like that, by the kind of light there was at those places? Can you feel certain that a man would not be mistaken? . . . Let us assume they were honest. Even then, are you so sure that they really took notice enough, that they had opportunity enough, to be able some days afterwards to swear with certainty to the man that they had driven?'

Was Steinie identified beyond reasonable doubt? This Darling called 'the deciding point of the case'. If the jury did not share that view by the time the judge had finished, it probably lay beyond the power of mortals to convince them.

23

The jury retired at eight o'clock that night. It was far from being an ideal time for grave deliberations. Weariness of the body promotes impatience of the mind; instincts and emotions usurp the place of judgment

Thirty-five minutes later they trooped back into their box. They had been absent the same length of time as Mrs Maybrick's jury and, upon such brief communion, delivered the same verdict.

The judge passed the only sentence sanctioned by the law. As he ended with the traditional words of solemn benediction, 'And may the Lord have mercy on your soul', Morrison's anguish found dramatic outlet. 'I decline such mercy,' he cried out in despair, 'I do not believe there is a God in heaven either.'

So the curtain fell on the trial of Steinie Morrison—fell, as it had risen, with the chief character declamatory in the centre of the stage, but renouncing the God he had formerly acknowledged.

24

There was to be an epilogue, however.

The authorities needed no prodding from the public to reconsider Steinie Morrison's fate. The verdict had been indirectly disapproved by all the trained intellects qualified to judge. Mr Justice Darling, on receiving it, had conspicuously abstained from expressing agreement and had recommended the accused to be guided by his lawyers 'as to anything you may have to say hereafter'. The Court of Criminal Appeal, to which Steinie had recourse, cast its decision in a most significant form : '*Bearing in mind that we are not entitled to put ourselves in the position of the jury*, we can only come to the conclusion that the appeal must be dismissed.'

To many, therefore, it did not come as a surprise when Mr Churchill, who then occupied the office of Home Secretary, advised the King to grant Steinie a reprieve. This was done; the usual course was followed; the death sentence was commuted to penal servitude for life.

It was merciful, if death be the greatest of all evils. But Steinie, behind prison bars, wished desperately to die. He was persistently violent, apparently in the hope that if he made himself intolerable the reprieve would be annulled. While his solicitors without were pressing for his release, the prisoner within was petitioning to be hanged. Finally, by long and drastic fasting he undermined his strength and died in Parkhurst prison at the age of thirty-nine.

25

Did Steinie die in the consciousness of innocence, the tortured victim of a terrible mistake? Or did he take the knowledge of his guilt, unconfessed and unrepented, to the grave?

In his admirable life of Mr Justice Darling, Derek Walker-Smith reveals the judge's own opinion. 'I had no doubt myself', he remarked to his biographer, 'that Morrison was guilty. But the view I took was that, had I been a juryman, the evidence that I had heard was not sufficient to prove to me beyond all reasonable doubt that he had committed murder.'

There lies the distinction between this case and Mrs Maybrick's. The verdict upon Steinie was doubtful, not outrageous. It was open to dispute, and will remain so for all time, because it failed to give the prisoner the benefit of a doubt, and was rooted in a trial that gave scant cause for satisfaction.

NORMAN THORNE

1

OF all the verdicts examined in this book, the least disputable, admittedly, is that on Norman Thorne. His trial was a
model of dignity and fairness; he was finely defended by a
notable defender; the issues and the evidence were handled
by the judge in a manner that drew praise from the Court of
Criminal Appeal. And indeed it is highly probable that, in
convicting Thorne of murder, the jury did no more than
register the truth. But a high degree of probability is not to
be equated with sufficient legal proof, and study of this case
makes one inclined to wonder whether the Crown did not
fall a fraction short of discharging the heavy onus that
rightly lies upon it.

2

On Friday, December 5th, 1924, Elsie Cameron, a young
London typist living with her parents, set off for Crowborough to see her sweetheart, Norman Thorne. She bought
her ticket, passed through the barrier, found a seat in a
third-class carriage, put her cheap little attaché case on the
rack above her head, and settled herself down for the short
journey, mercifully unaware that it was the last she would
make on earth.

The expedition was not prompted by romantic passion,
though Elsie Cameron was very much in love. At the
moment practical matters occupied her mind. She and
Thorne had been engaged since 1922; for more than a year
there had been signs that he was cooling; lately he had even

written of another girl. Now Elsie Cameron believed that she was pregnant by him, a state of affairs which would not brook vacillation or delay. She was going to Crowborough to claim her rights, to insist that her fiancé should marry her at once. It was an anxious, overwrought, but above all determined girl that drummed her fingers on the rough upholstery and watched the bleak winter landscape rolling by. . . .

Several days passed. Elsie Cameron did not come home, neither did she write. Her family's surprise soon turned to deep concern, and on the following Wednesday her father wired to Thorne. 'ELSIE LEFT FRIDAY. HAVE HEARD NO NEWS. REPLY.' Thorne wired back at once. 'NOT HERE. OPEN LETTERS. CAN'T UNDERSTAND.'

The letters in question were duly opened. There were two of them, each written by Thorne, each posted in Crowborough, each addressed to Elsie at her London home.

'Well,' asked the first, 'where did you get to yesterday? I went to Groombridge and you did not turn up.'

'I was expecting a letter today,' said the second, in mild but perceptible accents of reproach, 'especially after not seeing you and not hearing from you.'

The dates upon these letters confirmed the distracted parents in their fears. Thorne, it appeared, had written them to Elsie days after they had supposed that she was with him.

In yet a further letter, following up his telegram, Thorne shattered their last lingering hope of some misunderstanding. As it sets forth the substance of a story and conveys the essence of an attitude both of which he maintained during the subsequent six weeks, this letter merits quotation in full.

DEAR MRS CAMERON [it ran],

I have re-read the telegram over and over again and it has given me quite a shock. I presume from that

that Elsie left home on Friday. She wrote to me asking me to meet her at Groombridge on Saturday morning. I went but she did not turn up and I take it something had prevented her at the last moment.

I have been expecting a letter from her all the week and wondering why I did not hear. Apparently she has been gone six days now, and no delay must be made in making enquiries.

Send particulars of how she was dressed. I will try and get what information I can locally. It is an awful position and I fear the worst. What time did she leave and by what train? Why did she not write and say she was coming?

I cannot write any more, as needless to say I am very worried and upset.

With love to all,
Yours truly,
NORMAN

There was hardly a word of truth in this document. The telegram had not come as a shock to Norman Thorne. He had no need to deduce the day when Elsie left her home, or surmise why she did not present herself on Saturday. He *knew* the reason for her unaccustomed silence. He *knew* how many days—how many hours—she had been 'gone'. And as for her garments, he had had ample opportunity to study them in detail when he burnt them in his grate. . . .

But all this was a secret locked in his own breast, where he intended that it should remain. The Camerons, left without a clue to guide them in the mystery, reported the disappearance of their daughter to the police.

3

Investigation into the whereabouts of a missing person is seldom restricted to the immediate physical facts. Character, background and personal relations point out the paths where enquiry should prove fruitful. What was in the missing person's mind? Where would he want to go? What would he want to do? The answer, which may be critically important, can only be sought in the individual's history.

The history of Elsie Cameron was slowly pieced together. Bit by bit, the whole sad, tawdry business came to light : the courtship, the betrothal, the tentative attempts by Thorne to wriggle free, the girl's inflexible resolve to hold her man.

They had met, this hapless couple, under pious auspices, where the cold flame of Wesley casts its light on Kensal Green. Elsie was plain, fragile, inclined to introspection; Thorne was strong, healthy, good-looking in his way. What drew them together is not subject to analysis; one can only set on record that the formula did its work and held them in bond for a short, uneasy space.

Bad luck dogged them from the very start. In the slump Thorne lost his job as engineer; debilitated nerves kept Elsie unemployed. Throughout their engagement they were woefully short of cash.

Thorne's reaction at least showed enterprise. He turned his back upon the engineering trade and, with a small sum borrowed from his father, took a plot of land at Crowborough and began a chicken farm. But the farm failed to prosper. He lived there by himself in a hut twelve feet by seven : primitive, cramped, squalid beyond thought. Even so, Elsie refused to be discouraged. 'We can manage in a hut like yours,' she wrote, and urged the hesitating bachelor to marry. At every stage, it is clear, the girl had made the pace and the man had, in any given circumstance, recoiled. They were, in fact, a fundamentally ill-assorted pair, possessing nothing in common except a habit of chapel-going and the prospect of privation.

The Other Girl's appearance on the scene was an overt symptom of this underlying trouble. If no Other Girl had ever materialised, if the path of love had technically run smooth, the match would still have ended up in tragedy. It might have been a tragedy of the gradual, wearing sort : resentful husband and disillusioned wife unable or afraid to break their irksome ties. As it was, it turned into a tragedy of violence, where the pressure would not yield without the sacrifice of life.

4

Thorne had met The Other Girl about six months before. She lived near by. Elsie Cameron had seen her once when she was staying at Crowborough but does not appear to have regarded her as a potential rival. Such confidence was misplaced. Affection soon matured between The Other Girl and Thorne. Presently she took to visiting him at night and local gossip had it that 'there was something going on'.

Elsie remained in blissful ignorance of this and might so have continued but for Thorne himself. He deliberately chose to reveal his double-dealing, but, one may be sure, not at conscience's dictate. His confession was significantly timed. It was fired back as a counter to reports of Elsie's pregnancy, and was manifestly meant to stave off the immediate marriage for which his fiancée now more than ever pressed. Thus he had written to her on November 25th :

You seem to be taking everything for granted. . . . There are one or two things I haven't told you for more reasons than one. It concerns someone else as well.   I am afraid I am between two fires.

Perhaps Elsie's attention was fixed on other things; perhaps she closed her eyes to what she did not want to see. Her reply, which was by return, had expressed merely bewilderment.

Really Norman, your letter puzzles me, I can't make it out. Why are there one or two things you haven't told me and in what way does it concern someone else? . . . What do you mean by you are afraid you are between two fires. Oh I don't understand things at all.

Dismissing her lover's cryptic utterances, she had reverted to the theme that monopolised and obsessed her.

Well, Norman, please arrange about getting married as soon as possible. I feel sick every day and things will soon be noticeable to everybody and I want to be married before Christmas and Christmas Day is only a month from tomorrow. . . . Please do get married quickly.

Wilfully or guilelessly, she had not construed his meaning. He must make it plainer—so plain, so simple and so unequivocal that there would be no room for misinterpretation.

On the 27th he had written to her again.

What I haven't told you is that on certain occasions a girl has been here late at night, I am not going to mention her name, nobody knows. When you gave in to your nerves again and refused to take interest in life I gave up hope in you and let myself go; this is the result. I didn't know last week what I know now. . . . I must have time to think, she thinks I am going to marry her of course, and I have a strong feeling for her, or I shouldn't have done what I have.

Now was *that* straight enough? Not an ambiguous sentence in it except 'I didn't know last week what I know now', and surely even Elsie would grasp the drift of that.

She had grasped it, fully. Her next letter, again by return of post, was a genuine cry of anguish.

> You have absolutely broken my heart [she had written], I never thought you were capable of such deception. . . . So I am to take it that you have got this other girl into the same condition which you have got me?

But if Thorne had expected her outraged feelings to turn her from the project upon which she was set, he was doomed to disappointment. She reiterated her demand with emphasis.

> Your duty is to marry me. I have first claim on you. . . . I expect you to marry me and finish with the other girl as soon as possible. My baby must have a name, and another thing I love you in spite of all.

It is an ironical feature of this correspondence that neither allegation of pregnancy was true. Elsie Cameron's was honest but mistaken; Thorne's was a calculated lie. But that had not been known to Elsie Cameron when she started off to Crowborough and vanished into space. She saw herself confronting a desperate situation : a baby on the way, another girl in the same plight, Thorne torn between the two, and her rival being on the spot holding the advantage. Was it not natural, was it not inevitable, that this girl, who had at all times been clamouring for marriage, should hurry to the man by whom her fate was being decided . . . ?

94

The more the police found out, and the more they thought about it, the more they were driven to work from this conclusion : that nothing bar a catastrophe of the greatest magnitude would have sufficed to divert Elsie Cameron from her goal.

5

But Thorne stood in the way of this hypothesis. He steadfastly affirmed that she had not come to the farm, that he had not set eyes on her, that he did not know where she was. He behaved, too, exactly as a person should behave who is innocently suffering the torments of suspense. He wandered restlessly about with a troubled, harassed air, appearing to seek comfort in discussion with his neighbours. He canvassed the opinion of everyone he met, while frequently expressing his own melancholy forebodings. He was touchingly eager to assist with the enquiry and bombarded the police with little scraps of information. All in all, observing it in retrospect, his acting through this period was consummately skilled.

One thing robbed his bravura of its full effect. Two nurserymen came forward, one of whom at least knew Elsie Cameron by sight. They had been passing Thorne's gate, they said, on the evening of the 5th, and had seen Elsie Cameron going towards the farm.

It seemed very odd and they might both be mistaken, but of course the police could not afford to disregard this hint. Thorne was asked if he objected to an inspection of his farm, and at once spoke to the contrary with something like enthusiasm. 'I'm glad you're coming,' he said, 'to clear the matter up.'

A Superintendent and an Inspector went over the farm, looked into the huts, and found no trace of the girl. Before they left they took a statement from the owner. 'She did not come here,' Thorne again assured them, 'and I have not seen or heard from her.'

It was tempting to discount the nurserymen; it was tempting to accept the word of Norman Thorne. Who could be better entitled to belief? His character was unblemished, his record clear; he taught at Sunday School, worked for Temperance societies and spoke on occasion for the Band of Hope; no one could breathe a word to his discredit. Besides, if Thorne was wrong and the nurserymen were right, *where was Elsie Cameron now* ?

Come to think of it, that was the very thing they didn't know.

6

Meanwhile the public had grown intensely interested in Elsie Cameron's fate. It was almost a matter of principle. You could vanish without trace, no doubt, in the Sahara Desert or the Australian Bush or the upper reaches of the Amazon. But not between Kensal Green and Crowborough. Not in the close-knit network of communities that was southern England. Not where a highly trained, expensive staff of police guarded the safety of the humblest citizen.

It might be good news or bad, it might be life or death, it might be fair play or foul—but don't tell us that the woman can't be *found*.

So Britain grumbled and police efforts redoubled; a crack from Scotland Yard went down to help the Sussex force; but December passed and January began its chilly cycle and still they had made no appreciable advance. Already Elsie Cameron was like some figure in a myth; her name was familiar, her story known, but her existence half forgotten.

The case was approaching the edge of that abyss below which lies the limbo of mysteries unsolved.

Then, on January 1st, came the turning point.

Like so many turning points, in other fields besides detection, it did not appear outstandingly important in itself. It was merely that a Crowborough lady—who, one must conclude, saw newspapers but seldom—read for the first time a full account of Elsie's disappearance. She meditated on this singular event, so closely linked with local folk and places. Thorne's farm—she'd passed it more times than she could count. Whenever she went to visit Mrs Tester, she walked along that road right by his gate. She had been to Mrs Tester's, too, somewhere about the time they said this girl had vanished. Early in December it was, wasn't it? On a Friday afternoon. The first Friday afternoon . . . the first. . . .

And it all came back to her. Of course; on her way home that evening shortly after five, she had seen a young woman entering Thorne's farm. An ordinary young woman; nothing to distinguish her. One thing, though; she was carrying an attaché case

It was, in a sense, only the shadow of a story. She couldn't describe the person she had seen. She couldn't say she answered to Elsie Cameron's description. Being absolutely honest she couldn't say more than that she had seen *a* girl, in that place, at that time. But the police now had *three* people all of whom were saying that they had seen *a* girl, in that place, at that time. Sunday School and Band of Hope and Temperance notwithstanding, Thorne must be subjected to a further, final test.

No one could complain that this test was not rigorous—nor that, in the event, the rigour was unjustified. At half past three in the afternoon of January 14th, Chief Inspector Gillan of the Yard, together with other officers, arrived at the farm, where he found Thorne in his hut. Gillan explained in time-honoured phrases that he was making enquiries into Elsie Cameron's disappearance on December 5th, and that he had reason to believe she had been seen alive there on the evening of that day. Thorne was unshaken. 'I have heard remarks to that effect,' he said, 'but I don't believe them.' Gillan told him that he proposed to search; Thorne offered his assistance. Gillan asked him whether he would make a further statement; Thorne readily agreed. Gillan then suggested that, as accommodation was lacking in the hut, they might adjourn to the station, and take the statement there.

It might be thought that, however scanty its facilities, the living hut was at least equipped to fulfil this simple function. There were writing materials, there was a table, there were chairs. But perhaps Gillan was right. For this was to be a colossus, a mammoth, a marathon among statements. They began on it at eight o'clock that night: Thorne talking, a Sergeant writing, Gillan breaking off and coming back as other work allowed. When they finished, it was half past three next morning, and a tired Chief Inspector gazed on the fruit of their joint labours—an amplified re-echo of what Thorne had said before.

But meanwhile the new search was getting under way. Once again a squad of police descended on the farm, pledged to explore every inch for Elsie Cameron.

This time they carried spades.

7

At four minutes past eight on the morning of January 15th one of the policemen digging at the farm turned up an attaché case which had been buried near the gate. Inside it were a jumper, some shoes, and a broken pair of spectacles.

The part which Thorne had so far played with flawless plausibility was exposed in that instant as a fake and a sham. The gathering storm now broke over his head and it raged with unremitting fury till it had destroyed him.

8

In the station cell where he was now confined, Thorne spent the day pondering his next step. When Gillan had told him he would be detained and probably charged with Elsie Cameron's murder, he had held his peace and uttered not a word. But Thorne was no fool; he must have known that his game of wide-eyed innocence was up.

What could he put in place of all those lies that had served to shield him for so many weeks? A different fiction? Or the naked truth?

Which of the two he chose will never be known certainly. But by the evening he had made up his mind. He asked to see Gillan and, when that officer appeared, announced: 'I want to tell you the truth of what took place.' (The words are no criterion; they are common form when a suspect changes tune.)

And so another statement, the last and most important, made its laborious way towards the prisoner's file. Again Thorne talked; again the Sergeant wrote; again the Chief Inspector watchfully presided. But they no longer spoke and wrote and listened to soothing words of virtuous denial. Instead there was unfolded a tale so grisly that it sent a thrill of horror pulsating through the land.

Elsie Cameron, said Thorne, had indeed come to the farm on December 5th. She had walked into his living hut at tea time, taking him completely by surprise. She told him she intended sleeping in the hut and, moreover, staying till she was married. An argument had opened up at once; it continued on and off for several hours, till the last London train had gone and Elsie's persistence had temporarily prevailed.

Thorne was then in an uncomfortable dilemma. Earlier on, before Elsie's sudden advent, he had made an appointment to meet The Other Girl. At half past nine, as the hour was drawing near, he told Elsie this and made ready to go. She protested, he insisted, and on this occasion the advantage lay with him. He kept his appointment, leaving her behind him in the hut.

He was away about two hours. In simple, shocking words, he depicted his return.

'*When I opened the hut door I saw Miss Cameron hanging from a beam* that supports the roof, by a piece of cord as used for the washing line. I cut the cord and laid her on the bed. She was dead. I then put out the lights. She had her frock off and her hair was down. I lay across the table for about an hour. I was about to go to Dr Turle and knock up someone to go for the police and *I realised the position I was in*, and decided not to do so. I then went down to the workshop . . . I got my hacksaw and some sacks and took them back to the hut. I took off Miss Cameron's clothes and burned them in the fireplace in the hut. I then laid the sacks on the floor, put Miss Cameron (who was then naked) on the floor and sawed off her legs and the head by the glow of the fire. I put them in sacks, intending to carry them away, but my nerve failed me and I took them down to the workshop and I left them there. I went back to the hut and sat in the chair all night. Next morning, just as it got light, I buried the sacks and a tin containing the remains in a chicken run. It is the Leghorn chicken run, the first pen from the gate.'

The Sergeant laid down his pen. The statement was read out. Coolly Thorne affixed his signature.

Chief Inspector Gillan's face was grim. He had solved one problem, only to raise another. The case of Elsie Cameron was over; the case of Norman Thorne had just begun.

9

Important trials are usually held in important places—in London, or in one of the large provincial cities. But there are occasional exceptions. Several small towns still enjoy, by ancient heritage, the periodic pomp and pageantry of Assize. And now and again high drama visits one of these quiet spots in the shape of a trial that sets all England by the ears.

It happened in 1921 at Carmarthen when they tried Harold Greenwood, and crowds lined the streets to watch counsel going to court. It happened in 1922 at Hereford when they tried Herbert Armstrong, and those who failed to get into the building patiently waited in the snow outside. It happened in 1924 at Guildford when they tried the volatile, spade-bearded Vaquier. It happened in 1925 at Lewes when they tried Norman Thorne.

Throughout the five days of the battle for Thorne's life, Lewes was in a ferment of unwholesome curiosity. It is hardly fair, though, to blame the town itself for that. Norman Thorne was the talk of the whole country, and people flocked from near and far as to some prize entertainment. After all, even if you weren't one of the lucky ones who gained a seat in court, there were several fascinating ways of filling time: celebrity spotting, slandering the witnesses, gaping and goggling at the broken-hearted parents, and—most agreeable diversion of them all—booing and gibing at The Other Girl.

This lamentable atmosphere encompassing the courthouse was never permitted to penetrate within. That was assured from the outset by the character of the lawyers in whose hands the conduct of proceedings mainly lay. There was to be neither the weakness on the Bench that prejudiced Mrs Maybrick's trial, nor the disorder at the Bar that so disfigured Steinie's. Mr Justice Finlay was as clear-headed and capable as he was self-effacing. Sir Henry Curtis Bennett, chief prosecuting counsel, was as impartial in this rôle as he could be fervent when defender. And J. D. Cassels, who had accepted the brief for Thorne, was almost the prototype of modern criminal advocates: economy and point were his watchwords; verbiage and barnstorming he alike eschewed.

The lines of Cassels' plea were predetermined. Thorne's last statement did not admit of an alternative. 'When I opened the hut door I saw Miss Cameron hanging'; those were the words that governed the defence. They pointed not to murder, but to suicide—or at the very least, to death from shock in the attempt. And if that was once accepted, all the rest could be explained. The concealment, the lies, and even the dissection could then be attributed to overwhelming fear —a fear not unnatural in a man who quickly realised that appearances were against him and that he was likely to be blamed. 'I thought of the letters I had written. I remembered I had been telling people that I wanted to break the engagement. I remembered that it was known that another girl had been coming down to me and I had been walking out with her. In view of these things, I became afraid.' These were Thorne's words when he went into the box and one cannot deny them considerable force.

So the real battle in the trial of Norman Thorne was a battle to discover *how* Elsie Cameron died. If, as the defence was to maintain, she had died from shock while trying to hang herself, Thorne, whatever his conduct afterwards, was not guilty of murder and entitled to go free.

If, on the contrary, she had in fact been murdered, the jury could have no doubt who her murderer was.

10

Suicide isn't everybody's exploit. The majority of people go through the world without ever seriously contemplating self-destruction. Human capacity for suffering is immense, even more so in the female than the male. Pangs of jealousy, faithlessness of lovers, the prospect of social dishonour and disgrace—such agonising tortures are endured (and survived) by millions of young women in every generation. Only the neurotic prove unequal to the strain.

That Elsie Cameron was neurotic had been evident to her intimates; it was Cassels' task to make it evident to the jury. Much of his work on the first day of the trial was directed to this end. Scores of questions, skilfully placed and timed, ultimately united to compose a telling picture : a picture of Elsie at home, at work, at Crowborough; often depressed, sometimes hysterical, always plagued and harried by her 'nerves'. Her father, who was the first witness of substance, agreed that she had left employment because of 'nerve trouble', that on one occasion office colleagues accompanied her home because her 'nerves' were bad, that she had been treated by doctors, both in London and Crowborough, for 'nerves'.

'Did it ever come to your knowledge', Cassels asked him, 'that she had been brought from Crowborough to Victoria Station by the prisoner?'

'Yes,' Mr Cameron said.

'Did your other daughter meet her?'

'Yes.'

'Did your other daughter make any communication to you about a message she had had from the prisoner?'

'Yes.'

'Was the communication that your daughter Elsie had threatened to throw herself out of the train?'

'Something to that effect,' Mr Cameron admitted.

Presently Cassels handed up a letter and the witness identified the writing as his wife's.

'I put that letter in, my lord,' Cassels said, and the letter, thus formally introduced in evidence, was read out to the jury by the Clerk of Assize. Dated December 16th, it was addressed to Norman Thorne. 'The suspense is terrible,' it said, '. . . we get no rest night or day. *If it had been a week or two ago I should have thought she might have done something rash, poor girl.*'

That, then, was how Elsie had appeared to her own parents. Acquaintances in Crowborough had formed similar opinions. One, with whom she had lodged from time to time, spoke of her being 'nervy' and 'brooding over things'; another had remarked, soon after her disappearance, 'that there was no telling what might happen to a person who got so low'.

Cassels' cross-examination brought all these things to light. That first evening when the court adjourned and each man went his way, the barristers to their Mess, the judge to the stately solitude of his lodging, the prisoner to his cell—that evening saw Thorne's chances reach their highest mark. On the record up to December 5th he was not a likely murderer. Elsie Cameron was a not unlikely suicide.

11

This in itself did not constitute a case; it merely laid the foundations of a case. Suicide was possible, yes—but had it really happened?

The second day's hearing was largely taken up by the Crown's attempts to show that it had not; to dispose of any theories that might tend to show it had; and to prove, beyond that reasonable doubt which every prisoner lawfully invokes, that Elsie Cameron had lost her life under the violence of another's hand.

The method used was necessarily oblique. Of that dark and angry evening in the hut, Thorne was the sole survivor. The only eye-witness beside himself had been carefully buried underneath his farm. But the remains of that poor girl (divided and stowed away exactly as Thorne said) had been dug up, scrutinised, analysed, interred, dug up, scrutinised and analysed again. The tale that Elsie Cameron did not live to tell pathologists sought to read upon her decomposing flesh.

12

Speaking broadly, there are three kinds of evidence: direct, circumstantial and expert. It is direct evidence when one man says he saw a second plunge a dagger into the vitals of a third. It is circumstantial evidence when the knife of a lover is found, stained with blood, by the stabbed corpse of his mistress. But when test-tubes are mobilised and microscopes unleashed, when crimes are reconstructed and assaults revisualised, when the testimony of onlookers is scornfully swept aside by reference to a shred of skin or a dented metal bar—then the Experts have descended on the scene.

Each kind of evidence in turn can be disparaged. Eye-witnesses may lie. Circumstances may deceive. Experts may lack learning, err in observation, be faulty in logic or dogmatic in conclusions. Occasionally an expert has contrived to be all four.

Genuine experts, though, make few mistakes of fact. Disputes between them are generally confined to the interpretation that acknowledged facts should bear. In other words, they differ in opinion.

The experts in the Thorne case differed in opinion. A distinguished corps assembled at Lewes for the trial, and it was they who were to be the principal protagonists.

13

The real expert evidence, which was wholly scientific, followed semi-expert evidence on the subject of the beams.

There were two beams straddling the little living hut. If Thorne's story were true Elsie Cameron must have hanged herself with a piece of washing line secured to one of these. Her physique, of course, was slight—she weighed only eight stone—but the suspension, and still more, the jerk, might well have left a mark or nick on the beam that took the strain.

Three days after Norman Thorne's arrest, Gillan accompanied by an aide from Scotland Yard had been to the hut with this idea in mind. They observed no mark on either of the beams. Then they conducted two experiments with an eight-stone weight fastened to the beams by a length of washing line. First the weight was slowly raised and swung. Next, it was placed upon a chair which was kicked away to cause a sudden jerk. Both these experiments were said to have caused marks, which Gillan pointed out when the beams were exhibited in court.

No marks before the tests; marks as a result of the tests. The deduction invited was dangerously simple—that no comparable weight could have swung from there before.

There was some disagreement about the marks themselves,

about the character of the cord, about the possible effect of a
knot in the wood. But the defence's sharpest impact upon
this part of the case was packed into two questions which
Cassels put to Gillan.

'Was anyone present representing the defence when your
experiments took place?'

'No,' the Chief Inspector said.

'Had the defence any notice of the fact that you were making the experiments?'

'No,' the Chief Inspector said.

The effect of this admission ought to have been great. Experiments of the kind described depend on tiny details : the
balancing of the weight, the adjustment of the cord, the
direction in which the chair is kicked away. Exclusion of the
defence from even passive participation was a considerable
police error, conducing to offend a sagacious jury's sense of
right and fitness.

But how far did the Thorne jury merit this description?
That is impossible to say. A jury, that must perforce sit
silent till passing judgment with a simple yea or nay, pre-
serves its secrets as no prisoner can. The latter faces a twofold exposure—by the willing tongues of others and by the
loosening of his own. He cannot hope to pass wholly un-
scathed; some part, at least, of his soul will be stripped bare.
But a jury—every jury—is protected and remote, and remains
a complete enigma for all time.

It would be foolish, then, to set at naught the evidence of
the beams, since we cannot be sure that the jury did likewise.
But one may justifiably guess that it very soon sank into the
background of their thoughts. The beams were no more than
a penny-whistle overture, soon to be drowned in the crashing
chords of the mighty one-man orchestra on which the Crown
relied.

That orchestra dispensed a dance of death, scored and conducted with diabolic brilliance.

14

In almost every big trial there is a moment of transcendent crisis; a moment, as in Priestley's *Dangerous Corner*, that determines by remote control all the events to follow. It may come early or late; it may burst unheralded or have been long foreseen.

The crisis in the trial of Norman Thorne occurred on the second afternoon and it took the shape unanimously expected. Everyone in court and millions elsewhere had been waiting breathlessly upon the time when Sir Bernard Spilsbury would get up from his place and walk with calm assurance to the box.

Spilsbury was the Crown's sole expert witness. The defence had four or five, at least three of whom could boast qualifications on a par with Spilsbury's own. They agreed between themselves and disagreed with him, so that the defence enjoyed an easy lead on a mere counting of heads. How then did Spilsbury's evidence acquire such vast importance? Why was it being said by those conversant with the courts that, unless he were completely smashed in cross-examination, Spilsbury's opinion was certain to prevail?

The answer is simple. Juries are formed from members of the public, and the British public believed Spilsbury infallible.

Spilsbury had indeed done what few can hope to do; he had become a legend in his own lifetime. To the man in the street he stood for pathology as Hobbs stood for cricket or Dempsey for boxing or Capablanca for chess. By the middle twenties he had achieved a status merited by none—

not even by himself. His pronouncements were invested with the force of dogma, and it was blasphemy to hint he might conceivably be wrong.

This situation was not of Spilsbury's seeking. It arose partly because, as Home Office pathologist, he was constantly appearing in the most sensational cases; partly because his qualities were genuinely outstanding. Even so, it was a situation fraught with danger. As Cassels was to say in his final speech for Thorne: 'We can all admire attainment, take off our hats to ability, acknowledge the high position that a man has won in his sphere. But it is a long way to go if you have to say that, when that man says something, there can be no room for error.'

It *is* a long way to go; far beyond the territories of reason. But many a jury had gone that way before, and none knew better than Cassels himself how grave was the danger they would go that way again.

15

Spilsbury answered Curtis Bennett's questions in his own easy but authoritative style. Always matter of fact and unemotional, he spoke not as a champion of a cause but rather as an objective scientist announcing his conclusions. His courtesy, though, did not obscure the fact that he regarded these conclusions as indisputable.

Spilsbury's evidence-in-chief was damning against Thorne. He had examined the remains of Elsie Cameron; taken measurements, made slides, peered at them through magnifiers. He told the jury what he had observed: eight bruises on the head, face, arms and legs, *all of them inflicted shortly before death*, and one—on the temple—caused by 'a crushing blow'. ('One of those might have done it,' Spilsbury said,

referring to a pair of Indian clubs that the police had picked
up outside Thorne's living hut.)

Spilsbury also told the jury things he had noted by their
absence : signs of asphyxiation and scars or grooving in the
neck ('such as I should be certain to find if the woman had
been hanged').

How then, in his view, did Elsie Cameron die? From
shock; shock due to the combined effect of all the bruises. 'I
found nothing else to account for death,' said the Crown
expert oracularly—and if Sir Bernard could find nothing
else, what else could there be?

The effect of this was clear. There had been no hanging
and no suicide. Somebody had attacked the girl and injured
her so badly that she died.

Such an assumption would be fatal for the defence.
Cassels could not afford to let it stand; Spilsbury did not
make a habit of retraction. So the famous advocate and the
famous expert prepared to cross sharp swords while Thorne,
who knew the truth, sat quiet as a spectator.

16

Cross-examining a man like Spilsbury calls for special gifts.
He is not only an expert in the technique of pathology; he is
also an expert in the technique of giving evidence. He is not
only a professional lecturer and theorist; he is also a professional cross-examinee. He is as used as any counsel to the
atmosphere of courts; as trained in the rules, as familiar with
the tricks. The Bar thus forfeits its customary advantage and
joins battle with him on strictly level terms.

Half the art of cross-examination resides in knowing what
not to ask. Cassels' questioning of Spilsbury was in this respect a model. Seldom did the pathologist get a chance to

enlarge, expand, or re-emphasise his views. There was no direct attack on a broad front. With infinite delicacy Cassels moved one small step at a time, sometimes at this point, sometimes at that, consolidating instantly after an advance, covering up and switching in face of a repulse. It was not showy; the sensation seekers in the gallery may even have found it dull; but those who care for true forensic skill could seek no sounder exercise in craftsmanship.

The first major issue raised was that of the bruises.

'In no case,' Cassels asked, 'did you find a breaking of the skin?'

'No.'

'Would you think it possible that a heavy club like that' —Cassels made play with one of the Indian clubs—'could produce bruises and yet not break the skin?'

'Oh, certainly,' said Spilsbury. 'It depends upon the part of the body, of course.'

'Take the bruise on the temple. Do you think it possible for that bruise to have been produced with that instrument upon that part of the face?'

'May I show you?' Spilsbury said. The club was handed to him. 'Used *this* way, and striking *that*, it would produce the bruise without breaking the skin.' He demonstrated from the box.

The Indian club swished murderously. The sound of words was momentarily replaced by the sight of action. Such moments in a courtroom have the vivid glare of lightning and Cassels made full use of the impression thus produced.

'For the purpose of that answer are you assuming a blow with force?'

'Certainly.'

'Was the bone unbroken?'

'Yes.'

'With such an article as that, the weight alone is sufficient, is it not, to break the skin?'

'Certainly not.'

'If it were to drop, say, three feet on to wood, wouldn't it produce a considerable dent?'

'It would.'

'And yet you think it might produce that bruise on the human face without breaking either the skin or the bone?'

'Only on certain parts of the face, of course.'

It will be noted that, though Spilsbury had given nothing away, Cassels had none the less improved his position. The questions had been framed to bring out the inconsistencies—apparent or real—in Spilsbury's hypothesis.

Cassels now foreshadowed his alternative. The defence would contend—and their experts would affirm—that the bruises on the body were consistent with a fall. *Their* hypothesis was that Thorne returned to the hut just before Elsie died and that she sustained the bruises as he cut her down.

No conceivable expenditure of time or energy would ever make Spilsbury subscribe to this. It would mean utterly repudiating all that he had said. But minor reconciliations might be effected between the contradictory points of view. Treading warily as ever, Cassels sounded out the ground.

'The bruise which you found under the left eye—is that as consistent with a fall as with a blow?'

'Yes,' Spilsbury conceded, 'it might possibly have been caused by a fall.'

'And the one at the back of the head?'

'That is much more likely to be the injury produced by a fall.'

Cassels had taken the two safest examples. He prudently refrained from putting further specific instances and instead

asked a portmanteau question shrewdly designed to capital-
ise his gains.

'So several of the bruises might have been caused by falling
and striking a hard surface?'

There was but one answer to this. Spilsbury said yes.

Cassels crept a little further forward.

'The fall that produced the bruise under the left eye—
would it be a heavy fall?'

'It must have been.'

'The fall that produced the bruise at the back of the head
—would that be a heavy fall?'

'Yes.'

It was modest progress, but not unsatisfactory. Many able
counsel grappling with Spilsbury have found themselves
forced back behind their starting place.

'You found no injuries to the hands?'

'No.'

'Nor the forearms?'

'No.'

Another scoring point. Its virtue is apparent if one pictures how a woman would instinctively defend herself.

To have pressed Spilsbury harder, though, on the subject
of the bruises would have been to incur an unwarrantable
risk. The other half of the art of cross-examination resides
in knowing exactly when to stop.

In any event, Cassels' hardest task still lay ahead. While
both sides agreed upon shock as the cause of death, they did
not agree upon the cause of shock. The defence case rested
on an attempt at hanging—a supposition that Spilsbury had
pooh-poohed. Once again, there could be no thought of con-
verting the Crown expert; only of inducing him to qualify
his assertions. Using every resource of experience and talent,
Cassels embarked on this unhopeful venture.

'You found the cause of death, shock?'

Spilsbury assented, quickly adding 'Shock due to injuries.'

'Did you find anything to *demonstrate* the cause of death as shock? Or did you arrive at that conclusion because you could find no other cause?'

'It *is* conclusion,' said Spilsbury pontifically. 'It must be so.'

This was not one of his most ingratiating replies. Cassels followed up.

'Finding no other cause of death on the post-mortem examination, the conclusion which you arrived at—I am not contesting it—is that death was due to shock?'

'Yes,' Spilsbury said. These, he knew, were preliminary passes; he was all vigilance for the thrust itself.

'Can you get death from shock in an attempt at hanging?'

This time the approach was naked and direct.

'No,' Spilsbury answered, 'I do not think you can.'

'Why not?'

'Because the attempt at hanging is an asphyxial condition and death occurs from that.'

Deliberately or otherwise, this begged the question. Cassels, smoothly polite, declined to be put off.

'That is when death occurs from hanging?'

'Yes.'

'I'm asking you to deal with death occurring from shock due to an *attempt* at hanging.'

Spilsbury closed with the problem.

'I don't believe death could occur instantly from an attempt at hanging.'

'You get pressure on the neck, don't you?'

'Yes.'

'A very delicate part of the human frame?'

'Yes.'

'Containing the means whereby the communications pass from the brain to the rest of the body?'

'Yes.'

'Have you considered the effect of such circumstances upon a neurotic?'

'I have.'

'Do you still exclude the possibility of death by shock brought about by an attempt at hanging?'

'Certainly. If she died immediately after the cutting down, the death would be due, not to shock, but to asphyxia from hanging.'

Spilsbury had offered one of his rare openings. Cassels was not the man to miss it.

'You are *pre-supposing*, aren't you, that in all cases of hanging death *must* be due to the hanging?'

There can be little doubt that Spilsbury would have liked to recast his previous answer. But what he had said, he had said; he never shuffled; as he granted no favours, so he asked for none.

'Yes,' he replied.

A scientist might conceivably endorse his attitude, but the average man intuitively dislikes 'pre-suppositions'. . . .

The cross-examination neared its end without the slightest falling off in tension. The closing passages, fought out in the last minutes of the long spring afternoon, revolved around a point that bid fair to prove decisive.

Were there signs of injury visible on the neck, such as one would expect from the tight grip of a cord? Spilsbury gave an unhesitating no.

'On January 17th, when you performed your post-mortem, did you examine *microscopically* any part of the neck?'

'No.'

'Why not?'

'Because it was quite unnecessary. I made a thorough examination of the neck and found no mark.'

'Because *externally* you found no mark, you did not examine further?'

'Oh yes,' said Spilsbury, 'very much further.'

'But did you examine *microscopically*?'

'No. I deeply probed the tissues.'

'By the naked eye?' Cassels insisted.

'Yes.'

'Very well. On February 24th you were present at a further post-mortem conducted by two doctors who will be called for the defence?'

'Yes.'

'Was a section taken of the neck on this occasion?'

'Yes.'

'Did you have a part of that section for the purpose of microscopic examination?'

'I did.'

'And a part was retained by the other doctors?'

'Yes.'

'Slides would have to be made of them?'

'Yes.'

The defence doctors, sitting close to counsel and following every word, framed the next question in their minds before it had been asked.

'Did not microscopic examination definitely show extravasation of blood, consistent only with pressure?'

'No.' Spilsbury spoke in uncompromising terms. There was no extravasation to be seen, he said; indeed water had by then so soaked the tissues that all the elements of blood had been destroyed.

Here the very heart of the matter had been reached. If Spilsbury was cocksure, the rest were cocksure too; they believed they could see extravasation in their slides and were waiting their turn to say so upon oath.

17

The duel between Spilsbury and Cassels ended with honours even. Gains and losses on either side were small. Conflict remained on every major point, and in some cases was sharpened, but Cassels at least had cleared and mapped the ground for the group of doctors he was going to call.

They were eminent men, these doctors; rich in distinctions and respected by their colleagues. One was Director of the pathological department at Great Ormond Street Hospital; another, formerly professor at Glasgow University, was a medical legal examiner for the Crown; a third, as Crown Analyst for the government in Dublin, had been for many years the Spilsbury of Ireland. All of them were practising pathologists; all of them were adept in the use of slides. They were as definite in saying that there *was* extravasation as Spilsbury was definite in saying that there was not. Nor did a consultation held outside court hours, at which the rival experts met and examined each others' slides, shake them any more in their opinion than it shook Sir Bernard Spilsbury in his.

Count the three as one, and you still had a stalemate. But trials, unlike chess, are not determined mathematically. There was one name in the four the jury knew; to them the rest were as remote and strange as Einstein would be to a Hottentot. Spilsbury had spoken, and the idol, though at times hard pressed, had not been dethroned. Long before the defence experts were heard, even as Spilsbury stepped down from the box, the sensitive in court could tell which way the wind was blowing.

18

But there was still a chance for Thorne to be his own salvation. A prisoner in the box has curious powers which some times cancel out all other evidence. Let him but seem a worthy, decent man; let him appear 'a chap just like ourselves'; and, whatever the evidence on the charge preferred, a jury will be glad to wipe the record clean.

Thorne was in the box almost the whole of the third day. By academic tests, he was an admirable witness. He wooed the jury with the common touch; he challenged them with unexpected frankness. 'I absolutely lost my head and became frantic.   . I was trembling from head to foot and broke into a cold perspiration. . . . I flung myself on the bed and cried like a baby.' And again : 'I was trying to build up evidence. . . . I was trying to assume a rôle of knowing nothing about it. . . . I did not go for help as I should have done and consequently I had to go forward as I did.' One says he wooed them and he challenged them, but neither was necessarily the result of conscious art. It might—it *might*—have been the overwhelming impact of the truth.

Thorne laboured, however, under two great disadvantages which were inherent in the substance of his case. He was forced to proclaim himself a fluent, brazen liar, who could act and live as well as speak his lies. He was forced to recite a fearful inventory of horrors which would arouse more repugnance than homicide itself.

These were matters that refused to be forgotten. Thorne himself was their unwilling memorial. As they heard him tell his story with a host of vivid touches, the simplest would recall a different, earlier tale : equally credible and equally embellished with plausible minutiæ—such as letters to the dead. As they watched him in the witness box, so suave and almost gentle, the stolidest would conjure up a different, earlier scene : the darkened hut, the active crouching man, the body of the girl stretched out stark naked on the floor, the hacksaw flashing over neck and limbs, the whole ghastly tableau lit to a dim red by the glow and flicker of the tiny fire.

If a man had told such clever lies before, could he not tell such clever lies again? If a man was capable of dismembering his sweetheart, was there anything, *anything*, from which he would recoil?

19

Whatever chance Thorne had was lost in cross-examination.

Curtis Bennett stood out as a master of this art. Without bluster, bullying or other resort of the third-rate, he exerted a singular authority and power. He relied on the one legitimate weapon of a cross-examiner : the form and arrangement of the questions that he put. Because his skill in this respect fell not far short of genius, he secured his objects with the minimum of words.

The first four questions he addressed to Thorne were typical of his method and his gifts.

Curtis Bennett's aim was to elicit an admission that, by the day of Elsie Cameron's death, Thorne had transferred his affections to The Other Girl. It was not a matter of concrete fact, readily ascertainable, but a delicate enquiry into a state of mind. If the question had been baldly put without due preparation, Thorne would have been free to answer as he pleased.

Now consider the technique that Curtis Bennett used, not to trap him into falsehood, but to force him into truth.

'On the morning of December 5th were you still in love with Elsie Cameron?'

To answer 'No' would be to furnish forthwith superabundant evidence of motive. Thorne answered 'Yes.'

'On the morning of December 5th were you in love with the other girl?'

This was more tricky. To answer 'No' would be immediately expedient but there was his first statement to Gillan lying convenient to Sir Henry's hand. 'Almost every night from the middle of November she came to my hut . . . we had during this time gradually fallen in love.'

It was no use flying in the face of that. Again Thorne answered 'Yes.'

'On that morning which of these two girls that you were in love with did you desire to marry?'

'I do not know I was particularly desirous of marrying any just at that time.'

The evasion served to gain only a few seconds. Curtis Bennett's next question slammed and locked the door.

'Which did you intend to marry in the future?'

Which did he intend to marry in the future? If he said Elsie, there were his letters registering reluctance ('you seem to take everything for granted'). If he said neither, he would convict himself at once of double-dyed and callous caddishness in inducing both girls on to terms of intimacy without intending to play fair with either.

'Well,' he said, 'of the two, I suppose I thought more of the other girl.'

Four questions only, and each of them as compact as it was clear. A less accomplished cross-examiner might have asked four hundred without obtaining such a definite result.

The rest of this truly searching cross-examination bore the same hall-mark of precise economy. There was, for example, the so-called 'Piper incident.' A Mrs Piper, of Crowborough, with whom Elsie had often lodged, had been called as a witness for the Crown. She had told Cassels how one night Elsie refused to go to bed and, appearing 'stupefied . . . not normal', insisted on going back to Thorne from whose farm she had just returned after being there all day.

The defence dilated on the Piper incident to support their contention that Elsie was neurotic. Curtis Bennett sought to alter the motif from mental instability to passionate affection. It took him barely a dozen questions.

'Certainly after you were engaged,' he said to Thorne, 'Elsie Cameron was deeply in love with you, wasn't she?'

'Yes.'

'And being deeply in love with you, she was anxious to be with you as much as she could?'

'Yes.'

'And may I take it that you were very pleased to see her too at that time?'

'Oh yes,' Thorne answered promptly.

So often the form of Curtis Bennett's questions practically determined the reply.

'This incident when she was staying with Mrs Piper—at that time was she deeply in love with you?'

'Yes, passionately.'

'Upon that particular day she had spent the day with you?'

'Yes.'

'And you had been very happy together?'

'Oh yes.'

'She had then been engaged to you for about nine or ten months?'

'Yes.'

'She left you about half past ten at night; you took her back to Mrs Piper, and then she insisted on coming back to you to spend the night?'

'Yes.'

'Prior to that you had been intimate, had you not?'

'Oh yes.'

The purpose of this questioning was not to ferret out new facts but to create a new *atmosphere* round facts that had already been established. Curtis Bennett did this again, with certain variants, when he came to enquire about the reasons for dismemberment.

'When you made up your mind to dismember the body, was it because you were afraid that somebody might think that you had murdered her?'

'Not necessarily so.'

Used in such a context, the word 'necessarily' implies some hidden reservation.

'I want to know,' Curtis Bennett said. 'It must have been' some very strong impulse which would make you, there and then, dismember the body. What was it?'

'I cannot really explain,' Thorne said. 'My desire was to hide it, not to dismember it.'

'You had got nothing to be ashamed of?'

'No.'

'What was it that made you do it?'

'I suppose, as I've already explained, realising the position I was in, I was desirous of hiding her body lest I should be blamed for having caused her death by any means.'

The last phrase showed that Thorne still hoped to steer clear of full surrender.

'I do not want there to be any misunderstanding,' said Curtis Bennett calmly. '"For having caused her death"— you mean for having murdered her?'

'Through any means.' Thorne clung to his straw stubbornly.

Again a key question fell neatly into place.

'Did you want to hide the fact that she had committed suicide?'

'No,' Thorne answered. 'I thought they would perhaps think that she had not committed suicide.'

'Then it was because you thought they might imagine you had murdered her?'

'Yes,' said Thorne reluctantly.

It had taken a little time to get round to it. But they were there now.

20

The cross-examination was over, but before he returned to the immunity of the dock, there was still one last ordeal in store for Thorne. Mr Justice Finlay, biting his pen abtractedly and puckering his face, detained the prisoner a moment longer in the box.

'Just one or two questions, Thorne.'

There is room for a monograph on the one or two questions that judges have, from time to time, asked in similar circumstances, and which, coming with the weight of intervention from above, exercise immeasurable influence. Any such monograph would naturally begin with Darling's interrogation of the poisoner Armstrong, and perhaps follow up with Avory's inquisition of Frederick Guy Browne.

Finlay resembled neither of these judges; he had not Darling's hard and lacquered surface, nor Avory's reserve of cold remorselessness. He was a genial, kindly, unaffected man who spoke in a mild and almost diffident way. But his questioning of Thorne could hardly have been more deadly.

'When you came back to the hut, Thorne, your first act was to cut Miss Cameron down?'

'Yes, my lord.'

'Did you make any attempt to resuscitate her?'

123

'No. I thought she was dead.'

'Did you ever think of going to fetch a doctor?'

'Not until after I got up from the table.'

'That was about an hour later?'

'I should think it was about an hour.'

Then came three short, sharp and paralysing blows.

'You never thought of fetching a doctor *at once*, on the *chance* of her being revived?'

'No, I thought at once she was dead.'

'You have heard, I suppose, that people who are apparently dead are sometimes revived?'

'Yes, I have heard of such things.'

'But you never thought of getting a doctor, and you did not get one?'

'No.'

The judge bit his pen again and nodded a dismissal.

21

There was an eloquent closing speech by Cassels, a massive reply by Curtis Bennett, a careful, thorough summing up by Finlay—perfectly fair, but not disguising his own belief that the Crown case had been proved.

At twelve minutes past five on the fifth day the jury withdrew, and at twenty minutes to six returned to pronounce the prisoner guilty.

22

Many murder appeals are devoid of substance; few have any real hope of success. But Norman Thorne's application for leave to appeal at least raised a novel and interesting point.

The Criminal Appeal Act of 1907 (which, among other things, founded the Court of Criminal Appeal) provides that where any question arising on appeal involves scientific investigation or expert knowledge either it may be referred to a Special Commissioner for enquiry and report, or else a skilled assessor may be appointed to assist the court. Although the best part of two decades had passed, these powers had never previously been invoked. It was the defence's argument on appeal that they precisely fitted a case like Norman Thorne's. The bruises, the neck marks, the state of Elsie Cameron's nerves and mind, were all put forward as proper subjects for the special procedure which the Act envisaged.

There was much to be said for the defence's proposition. The whole trial may have turned on the interpretation of a slide showing a fragment of the skin of a person three months dead. Expert One looks at his slide and says he can see nothing. Expert Two looks at his and says he can see something—and the something he can see is extravasation of blood. Expert One looks at the slide of Expert Two and says, ah yes, he sees what the other means; there *is* something there, but it is not extravasation; it is the degenerated remains of some sebaceous glands.

Is any layman competent to judge between them? Should any man's life be at the mercy of such a judgment? If there could ever be a case for a Commissioner or assessor, was it not the case that now occupied the Court?

How a Commissioner would have reported, or an assessor advised, is a point which can only offer material for conjecture. They were never given an opportunity to show. The appeal court of three judges—two of whom were not among the ablest—dismissed the application without calling on the Crown. The usual petition was presented and refused, and in due course, like his jilted love, Thorne died a violent death.

23

No one now will ever know what happened in Thorne's living hut that winter evening many years ago. Did he, as the jury evidently believed, wilfully murder Elsie Cameron to avoid the unwelcome necessity of marriage and free himself for pursuit of a new passion? Or was there a struggle when he tried to leave the hut, with this dreadful but unpremeditated consequence? Or—and this is the most terrible alternative—did Thorne in the last resort speak nothing but the truth?

One thing alone is certain. However Elsie Cameron died, it was Thorne who slashed and hacked her corpse and cunningly concealed the severed fragments. Assuming that this had never been found out, one is tempted to speculate on what he meant to do. Perhaps, after a decent lapse of time, he would have gone abroad and lost his identity in some far-off land. Perhaps he would have wed the other girl and moved from his farm to less evocative surroundings. Perhaps he would have stayed on where he was, feeding his chickens, attending Sunday school, and sleeping sound and dreamlessly at night while Elsie mouldered in the quiet earth.

Any and every course would have required a heart of marble and a nerve of steel. Both these attributes were possessed by Thorne, as he had proved in the weeks before arrest. It is this inhuman streak in the man's character that bedevils assessment of the evidence and makes him one of most baffling of all convicted murderers.

EDITH THOMPSON

1

THE case of Edith Thompson caught the British legal system on its weakest side. That system is an admirable instrument for ascertaining *facts*; it is much less efficient in dealing with psychology. The fault lies less with the machinery itself than with those who operate and supervise it. Imagination is the lawyer's bugbear and literalism his occupational disease. For him life is governed not by passions but by statutes, and he likes to interpret individual actions as if each had its origin in icy reason. The dismal consequences may be seen in a string of bad decisions. The human mind cannot be read like a charter-party or a bill of sale.

Great advocates, of course, are in a class apart. Their success with witnesses and their command over juries are based upon the most penetrating insight. A Carson or a Russell, a Hastings or a Birkett, possesses powers to grasp and understand the thoughts of others which sometimes seem to verge on the uncanny. But in any generation great advocates are few, while stereotyped lawyers are always two a penny. Rigid, narrow, formalistic and self-righteous, they are particularly ill-suited to present or sit in judgment on a case which calls for sympathetic knowledge of the world.

2

Edith Thompson was charged with murdering her husband, but not by direct act, and not alone. At no time was it suggested that she played a physical part; the Crown acknow-

ledged that she did not lift a finger. Their case was that she
urged murder on her lover; that the latter in her presence
carried out the wicked deed; and that these two factors
taken in conjunction made her under English law a principal in the crime.

Much of this thesis was not seriously contested. The lover
at least admitted having fought and stabbed the husband;
Mrs Thompson admitted being present when he did; the
legal proposition was unarguably sound. So if, as appeared
likely all along, Mrs Thompson's lover was found guilty of
murder, her own neck would be forfeit if the jury were convinced that she had spurred him to it with malice and design.
This in its turn depended upon whether, in their estimation,
words that she had used constituted—and were *meant* to
constitute—incitement.

Words exist to communicate a meaning. But the meaning
inferred by the listener or the reader is not always that intended by the speaker or the writer. There are primary and
secondary senses; there are overtones and undertones that
are idiosyncratic; there is hyperbole and satire; there is un-
trammelled fantasy and deliberate make-believe. It is absurd
to suppose that every phrase should be literally construed.
The man who says 'I thought I'd die' when talking of an
illness may well mean that he really anticipated death, but
the man who says 'I thought I'd die' about a comic story is
merely conveying that it gave him a good laugh. It is only
by reference to the character of their author and to the circumstances in which they were employed that one can hope
to extract the true significance of words. They must be related, not only to the dictionary, but to life.

The lawyers in the Thompson trial brought dictionaries
to court, but carefully closed the doors upon the teeming
life outside.

3

Few are unfamiliar with the outline of the tragedy that cast a City bookkeeper and Ilford housewife for a rôle befitting Bernhardt or Réjane. Beneath a commonplace plot of jealousy and intrigue lay hidden drama of such spiritual intensity that it fascinates even those most repelled by crime. The story has been told by many practised pens, and several works of fiction owe to it their inspiration. But the latter, not improperly, have claimed artistic licence; recapitulation of the facts may not be out of place.

Late in the evening of October 3rd, 1922, Mrs Thompson was walking along a quiet road in Ilford with her husband, a respectable shipping clerk, at her side. They were returning from a visit to a West End theatre. As they neared their home, a man overtook them; he pushed Mrs Thompson to one side, stabbed her husband several times and swiftly disappeared. Mrs Thompson shrieked and ran for help. A doctor lived near by; he hurried to the spot, but Percy Thompson was already beyond aid.

The police arrived, the body was removed, and a Sergeant escorted Mrs Thompson home. She was much distressed and apparently bewildered. She spoke as though her husband had had some kind of fit, and made no mention of an attack or an attacker.

But meanwhile at the mortuary they were examining the corpse. Natural death could be instantly ruled out. There were cuts in the ribs, on the chin and lower jaw, and at the right elbow on the inside of the arm. At the back of the head there were two vicious-looking stabs, one of which had severed a great artery in the neck. It was this last wound that had caused Percy Thompson's death and established beyond doubt that the hapless man was murdered.

Taking all into account, it was difficult to believe that Mrs Thompson had told them the whole truth. Not unnaturally the police began to wonder whether the murder had its roots in her domestic life.

An enquiry on these lines immediately bore fruit. It led them to a young man by name of Frederick Bywaters, a P. and O. employee of excellent repute. They discovered, with commendable energy and speed, that this boy—he was but twenty—had been linked with Mrs Thompson in one form or another for a considerable time. He had known her family since he was a schoolboy. In 1921 he had been on holiday with the Thompsons and afterwards had stayed with them for several weeks at Ilford. He had left as a result of a dispute with Percy Thompson about the latter's behaviour to his wife. Since then he had corresponded with Mrs Thompson when he was at sea and seen her surreptitiously when he was at home. He had in fact met her in an Aldersgate Street tea shop less than seven hours before the murder was committed.

The police concluded—and their conclusion was well founded—that Frederick Bywaters was Edith Thompson's lover. He was obviously a man who 'might be able to assist them in their investigations.' On the evening of October 4th Bywaters was taken to the police station for questioning.

When he got there he found, among others, Mr Wensley —Inspector Wensley of the Steinie Morrison case, much older now and more exalted in the hierarchy, but just as shrewd and eagle-eyed as ever. While Bywaters denied all connection with the crime and adopted an aggressive, irritated air, Wensley was scrutinising him minutely. 'There are spots on the sleeve of your overcoat,' he suddenly remarked. 'They look to me like blood.'

The overcoat was confiscated for chemical examination

(which ultimately confirmed the detective's diagnosis) and Bywaters, still protesting, was provisionally detained.

A little later the same evening the police brought Mrs Thompson to the station. She was not officially placed under restraint, but, in Superintendent Wensley's felicitous phrase, 'it was *convenient* to have her at hand while we were looking for something that would give us a line'. So, unbeknown to each other, in the interests of 'convenience', lover and mistress slept under the same roof.

Mrs Thompson had not implicated Bywaters at all. Next day, when she was invited to give 'further information', she still maintained she had seen nobody approach. Bywaters for his part made no change in his attitude. The enquiry, which had opened with such impetus and promise, was now merely ticking over and showed signs of being stalled.

Late that afternoon, though, an incident occurred that set the wheels back again in motion. It has been described by Wensley as 'a dramatic interlude' and by at least one famous lawyer as 'a little trap'. Whether by accident or whether by design, Mrs Thompson was conducted along a corridor where, through an open doorway, she caught a glimpse of Bywaters.

The shock cracked her nerve. She broke down, crying, 'Oh God, oh God, what can I do? Why did he do it? I did not want him to do it.' Mrs Thompson was at this moment admittedly hysterical and it is not without interest to dwell upon her words. 'Why did he do it? *I did not want him to do it.*' That could not have been a calculated stratagem; that was uttered in the agony of impulse, a cry wrung against her will out of the woman's heart. Yet one would be hard put to it to draft another sentence expressing so precisely the gist of her defence.

But, understandably, the police were not concerned with

her defence; they were only concerned with the effect of this on Bywaters. 'Why did he do it?' That was all the lead required. The notebooks were whipped out, the formal warning given, and within a few minutes Mrs Thompson signed a statement naming Bywaters as the man who had 'scuffled' with her husband.

From that moment Bywaters was halfway to the gallows. Faced with this complete reversal of the situation, he made a further statement from which he never struggled free.

'I waited', he said, 'for Mrs Thompson and her husband. . . . I pushed her to one side, also pushing him further up the street. I said to him, "You have got to separate from your wife." He said, "No." I said, "You will have to." We struggled. I took my knife from my pocket and we fought and he got the worst of it. Mrs Thompson must have been spellbound for I saw nothing of her during the fight. I ran away. . . . The reason I fought Thompson was because he never acted like a man to his wife. He always seemed several degrees lower than a snake. I loved her and could not go on seeing her leading that life. I did not intend to kill him. I only meant to injure him.' Bywaters prefaced this statement with an important affirmation : 'Mrs Edith Thompson was not aware of my movements on Tuesday evening, October 3rd.'

It may have been true, but one should say this about Bywaters; he tried his best to shield Mrs Thompson (and continued to do so gallantly, though clumsily, to the end).

His efforts, however, met with no success. The police had made their minds up to bring them both to trial, and each was duly charged with Percy Thompson's murder.

4

The case against Bywaters was simple, factual and tolerably clear. Apart from noting that on trial he introduced somewhat belatedly the theme of self-defence, it need not concern us further.

The case against Mrs Thompson had at first been non-existent. All that could be said against her was that she had lied in a futile attempt to protect and cover Bywaters. That might make her an accessory after the fact. It could not bring her into danger of the rope.

What could? At the Old Bailey the judge was to express it in these words. 'You will not convict her,' he enjoined the jury, 'unless you are satisfied that she and he *agreed* that this man should be murdered when he could be, and she *knew* he was going to do it, and *directed* him to do it, and *by arrangement between them* he was doing it.'

There had been nothing whatever in Mrs Thompson's conduct to suggest that she possessed foreknowledge of the crime. She had seemed serene and normal to companions at the theatre. She had made frantic exertions to procure medical aid. Most striking touch of all, a householder who lived close by the scene of the assault had heard her cry, 'Oh don't! Oh don't!' in a most piteous tone. If that was merely play-acting to impress an unseen audience, to dissociate herself from Bywaters' attack, why did she say afterwards she had seen nobody there?

How could the police prove Mrs Thompson's complicity? How could they establish the existence of a plot? How could they show, with the material available, that Bywaters had acted at her bidding and direction? The answer is, they couldn't; and if nothing had turned up the prosecution of the woman would have been quietly withdrawn. No self-respecting counsel would have agreed to open it.

But something did turn up. In a routine inspection of Bywaters' belongings the police unearthed and seized sixty-five letters written by Mrs Thompson to her lover and sometimes couched in extraordinary terms.

These letters became the salient feature of the trial and were certainly the arbiter of Edith Thompson's fate. One must now turn aside from the action of the story. It is the letters one must study—the letters and their writer, for they throw light on her just as she throws light on them.

5

Edith Thompson was no ordinary woman of the suburbs, occupied and satisfied by the dreary daily round. She was a remarkable and complex personality, endowed with signal attributes of body and of mind. She had intelligence, vitality, a natural grace and poise, sensitiveness, humour and—illumining all these—that quintessential femininity that fascinates the male. If the list had only ended there her tale would have been different; she might not have found happiness, she would not have met her doom. But there was one further element in Edith Thompson's make-up; she had the instincts of an artist and, lacking the artist's outlet, she used them in a manner that led to her undoing.

The friends and acquaintances of her own social circle doubtless envied Edith Thompson the good fortune of her lot. She had a sober, thrifty husband; a pleasant little home; a responsible and well-paid job she had held for several years. Indeed, she earned as much as or perhaps more than did her husband, which could hardly fail to gratify her taste for independence. 'She is a very capable woman,' said her employer at the trial. 'With her business capacity she could get employment anywhere.'

But the comfortable monotony of Ilford and the City did not appease the restlessness in Edith Thompson's soul. There was nothing in either to fire imagination, as the artist in her so avidly desired. Her existence was prosaic and uneventful; her husband unresponsive and humdrum. She lived in and through novels which she devoured till they were part of her; but what were other people's novels, after all? Time was slipping by; in 1921 she had been married six whole years; soon, all too soon, she would be an old, old woman without even the solace of remembered joys. Unconsciously but ardently she sought some focus, some rallying point and symbol of her appetite for life.

She found it in Bywaters. He was eight years her junior; hardly more than a youth, but conspicuously virile and handsome in a heavy, sensual way. She raised this earthy lover to the heights. She breathed into their love a flame so fierce that even Bywaters was transported and transfigured. It was Antony and Cleopatra, it was Romeo and Juliet, it was every great romance in the chronicles of time.

Fact and reality were no more than a cue for the exuberant fancy of Edith Thompson's mind. When the true story fell short she improved it in her letters, until it was a story worth an artist's while; a story replete with sacrifice and violence, with colourful suitors and relentless poisoning wives, with all the trappings of the novels she had read and all the delirium of the love she had imagined. This was the driving force behind the famous letters which the prosecution used to get their writer hanged.

One does not seek to whitewash Mrs Thompson nor to try to gloss over whatever were her sins. But none can understand her who fails to realise that she was a woman of quality whose talents were frustrated.

6

A notion has found currency that Mrs Thompson's letters contained little else but equivocal and sinister allusions. This notion runs quite contrary to the fact.

From August 1921 to October 1922 she wrote to Bywaters several scores of times. The letters she received from him during the same period were, with three exceptions, prudently destroyed. Of the sixty-five from her remaining in existence, more than half were not introduced in evidence by the Crown—because there was nothing in them, no reference, no phrase, which could possibly be quoted to Mrs Thompson's detriment. Of those that were exhibited— thirty-two in all—only fractions consisted of disputable stuff; more than nine-tenths was as transparently innocent of crime as is the private talk of lovers anywhere on earth.

Most love letters, however skilled the writer, are unreadable except by those to whom they are addressed. In making herself an exception to this rule, Mrs Thompson gave a further proof of her peculiar gifts.

Sometimes she looked forward to Bywaters' return :

It is four whole weeks today since you went and there is still another four more to go—I wish I could go to sleep for all that time and wake up just in time to dress and sit by the fire—waiting for you to come in on March 18th. I don't think I'd come to meet you darlint it always seems so ordinary and casual for me to see you after such a long time in the street, I shall always want you to come straight to our home and take me in both your arms.

Sometimes she looked back into the past, half gratified, half fearful:

I'll always love you—if you are dead—if you have left me—even if you don't still love me—I shall always love you.   If things should go badly with us, I shall always have this past year to look back upon and feel that 'Then I lived!' I never did before and never shall again.

Sometimes she is despondent and reproachful: he does not write (or 'talk' as she always calls it) often or expansively enough.

What an utterly absurd thing to say to me, 'Don't be too disappointed.'

You can't possibly know what it feels like to wait and wait each day—every little hour—for something that means life to you and then not get it.

You told me from Dover that you were going to talk to me for a long time at Marseilles and now you put it off to Port Said.

You force me to conclude that the life you lead away from England is all absorbing, that you haven't time nor inclination to remember England or anything England holds.

There were at least five days you could have talked to me about—if you only spared me five minutes out of each day. But what is the use of me saying all this—it's the same always—I'm never meant to have anything I expect or want. If I am unjust—I'm sorry—but I can't feel anything at present—only just as if I have had a blow on the head and I'm stunned—the disappointment—no, more than that—the utter despair is too much to bear—I would sooner go under today than anything.

All I can hope is that you will never feel like I do today.   Perhaps I ought not to have written this, but how I feel and what I think I must tell you always.

There is no mistaking the dynamic of her passion, nor her untutored power of conveying it in words.

Let's be ourselves—always darlingest there can never be any misunderstandings then—it doesn't matter if it's harder—you said it was our Fate against each other— we only have will power when we are in accord, not when we are in conflict—tell me if this is how you feel. With you darlint there can never be any pride to stand in the way—it melts in the flame of a great love—I finished with pride, oh a long time ago.

The City bookkeeper's pen flew over the paper; she was buoyant, depressed, ecstatic, apprehensive. But over and over again a bogey rose to scare her. He was twenty. She was twenty-eight.

My veriest own lover, I always think about 'the difference'. . . . Sometimes when I'm happy for a little while I forget—but I always remember very soon. . . . Shall I always be able to keep you? Eight years is such a long time—it's not now—it's later—when I'm Joan and you're not grown old enough to be Darby. When you've got something that you've never had before and something that you're so happy to have found—you're always afraid of it flying away—that's how I feel about your love.

Don't ever take your love away from me darlint. I never want to lose it and live.

Life, it is clear, inflicted many torments on this burning spirit with aspirations unfulfilled. But there was always one escape.

Aren't books a consolation and a solace? We ourselves die and live in the books we read while we are reading them and then when we have finished, the books die and we live—or exist—just drag on through years and years, until when? Who knows—I'm beginning to think no one does—no, not even you and I, we are not the shapers of our destinies.

I'll always love you darlint.

'We are not the shapers of our destinies.' It has a terrible and prophetic ring.

She wrote always a great deal about the books she was reading or wanted him to read. She did not merely tell him whether she had enjoyed them; she did not even confine herself to mentioning the theme; but habitually made minute analyses of the characters and discussed the motive springs that underlay their actions. She formed and ventilated fervid views about these fictional creations.

The man Lacosta in *The Trail of '98* . . . he was so vile I didn't think of him at all, and I'd rather not now darlint.

I enjoyed John Chilcote ever so much, I admire the force in the man that made him tackle such a position against such odds.

No I don't agree with you about Bella Donna darlint—
I hate her—hate to think of her—I don't think other
people made her what she was—that sensual pleasure-
loving greedy Bella Donna was always there. If she had
originally been different—a good man like Nigel would
have altered her darlint—she never knew what it was
to be denied anything—she never knew 'goodness' as
you and I know it—she was never interested in a good
man—or any man unless he could appease her sensual
nature. . . . She doesn't seem a woman to me—she
seems abnormal—a monster.

A reply to some stricture on the ending of a novel shows the
depth of her absorption in imaginary worlds.

The endings are not the story. . . . Do as I do. Forget
the end, lose yourself in the characters and the story,
and in your own mind make your own end.

Such was the prevailing mental climate of these letters that
are passed down to posterity as the effusions of a murderess.
One must now examine a few specific passages selected by
the Crown as indicative of guilt. These passages of course
should not be read in isolation. They ought to be read—as
the lawyers did not read them—within the context of the
letters as a whole. Then and only then one has a chance of
judging whether, according to the precept she herself laid
down, it was in her own mind that Mrs Thompson made
her end.

7

The compromising words, faithfully copied into counsels'
briefs by thrilled and awestruck typists, were singularly art-

less if they ministered to crime. Does a cold-blooded con-
spirator, pondering every move, ignore the risk of letters
getting lost or going astray? Does a party to a plot, receiving reckless letters, studiously preserve the evidence of guilt?

Such modifying reflections usually come as afterthoughts.
First interpretations are rigorously literal. One can well
imagine detective eyes popping out of detective heads when
they originally lighted upon passages like this.

> I used the 'light bulb' three times, but the third time—
> he found a piece—so I have given it up—until you come
> home.

Who is 'he'? Who could it be except the lady's husband?
What was the 'light bulb' and in what way was it used?
The light bulb; he found a piece. Wasn't powdered glass a
familiar form of poisoning?

As they read on, letter after letter, Scotland Yards's suspicions deepened into certainty.

> I was buoyed up with the hope of the 'light bulb' and I
> used a lot—big pieces too—not powdered—and it has
> no effect—I quite expected to be able to send that
> cable—but no, nothing has happened from it. . . . I
> know I feel I shall never get him to take a sufficient
> quantity of anything bitter.

References to a bitter taste frequently recur.

> He puts great stress on the fact of the tea tasting bitter
> 'as if something had been put in it', he says. Now I
> think whatever else I try in it again will still taste bitter
> —he will recognise it and be more suspicious still and
> if the quantity is still not successful it will injure any
> chance I may have of trying when you come home.

Though other extracts gained equal prominence at the trial, one surmises that in the initial stage these furnished the key. They laid a firm-looking foundation for a practicable theory which was confidently applied to unriddle ambiguities. By the aid of this explanatory touchstone, each could be resolved to favour the Crown case.

> This time really will be the last you will go away—like things are, won't it? We said it before darlint I know and we failed . . . but there will be no failure this next time darlint, there mustn't be—I'm telling you—if things are the same again then I'm going with you—wherever it is—if it's to sea—I am coming too—and if it's to nowhere—I'm also coming darlint. You'll never leave me behind again, never, *unless things are different.*

What did Mrs Thompson mean, 'unless things are different'? Obvious, said the Crown; she meant, unless we've done the murder.

> I ask you again to think out all the p*lans and methods* for me.

What did Mrs Thompson mean, 'plans and methods'? Obvious, said the Crown; she meant ways and means of murder.

> Yes, darlint, you are jealous of him—but I want you to be—he has the right by law to all that you have the right to by nature and by love—yes darlint be jealous, so much that you will *do something desperate.*

What did Mrs Thompson mean, 'do something desperate'? Obvious, said the Crown; she meant, brace yourself for murder.

If some of these inferences seem prejudiced or forced, this must be said in fairness to the Crown. Make one assumption, and it is true that all else follows. If what one terms the key passages are taken at face value; if every statement in them is accepted as a fact; if each of the incidents described by Mrs Thompson is assumed to have occurred exactly as she says—then there can be only one possible conclusion. Mrs Thompson had herself tried to kill her husband and had been imploring Bywaters to succeed where she had failed.

That was the conclusion, granted the assumption. But was the assumption justified that Mrs Thompson never indulged in flights of fancy and that all her reporting was meticulously exact?

The trial, so far as she was personally concerned, became a committee of inquiry to decide this single point.

8

The case of The King against Bywaters and Thompson began at the Old Bailey on December 6th, 1922. A row of well-known counsel faced Mr Justice Shearman. Sir Henry Curtis Bennett, then rivalling Marshall Hall in public esteem as a defender, was instructed to appear on behalf of Mrs Thompson. Mr Cecil Whiteley, an agile-minded and energetic advocate, undertook the well-nigh hopeless task of representing Bywaters. The Crown had thought fit to nominate a Law Officer—a move which secured for them the right to the last word. Their choice fell on Thomas Inskip, a learned abstract lawyer, who in the whirligig of politics had been made Solicitor-General. This case was not, one may conjecture, an assignment Inskip relished. His capacities were misemployed, his shortcomings exposed. He displayed as little grasp of human impulses and frailties as he later did of strategy when Minister of Defence.

Interest in the trial was not confined to those who, through craving for sensation or mere prurient curiosity, can never resist the double bait of murder and of sex. The unusual issue that had to be determined; the fact that the solution lay in the temper of a mind; a feeling that Mrs Thompson was a highly gifted woman who, innocent or otherwise, would repay attentive study—this made a gulf between the case and the average murder trial like the gulf between the average thriller and one by Graham Greene. The best, as well as the worst, were attracted into court, and some notable figures from literature and Fleet Street took their place among the audience assembled for the drama.

9

The drama opened in most undramatic circumstances.

The scene had been set and the characters introduced. Bywaters and Mrs Thompson had been brought into the dock and eyed from every angle like a pair of movie stars. The twelve who were to try them had answered to their names and all had seemed in readiness for a great forensic battle.

Then Sir Henry Curtis Bennett spoke in quiet, even tones. The judge gave a brief order. An official led the puzzled jury out of court. The defence were raising a preliminary objection; they wished to argue on a point of law.

This argument took place, as such arguments do, in a deceptive atmosphere of academic calm. Points of law are not contrived to gratify the public thirst for clamour and excitement. They may be as fateful, though, as contests more spectacular. The routine seldom varies. An erudite submission by one counsel, an erudite counter-submission by another, much reading out of large books, a Latin tag or two—and then a gentle pronouncement by the judge, which may create a precedent and terminate a life.

The significance of Sir Henry's point of law cannot be overstated. He was contending that the letters, the all-important letters, were not admissible as evidence and should be excluded from the trial.

The rules governing the admissibility of evidence are something of a mystery to the man in the street, who is apt to think of them as lawyers' hocus-pocus. This view is unwarranted. Though they sometimes seem—and sometimes are—mechanical and arbitrary in operation, such rules are based on long and rich experience of what is required to protect the individual. Reliance upon them betrays neither guilt nor weakness; it is a claim upon the birthright of a British citizen.

To invoke the aid of any rule which might shut out the letters was the plain duty of Mrs Thompson's counsel. Success in this would be decisive. There would be no evidence, no need for further argument, no element of risk. If the Crown could be deprived of the right to read and use the Correspondence bundle in Sir Thomas Inskip's brief the case against Mrs Thompson would be virtually at an end.

Curtis Bennett's submission was necessarily technical, and interesting only to scholars of the law. Briefly, he said this: that the letters, by their nature, could only throw light upon *intent*; that intent is not an issue unless there is an *act* to be explained; that the Crown could not prove, and did not set out to prove, that Mrs Thompson committed any act in the murder. Hence, said Curtis Bennett, the letters were irrelevant; hence they ought not to be admitted into evidence.

'But,' said the judge, 'it is alleged that the lady was

present at the murder. Are the letters not *then* evidence of her felonious intent?'

'No, my lord,' said Curtis Bennett, 'not on this indictment. I agree', he added, 'that I should not be able to object to the letters on the *second* indictment.'

(In fact five separate charges stood against Mrs Thompson—charges of murder, of soliciting to murder, of inciting to conspire to murder, of administering poison with intent to murder, and of administering a destructive thing with intent to murder. The last four had been deferred pending the verdict on the first, though it might be assumed that in the event of an acquittal the Crown would not proceed with the subsidiary charges.)

Cecil Whiteley who, at Bywaters' desire, accorded all support throughout to Mrs Thompson's case, also objected to the admission of the letters. In reply, the Solicitor-General said that the letters were evidence not merely of intent, but of incitement. 'This is a crime', he declared, 'where one hand struck the blow, and we want to show by these letters that Mrs Thompson's mind conceived and incited it.'

The judge accepted this submission and rejected those of the defence. 'The question is a very difficult one,' he said, 'but I think that these letters are admissible.'

It was a decision firmly based in law, but it proved in the long run inimical to justice.

10

So the letters were 'in', as lawyers say colloquially, and the Crown exploited them down to the last syllable. The Solicitor-General made them the burden of his somewhat undistinguished opening address. At the prosecution's close they were read in their entirety—a proceeding which occupied most of the second day. They were put piecemeal to the prisoners when they went into the box; not only to Mrs Thompson, but to Bywaters as well. She was invited to explain what she had meant, he to explain what he had taken her to mean.

In the course of this repetitive and time-consuming process the jury could have learnt the key passages by heart, together with the innuendoes proffered by the Crown. But there was another consequence that favoured the defence. As the background gradually filled in and a fuller, clearer picture of the tragedy took shape, much that had been quoted acquired a fresh perspective.

It transpired, for instance, that the lovers, faced with the barrier of Mrs Thompson's marriage, had together discussed the possibility of suicide. One strongly suspects that this was just another piece of Mrs Thompson's mania for self-dramatisation, and that there was no real intention of carrying it out. But the vital point to mark is that it was at least *discussed*; there were expressions in the letters not susceptible of any other meaning.

All I could think about last night was that compact we made. Shall we have to carry it through? Don't let us darlint. *I'd like to live* and be happy—not for a little while but for all the while you still love me. Death seemed horrible last night—when you think about it darlint, *it does seem a horrible thing to die, when you have never been happy really happy for one little minute.*

They had also canvassed the idea of persuading Percy Thompson to separate from his wife.

I said exactly what you told me to and he replied that he knew *that's what I wanted and he was not giving it to me*—it would make things far too easy for both of you (meaning you and me) especially for you he said.

Mrs Thompson had been ready—or had said that she was ready—to run away without warning from her husband and her home.

Darlingest find me a job abroad. I'll go tomorrow and not say I was going to a soul and not have one little regret.

Suicide. Separation. Leaving England with her lover. Might it have been these objects, and not murder at all, that had taken such a grip of Mrs Thompson's mind? 'I ask you to think out the plans and methods for me.' Plans and methods for killing her husband—or herself? 'You'll never leave me again unless things are different.' Different because Percy Thompson had been killed—or because he had at last agreed to separation? 'Be jealous so that you will do something desperate.' Murder the husband—or take away the wife? It became glaringly, almost embarrassingly, apparent that many of the phrases which the Crown had singled out were open to quite credible alternative constructions.

But this merely trimmed the edges of the sprawling, straggling case which the Solicitor-General had placed before the jury. The key passages were not affected nor dislodged. 'I used the light bulb three times, but the third time he found a piece.' 'I feel I shall never get him to take a sufficient quantity.' 'Whatever else I try in it will still taste bitter.' No stretching of the sense could make these refer to suicide, or matrimonial separation, or slipping off abroad. For these there was but one excuse conformable with innocence—that they were fabulous, air-drawn, fantastical inventions, the figments of Mrs Thompson's over-fertile brain.

This in a sentence was the case for the defence. It was not a case that could be built up far in cross-examination. It was not a case that could be tested much by pondering the facts. The problem was to estimate a woman's imagination, and to solve it the jury were thrown back upon their own.

There were, however, two solid tangible realities to guide them in their psychopathological explorations.

11

The first was more revealing of her character than anything Mrs Thompson could have said about herself.

In one of her letters she had treated Bywaters to a particularised description of a family upset. Her sister Avis had informed her, she declared, that her indignant husband had been down to see her father and told him 'everything—about all the rows we have had over you. But'—observe the painstaking reverence for detail—'she did not mention he said anything about the first real one on August 1st—so I suppose he kept that back to suit his own ends.'

Mrs Thompson's father (Avis was alleged to have reported) had expressed an intention of 'talking to' his daughter. 'But I went down and nothing happened.   I told Avis I should tell them off if they said anything to me.'

Now Mrs Thompson's father and sister were witnesses at the trial—the latter for the defence, the former for the Crown. Curtis Bennett questioned them both about this highly circumstantial story.

'Did Thompson', he asked the father, 'ever come to you and make a complaint about the conduct of Bywaters with your daughter?'

'Never,' was the reply. 'That is the purest imagination.'

'Is there any truth whatever in this story?'

'There is none. As a matter of fact, I had no idea that my daughter and her husband were not on good terms.'

The sister in turn was equally emphatic. Curtis Bennett read aloud the passage from the letter with its constant and plausible mention of herself. 'I rang Avis. . . .' 'Dad was going to talk to me, Avis said. . . .' 'I told Avis I should tell them off. . . .'

'Is there any truth in that at all?' Curtis Bennett enquired of Avis.

'There is none whatever.'

'Did you ever tell her anything like that?'

'I did not.'

'Did it ever happen?'

'It did not.'

It had never happened and Avis had never told her. Yet Mrs Thompson's account of this imaginary incident has a realism few can infuse into the truth. What a little miracle of unconscious art prompted that reference to 'the first real row' in August! Who could believe that a story so minutely related wasn't true? Almost certainly it half convinced its author, and this I have no doubt was its principal design. More important than anything, more important even than her hold upon her lover, was the endless romantic tale that Edith Thompson spun, and deep in the heart of which she lived a life apart.

12

The second signpost was erected by a witness of great influence whose word, as we have seen before, was magical with juries.

There had been an exhumation of Percy Thompson'

body with the express object of examining for poison. Bernard Spilsbury conducted the post-mortem.

He found precisely nothing. There was no trace or sign of any poison. There was no trace or sign of any glass. There was no indication that either one or the other had ever been administered.

The Crown produced this tremendous piece of evidence in a shabby, grudging, discreditable way. They tried to make it seem that the post-mortem was nugatory by stressing that all traces might have disappeared. But the exhumation wasn't made without hope of finding something; the most famous of pathologists had said that there was nothing; and the Crown would have done better to have faced up to the fact and not tried to look as though they expected nothing anyway.

All those pieces of glass ('I used quite a lot'), all those light bulbs, all that stuff that tasted bitter. Like the story about Avis and the family upset, its unaffected naturalness insisted on belief. But Science—unimpressionable Science— using its steely, material approach, could find no evidence that this transpontine melodrama had ever been performed except in Mrs Thompson's mind.

13

The Crown case had closed. Bywaters had given evidence with the pugnacity of despair and tightened the noose already slung around his throat. Now Curtis Bennett faced a grave and vexing question. Ought Mrs Thompson to go into the box?

Criminal charges must be strictly proved. It is not enough for the Crown to say, 'Look, we have kicked up a great dust of suspicion; you, the accused, are bound to lay that dust; you must take the oath and submit yourself to cross-examination.' A more exacting onus lies upon the Crown: to establish guilt beyond reasonable doubt. If they are incapable of doing that unassisted, the prisoner will be well advised to hold his peace.

As matters stood, had the Crown discharged this onus on the trial of Mrs Thompson? Their case against her was based solely on her letters. Suppose Curtis Bennett had adopted a bold line; suppose he had called no evidence, addressed the jury, pointed to Mrs Thompson's bent for vivid storytelling, and challenged them to convict her on the letters by themselves. Would they have dared?

Curtis Bennett's dilemma has been that of many advocates since the Criminal Evidence Act was passed in 1898. Until then, as noted in the case of Mrs Maybrick, no prisoner could give sworn evidence in his own behalf. That often placed him at a disadvantage—a disadvantage that the Act was intended to remove. But in removing one, it introduced another. In theory, the prisoner now enjoys an option; he gives evidence or not, exactly as he likes. But in practice, his election to keep out of the box will generally result in adverse comment by the judge and an assumption by the jury that he has got something to hide.

All this had to be weighed. If the final decision had been wholly Curtis Bennett's, if his client had placed herself entirely in his hands, one is disposed to guess that she would never have been called. But heavy pressure was brought to bear upon his judgment.

Mrs Thompson herself had decided to give evidence. She would hear no advice and brook no denial.

14

Mrs Thompson's appearance in the box did her irreparable harm.

It was not that she offended in style or personality; nothing could divest her of her native distinction. It was not that she brought forward any new and dreadful fact; hardly once during her testimony did she break onto fresh ground. She certainly did not succumb to the acumen of Inskip; his cross-examination, although long, was uninspired.

The cause of Mrs Thompson's failure as a witness must be sought in some sphere less obvious than these. I myself think that, despite the seeming paradox, it was due to the acuteness and the strength of her perceptions.

One may follow the thought process that set her on her course. The jury must be made to see the motive for the letters. She knew the motive best, so it was best that she should tell them. Looking on each day from the seclusion of the dock, or brooding at night in the fastness of her cell, she felt certain—*certain*—she could make them understand. But once face to face with the unforthcoming twelve, hope drained suddenly like blood out of her heart. It is my belief she realised, in the moment of essaying it, the utter futility of her self-appointed task. She learned the last agony afflicting those on trial—knowing it is impossible to get oneself believed.

How could she put it? How could she find words? How could she convince them that those letters to her lover consisted in part of sheer escapist fiction, invented and written to compensate a little for the drab dull existence to which the twelve belonged?

She perceived this and she faltered. Her mind refused to act. She pathetically took refuge in the barest of denials.

'Did you ever put anything in your husband's tea?'

'No.'

'Did he ever complain that his tea tasted bitter?'

'No.'

'Did you ever intend to use an electric light bulb?'

'No.'

'Did you ever use one?'

'Never.'

But why write and say you had? That was the point, and it was never really dealt with. Vaguely and feebly, when pressed upon the matter, Mrs Thompson talked of 'holding Bywaters' affection'. This does not convey to me the ring of authenticity, and doubtless it appeared even more inadequate at the time. It sounds hollow and would leave the jury still demanding, why? Why the *fantasy*? Why the *make-believe*?

Mrs Thompson could not tell them—she who knew so well.

15

Responsibility lay heavy on Sir Henry Curtis Bennett. Four days of prim sententiousness and virtuous moralising could not fail to magnify that attitude of censoriousness so readily adopted by humans in the mass. It was on the whole an unfavourable atmosphere in which Mrs Thompson's counsel began his final speech.

He made an admirable and sustained attempt to dissipate this atmosphere, to rescue his client from the dead hand of the law. He projected Mrs Thompson as she could not project herself.

'Am I right or wrong', he asked, 'in saying that this woman is one of the most extraordinary personalities that you or I have ever met? Bywaters truly described her, did he not, as a woman who lived a sort of life I don't suppose any of you live—an extraordinary life of make-believe in an atmosphere created by something which has made an impression on her brain. She reads a book and she imagines herself one of the characters. She is always leading an extraordinary life of novels.'

At last the real Mrs Thompson was being put before the jury. With unpretentious force Curtis Bennett drew a portrait of a woman whose mental horizon did not end at Chancery Lane. He took the letters themselves as the best corroboration of this reading of her mind.

'Have you ever heard more beautiful language of love? Such things have been very seldom put by pen upon paper. *This* is the woman you have to deal with, not some ordinary woman. She is one of those striking personalities that stand out.'

Tactfully the defender endeavoured to diminish the whipped-up prejudice of moral disapproval.

'Thank God,' he cried, 'this is not a court of morals, because if everybody immoral was brought here I would never be out of it, nor would you. . . . We are men and women of the world.'

When Mrs Thompson had stepped down from the box, the darkness of doom enwrapped her like a mantle. Now it was growing lighter with every passing minute. As Curtis Bennett developed and enlarged upon his theme, his words always homely, his voice always sonorous, his burly figure like a tower of strength incarnate four-square to the world, he produced an immense and discernible impression on the throng of spectators crammed into the court.

The jury's response was more difficult to gauge, because juries, in the limelight's glare, try to be impassive. But at the afternoon's end, when he broke off his speech upon the bidding of the clock, Curtis Bennett had good cause for self-congratulation. There was reason to think he had made substantial headway. It was a Saturday, and all through the weekend recess it would be his words that were ringing in the jury's ears. He had done much to reverse the drift towards disaster, and he could confidently look forward to resuming on the Monday in a court altogether more cordially inclined.

It seems that this transformation had also struck the Bench, and that the Bench did not look upon the change with satisfaction. For, as counsel and solicitors were tying up their papers and the crowd was shuffling in readiness to move, Mr Justice Shearman delivered a last word.

It is not uncommon for a judge to warn the jury against jumping to conclusions before hearing both sides. It is very uncommon—one would have liked to say, unheard of—for a judge to interject antagonistic comment in the middle of a closing speech by counsel for the prisoner.

Mrs Thompson's evil star accorded her that judge.

'Members of the jury,' said his lordship, 'before the court rises for the day I wish to offer you this advice. Of course, you will not make up your minds until you have heard the whole case.' (In fact, the evidence had long since been completed; all that remained before the jury's verdict was the Crown's reply and the judge's summing-up. If this piece of 'advice' meant anything at all, it meant 'Don't decide about Sir Henry's plea until you have heard Sir Thomas Inskip and me.') 'The only other thing is, having regard to the surroundings for so many days, by all means look at the atmosphere and try to understand what the letters mean, but you should not forget that you are in a court of justice trying *a vulgar and common crime.*'

16

In describing this amazing case as vulgar and common, Mr Justice Shearman spoke for the profession he adorned.

Curtis Bennett and those like him are rich and rare exceptions; rich in their humanity, rare in their comprehension. The representative lawyers, seeing no further than their notebooks, one after the other expressed agreement with the judge. 'I ask you', said Inskip in his last speech to the jury, 'to treat this as an *ordinary* case.' 'It is squalid and indecent,' said the Lord Chief Justice later, presiding in the Court of Criminal Appeal. 'It is essentially a *commonplace* and unedifying case.'

These inane pronouncements, uttered in all solemnity by grown men, are a measure of the lawyers' incapacity to fathom the depths beneath the surface that they skim. They had missed or ignored the vital feature of the case—that it was highly unusual and possibly unique because of the character of the feminine protagonist. But the whole affair provoked their sour displeasure; it didn't fit inside a legal frame; it raised vast questions of sex and of psychology foreign to their experience and repugnant to their tastes. Because it was beyond them, they took refuge in aloofness; they branded it contemptuously as 'ordinary' and 'common'.

Lawyers react thus to every manifestation of imaginative artistry or passionate desire. It is their sole defence. You can hear them crying 'commonplace' after Beatrice and Dante, and stigmatising Héloïse as a vulgar little slut.

17

These legalistic preconceptions were painfully apparent in Mr Justice Shearman's long and ill-phrased summing-up. He was bitterly hostile to Mrs Thompson from the start. He dismissed her letters breezily as 'gush', though if his own command of language had been comparable with hers he would not have dropped so often into slipshod imprecision.

But his drift was plain enough. 'It's a common or ordinary charge', he told the jury, 'of a wife and an adulterer murdering her husband. . . . You are told that this is a case of a great love. Take one of the letters as a test.' He took one and pointed out this solitary sentence : 'He has the right by law to all that you have a right to by nature and by love.' This had excited the judge's indignation. 'If that means anything,' he said, 'it means that the love of a husband for his wife is something improper because marriage is acknowledged by the law and that the love of a woman for her lover, illicit and clandestine, is something great and noble.'

That, needless to say, is not what it means at all. Mrs Thompson was not *generalising* about love and marriage; she was writing particularly and solely of herself. In *her* life the only love that mattered was unlawful, but where does she suggest this is a universal rule?

Even fellow lawyers might be loath to defend this singular specimen of Mr Justice Shearman's logic. But its author had no qualms, and the full force of his moral reprobation was visited on Mrs Thompson's head. 'I am certain', he said to the jury, 'that you, like any other right-minded persons, will be filled with disgust at such a notion. Let us get rid of all that atmosphere and try this case in an ordinary, commonsense way.'

Calls for 'common sense', 'plain common sense', 'commonsense principles', and 'commonsense considerations' were repeated at intervals like ritualistic incantations. No one of course objects to common sense, but the judge's application of it was frequently bewildering. It was apparently common sense that made him warn the jury against Curtis Bennett's 'flights of imagination' when imagination on the part of others was so sorely needed and so sadly lacking. It was apparently common sense that enabled him to see why 'two people agreeing to murder don't make that agreement when anybody is listening,' but prevented him from seeing the parallel presumption that they don't put their agreement into writing either. It was apparently common sense that made him speak of 'this silly, but at the same time wicked, affection'; wicked possibly, but was silly the apt term for a passion so compelling that it drove a man to kill?

In any event, and contrary to popular belief, it is not every problem that common sense can solve. Some require uncommon sense, and Mrs Thompson's case was essentially one of these. The jury should have received an impartial direction, free from irrelevant lectures upon ethics, and emphasising that their primary concern was to grasp the tendencies of Mrs Thompson's mind. Instead they were fobbed off with a good many opinions that had been better unexpressed, a string of pious platitudes on sexual behaviour, and a total disregard of the question of psychology.

The result could be foreseen.

18

It may be said: you blame Inskip, who was subject to the judge; you blame the judge, who was subject to appeal; why not blame the jury, which was not subject to anything?

I do, but to a much smaller degree, for reasons which involve a short excursus upon juries. . .

The twelve average people who occupy a jury box are, almost always, twelve frightened people too. They are little folk, leading little lives, scared of policemen and respectful to solicitors, who are suddenly called to responsibility and power. They are generally one-quarter proud, three-quarters apprehensive, and desperately anxious for guidance from the Law.

To them the Law is embodied in the judge. Counsel, with their wigs and gowns and sprucely starched white bands, inevitably take rank as superior beings, but they are identified with the fortunes of a side. His lordship has a pure and godlike quality; placed physically and spiritually above the sordid strife, his lightest word reverberates around Mount Sinai.

It follows that, in the overwhelming majority of cases, juries follow the judge when he gives a definite lead. There are exceptions. Occasionally a judge will overdo it; he will espouse one party's cause so heatedly and fiercely that the jury find against him because they don't think it fair play. Even this happens only with a panel of strong jurors—or one strong juror who dominates the rest. For the most part judges get the verdicts that they want.

It is all the easier for a jury to accept the judge's promptings if these coincide with their own spontaneous instinct. And instinct in a jury is generally clear cut; it urges them to vindicate their corporate rectitude. They like to distribute penalties and rewards, and to uphold good morals as a by-product of verdicts.

There is one further element in the average jury's make-up; a propensity to condemn what they cannot understand. An unseen handicap rests upon a prisoner who in life or mind or habit appears alien to themselves. They are more at home, and therefore more forbearing, with bookmakers and licensees than with prophets or with poets.

It will be seen that Mrs Thompson had the worst of every deal. The judge was against her; she was technically dissolute; her own counsel had described her as living 'a sort of life I don't suppose any of you live'. What chance had she against this combination of misfortunes?

They gave her longer thought, though, than had been

given Mrs Maybrick. For two hours and ten minutes the jury remained out, striving to do justice according to their lights.

19

Even when she cried out, 'Oh God, I am not guilty,' even when the judge assumed the black cap of her novels, even when she found herself receiving the sad privileges imposed on the condemned, Mrs Thompson cannot have believed that she would die. Nor did a host of others. She had struck no blow; she had played no part; the intention of her letters was in strenuous dispute. A petition raised on her behalf was signed by many thousands and most people confidently expected a reprieve.

It never came. The legal system and its affiliated offices continued to react with a species of cold frenzy at Mrs Thompson's name. No yielding to clamour; an example must be made.

And so it came about that the British Home Secretary, whose forerunners and successors have restored to society so many brutalised and violent murderers, turned a deaf ear to the plea of Edith Thompson and permitted her to hang for the glory of the law.

'We ourselves die and live in the books we read while we are reading them and then when we have finished, the books die and we live . . . until when. . . ? Who knows. . . ? We are not the shapers of our destinies.'

20

The Thompson verdict is now recognised as bad, and the trial from which it sprang stands out as an example of the evils that may flow from an attitude of mind.

There was no failure of law; there was no failure of procedure; there was no failure to observe and abide by all the rules. It was from first to last a failure in human understanding; a failure to grasp and comprehend a personality not envisaged in the standard legal textbooks and driven by forces more powerful and eternal than those that are studied at the Inns of Court.

1

The Wallace case was a highly professional affair. It was planned with extreme care and extraordinary imagination. Either the murderer was Wallace or it wasn't. If it wasn't, then here at last is the perfect murder. If it was, then here is a murder so nearly perfect that the Court of Criminal Appeal, after examining the evidence, decided to quash Wallace's conviction.—James Agate in *Ego 6*.

2

AGATE was fascinated by the Wallace case. He made it one of his constant bedside books. He wrote on it from time to time in his famous published diary. And if he ever felt depressed or bored he would telephone and say: 'Come over, my dear boy; let's have a good talk about Wallace.'

Those good talks about Wallace were spirited but exhausting. I have often sat up with him half the night probing the mystery of Menlove Gardens East. . . .

Agate's interest in Wallace was not at all surprising. It was a case to delight that hard and lucid brain which had allied itself so oddly to a subtle sense of art. The latter had become the instrument of his profession; the former he made the foundation of his hobby, and he loved to dedicate his scanty leisure hours to exercising a prodigious gift of logic. He doted on detective problems of the higher type; he could meditate for hours over a cunning move in chess; he was in fact a devotee of scientific puzzles.

And Wallace is the perfect scientific puzzle. Perfect

because it hasn't a solution—and, so far as anything in this world can be certain, never will have now. Other crimes have other qualities in far greater abundance; more psychological interest, wider human appeal, greater social significance. But, as a mental exercise, as a challenge to one's powers of deduction and analysis, the Wallace murder is in a class by itself. It has all the maddening, frustrating fascination of a chess problem that ends in perpetual check.

3

At the time of the tragedy that broke up his home and ruined his life, William Herbert Wallace was fifty-two years old. A placid, good-tempered, gentle individual, he incurred no enmities if he attracted few close friends. Integrity and stability were the distinguishing marks of his modest and respectable career. For sixteen years he had been a valued whole-time agent of a famous insurance company—the Prudential. For sixteen years he had rented the same small house in Liverpool, one of a dull and featureless row in a dull and featureless district. For more than eighteen years he had shared married life with a woman as unassuming as himself. His business accounts were always in good order; his rent was always punctually paid; he and his wife enjoyed a relationship of uninterrupted concord and affection. 'A very loving couple,' said their next-door neighbour, and this judgment has never been challenged or gainsaid.

In one respect only Wallace sharply differed from the average worthy man of provincial middle class. He was remarkably studious and intellectual in his tastes. He enjoyed a wide range of cultivated interests which his wife either encouraged or participated in. There was chess, which he played regularly at the Liverpool Central Chess Club. There was chemistry, which he practised in an amateur laboratory he had rigged up for himself in the back part of his house. And there was music; Mrs Wallace was accomplished at the piano, Wallace had taken lessons on the violin, and they often entertained themselves by performing duets in the comfort and privacy of their sitting room.

It was this harmonious and inoffensive couple that became involved in 'the perfect murder case'; she as the victim, he as the accused. For of all men in the world, Wallace, the mild, peaceable, easy-going Wallace, was to face a charge of murdering his wife. Murder—if it were done by him—not in sudden heat or rage but by cold and brilliant and calculated plan; murder not committed with the minimum of violence, but with vicious, wasteful and horrible brutality; murder not prompted by some clear and powerful motive but without the slightest purpose and without the slightest gain.

4

The first overt move in the deep-laid plot to murder Julia Wallace was taken almost exactly twenty-four hours before she died. A telephone call, which at the time appeared commonplace, is seen in retrospect to have presaged her end.

It was Monday, January 19th, 1931. There was a match that evening at the Liverpool Central Chess Club, and Wallace was among the members scheduled to take part. Shortly after seven o'clock, when the players were assembling but before Wallace had arrived, someone telephoned the club and left a message with the captain. Would Mr Wallace go out at 7.30 the next night and visit Mr Qualtrough—Mr R. M. Qualtrough of 25, Menlove Gardens East? 'It is something', said the caller, 'in the nature of his business.'

If we knew for certain who this caller was, the Wallace

puzzle would be solved at once. For whoever left that message did it for the purpose of advancing a murderous design.

When Wallace arrived, about half an hour later, he seemed somewhat puzzled by this telephoned request. 'Qualtrough, Qualtrough, who is Qualtrough?' he said. 'I don't know the chap. And where is Menlove Gardens East?' None of the club members were absolutely sure, but they all—Wallace included—knew of Menlove Avenue. Menlove Gardens East, they thought, must be in the same neighbourhood, and Wallace accepted this plausible supposition. 'After all, I've got a tongue in my head,' he said. 'I can ask when I get in the vicinity.'

5

The Wallaces had no children and no servants. They were very seldom visited by relatives or friends. So if Wallace went out at night, almost certainly Mrs Wallace would be in the house alone. The case turns on this fact.

On the evening that followed the chess match and the message Wallace returned home from work at about six. At half past, or thereabouts, a milk boy called, and Mrs Wallace responded to his knock. Very soon after seven Wallace was on a tramcar, travelling in the direction of Menlove Avenue, which was a distance of three or four miles from his home. A few minutes later he had reached 'the vicinity' and began asking for directions to Menlove Gardens East.

In Liverpool there is a Menlove Gardens South; there is a Menlove Gardens North; there is a Menlove Gardens West. There is no Menlove Gardens East. And the Mr R. M. Qualtrough who should have lived at Number 25 and who ought to have been waiting to discuss insurance business has never been discovered to this day.

Wallace undoubtedly made numerous enquiries and roamed round the neighbourhood for the best part of an hour. At last he gave up and, without visible recompense for his errand, quitted 'the vicinity' and started off for home.

At about a quarter to nine it so happened that his neighbours came out of their back door. In the alley they saw Wallace who, they thought, looked 'anxious', and who asked them whether they had heard anything 'unusual'. He couldn't get into his house, he said; both the front door and the back were locked against him. At their suggestion he tried the back door again. 'It opens now,' he called, and they waited, neighbour-like, while he went inside to look around.

A minute or two later he came out to them again. 'Come and see,' he said. 'She has been killed.'

Horrified, they followed him through the house to the front parlour. Mrs Wallace lay there, stretched across the floor. Her brains had been dashed out and her blood was spattered everywhere.

6

There was no sign that the murderer had broken in by force. There seemed to be nothing missing except, so Wallace said, four pounds in cash from a box kept in the kitchen. One bedroom, it is true, was found in some disorder, but, to the expert eye of a Detective Superintendent, it did not look as though a thief had been searching round for valuables. The Superintendent formed an exactly contrary opinion: that the place had been deliberately upset in order to mislead.

Robbery, then, could be virtually excluded. It was not a crime of sex. What feasible hypotheses remained? Who could have nourished such malignant hatred against this amiable and harmless lady that he painstakingly evolved a plot the aim of which was to bring about her death? For the murder was unquestionably linked with the phone call to the chess club on the evening before.

But linked in what respect? Either—and this was the obvious conclusion—someone had wanted to get Wallace out of the way; or—and this was a more circuitous approach —*Wallace himself* wanted people to *think* that someone had wanted to get him out of the way.

After diligent enquiries, spread over a wide area and lasting many days, the police threw their weight behind the second of these alternatives. They believed that Wallace had made the telephone call himself. They believed that on the following night, shortly after half past six, he had murdered his wife in the front room of their home. They believed that he had then gone out and conspicuously engaged in an elaborate search for a place that he knew did not exist in order to equip himself with a strong and well-knit alibi.

On February 2nd Wallace was arrested. The detectives stood ready to take down any statement. But 'What can I say', asked Wallace, 'to a charge of which I am absolutely innocent?'

7

The trial at St George's Hall was presided over by Mr Justice (afterwards Lord) Wright, one of the greatest of contemporary judges, and fought out by two redoubtable King's Counsel, E. G. Hemmerde and Roland Oliver.

Roland Oliver had played a minor part in two of the cases already examined in these pages. At the trial of Steinie Morrison he had been second junior to Abinger; at the trial of Mrs Thompson he had been second junior to Inskip. By the time of the Wallace case, where he led for the defence,

Oliver was in the front rank of English advocates. He was an all-round man, equally effective and constantly briefed in 'fashionable' jury suits, 'society' divorces, and so-called 'heavy' crime.

Hemmerde was something of a stormy petrel. At the fiercely competitive Liverpool Bar of the early nineteen hundreds he had established himself with such rapidity and brilliance that there were those who predicted an even greater future for him than for his dashing colleague, F. E. Smith. He took silk early, entered politics, and for a while his youthful promise looked certain of fulfilment. But in later years his career went awry. Private transactions, ill-judged or unlucky, did him grave and permanent disservice; irrepressible combativeness and an outspoken tongue involved him in injurious dissensions; an honourable but unbending pride did nothing to win back those he had estranged. His practice suffered, and though he always could command a fair volume of work upon the Northern Circuit, there is not the faintest doubt that in the twenties and the thirties his status did not equal his professional capacity.

It is important to bear this in mind when studying the trial. Both through technical skill and sheer personal dominance, Hemmerde's impact on a jury was immense. He was a remarkably handsome and imposing-looking man, to whom ripening age had lent additional authority. If he believed—and he usually did quite genuinely believe—that the side he represented was the side of right and truth, he threw into a case his very heart and soul. He conducted this prosecution with his customary fairness, but in a trial there are imponderables to take into account. In the Wallace case, one of them is the effect that would be produced by this able, forceful and convincing personality presenting a charge that he himself felt sure was true.

8

Hemmerde opened his case characteristically 'high'; that is, he spoke as though all his witnesses would come right up to proof, and none would retreat or qualify under cross-examination.

Opening 'high' has one serious disadvantage. If your opponent has any real success, he may induce a violent swing in his direction merely because the Crown case has been patently over-stated. What remains may be discounted because of what has gone.

But there is also a corresponding advantage in the method. At the very outset the jury get the Crown version in one solid and coherent piece. Its destruction can only be accomplished in distinct and maybe widely separated stages. The first impression, if deep enough, may be difficult to dislodge.

In the Wallace trial, which depended more than most upon the accumulation and interpretation of a mass of tiny details, opening 'high' was likely to pay dividends. This is not to say that Hemmerde acted on design. Given the circumstances and his temperament, a 'high' opening was inevitable.

Certainly the Crown case never afterwards appeared quite so formidable as it did at the end of Hemmerde's opening speech.

9

'The evidence for the Crown', said Hemmerde, slowly and emphatically, 'will not show you any motive. Nevertheless I suggest it will carry you almost irresistibly to the conclusion that, in spite of all the happiness of that little household, in spite of everything that one knows about the relations of these people, this woman was murdered by her husband.'

Almost irresistibly. The keynote had been struck in the first minute, and thereafter Hemmerde held the court enthralled while he gave chapter and verse in a masterly oration.

He plunged into the story with the telephone call, and straight away created a sensation. 'We know where the call came from,' he asserted. 'In the ordinary way, it would not be possible to tell, but in this particular case difficulty was experienced.' In fact, there had been some hitch in the automatic machinery and the operator had had to intervene. 'As a result, we can trace the call to a call-box four hundred yards from Wallace's house—the nearest call-box to his house there is.' Hemmerde paused for a moment. 'You may think it curious that a total stranger to the prisoner speaking from a place four hundred yards from his home—where, according to him, he actually was—should have rung up the chess club.   It is a club that does not advertise; a club the meetings of which are known only to its few members. . . . There he leaves a message that Wallace is expected to call next night on someone he does not know at an address which does not exist.' The ground was prepared for Hanging Point Number One. 'You will have to consider whether this was part of a cunningly laid scheme to create an alibi for the next night.'

After a reference to Wallace's insistence at the club that he did not know either Qualtrough or Menlove Gardens East ('You may think that this ignorance was assumed to draw attention to the fact that next night at half past seven he was going some miles from his house'), Hemmerde passed to Hanging Point Two : Wallace's conduct that next night as he went upon that journey. He made much of this, and legitimately so, for everything that Wallace did seemed perfectly consistent with the prosecution's theory that he was out procuring witnesses. 'Does this car go to Menlove Gardens East?' he asks one tram conductor. 'No,' says the man, 'but you can get on and I can give you a penny ticket or a transfer.' 'I am a stranger in the district,' Wallace volunteers, 'and I have important business.' ('You will remember', Hemmerde commented acidly, but not altogether justly, 'that he did not know Qualtrough or what his business was.') Presently the conductor goes upstairs to collect fares. 'You won't forget,' Wallace calls after him, 'I want to get to Menlove Gardens East.'

He changes cars; there is another conductor; Wallace goes through the self-same hoops. He asks to be put off at Menlove Gardens East; the conductor does his best and puts him off at Menlove Gardens West; Wallace says 'Thank you, I am a complete stranger round here.' 'You may think', observed Hemmerde, with significant inflection, 'that these conversations with the conductors are natural—or unnatural.'

But this was only the beginning; there was more, much more, to come.

From twenty past seven until after eight that night Wallace is busy in the Menlove Gardens region. He starts by enquiring of a passer-by, who tells him flatly 'There is no Menlove Gardens East.' He rings the bell of 25, Menlove Gardens West and asks the lady who answers it if Mr Qualtrough lives there. He gets into conversation with a policeman, who, having added his official reassurance that Menlove Gardens East is non-existent, receives in return an account of the whole episode—how Wallace is an insurance clerk, how a Mr Qualtrough had rung up his club, how a message had been taken for him by his colleague. Then Wallace pulls out his watch. 'It isn't eight o'clock yet,' he remarks, 'it's just a quarter to.' The policeman inspects his own watch and confirms. 'You may think', said Hemmerde, 'all this is perfectly natural—or you may think it over-elaborated. The taking out of the watch, so that the police-man should know exactly when he was there, you may think is of some importance.' (The harmless, non-committal 'you may think' can shoot like deadly poison from a rhetorician's tongue.)

Even this was not the end of Wallace's researches. He goes into a newsagent's and asks for a directory. It is given to him; he looks through it; and then—'Note this', Hemmerde interjected sharply—'he says to the manageress, "Do you know what I am looking for?" "No," she not un-naturally replies. "I am looking", says Wallace, "for Men-love Gardens East."'

10

The gathering power of this narration could not fail to im-press even a neutral and impartial jury. It is to be doubted, though, whether the ten men and two women appointed to sit in judgment upon Wallace qualified for this commenda-tory description. All provincial towns smack of the parish pump, and Liverpool had hardly changed since the days of Mrs Maybrick. The buzz of voices and the clack of tongues were never stilled in the weeks before the trial, and Wallace had been prematurely tried in every local shop and public house. The verdict of these crude tribunals was seldom in his favour.

One may surmise that not all the jurors were unenthusi-astic as Hemmerde developed his indictment.

He followed his stirring and tendentious curtain-raiser with a devastating commentary on Wallace's return.

'The next we know of him is at 8.35, when he is seen

just outside his house, at the back.' Hemmerde recounted Wallace's talk with his neighbours and his statement that the doors were 'locked against him'. 'Now supposing you came to the conclusion'—oh, the guilelessness of counsel with their decorous 'supposings' and forbearing 'you may thinks'—'supposing you came to the conclusion that the doors were never shut against him, and that you then find a man who could get in if he wanted to, pretending that he couldn't. There he is'—it's axiomatic now—'there he is, able to get in when he is there alone—but the neighbours are not there.'

So it was settled, wasn't it? Wallace could have gone straight in. There was nothing to stop him. The whole business was a fake. Hanging Point Three.

The flood mounted and quickened. 'He goes in and the neighbours follow his course. If you went into a house like that, where would you go? You have left your wife downstairs; would you have looked in the downstairs room, or would you have gone upstairs? . . . First of all, *he* goes upstairs, then he comes down into the *kitchen*, and *then* goes into the front sitting room. Then—then—he finds his wife lying dead.'

And his demeanour when confronted with this shocking tragedy? Hemmerde was rising to the heights. 'You might have expected a cry of agony, bitter sorrow—but what happens?' Well, *what* happens? Wallace, says the Crown, is calm, cool, collected, realistic. Too calm and cool for a man in his position.

From calmness it is but a step to callousness, which slips into its place as Hanging Point Number Four.

11

Hanging Point Number Five depended on the mackintosh
—one of the most bizarre and puzzling clues that ever
stepped outside detective fiction.

When Mrs Wallace's body was discovered, she was lying
in a twisted position on the rug. Pressed close against her,
rolled up and half hidden, was a blood-drenched mackintosh
that had been partially burnt. It was Wallace's mackintosh,
as he did not deny.

'Now,' said Hemmerde, with a glance at the jury which
could and did speak volumes, 'just let me draw your attention to this. The mackintosh is found there after some
attempt has been made, if it was not an accident, to burn
it. Just consider. Who had an interest in burning that mackintosh? Assuming that someone had broken into the house
—there is no trace that anyone did—such a person might
have taken down the raincoat and put it on to prevent the
blood getting on his clothes. But having done so, why should
a stranger want to destroy it? Why should he want to destroy
someone else's mackintosh?'

It was a persuasive argument, at its most deadly in reverse
—the mackintosh's owner, by the same token, *would* want
to destroy it. Having placed this implication in every juror's
mind, Hemmerde offered a most ingenious reconstruction of
the crime.

Mrs Wallace, he stressed, was lying in a pool of blood.
Blood had spurted on to the furniture and walls. But
although the murderer had gone upstairs directly afterwards,
there was not a trace of blood detected on his route. With
one tiny exception, irrelevant for this purpose, the only blood
found anywhere outside the room of death was a single clot
in the water-closet pan which stood by the side of an ordinary

wash bowl. 'One of the most famous criminal trials', Hemmerde said, 'was of a man who committed a crime when he was naked. A man might perfectly well commit a crime wearing a raincoat, as one might wear a dressing gown, and come down when he is just going to do this with nothing on upon which blood could fasten; and with anything like care he could get away, leaving the raincoat there, and go and perform the necessary washing.'

A jury, like an audience of children, always responds to a really vivid picture. Here was conjured up an entire series of pictures, each with its own hard outline and effect. Wallace upstairs, coolly putting on his mackintosh; Wallace descending, step by step, to his unsuspecting victim; the fierce and bloody act of swift annihilation; Wallace slipping off the saturated mackintosh as a boxer in the floodlit ring might shed his dressing gown (how apt and telling was Hemmerde's simple phrase); Wallace trying to burn the mackintosh and finding his carefully plotted time-table in arrear; Wallace doing the best he could and bundling the mackintosh underneath the inanimate body of his wife; Wallace stepping out of his house into the street—wicked, triumphant, satisfied, and free.

Wallace; always Wallace. For who else—who else—could have wanted to destroy that mackintosh?

In order of chronology this was Hanging Point Five. In order of effectiveness, it may have been Number One.

12

The biggest shots had now been fired; Hemmerde followed with a fusillade of shrapnel.

There was 'an iron sort of poker thing' which had lain by the parlour gas stove from time immemorial, according to a woman who came in to do the cleaning. It had been there on her last visit; after the murder it was missing. It was, said Hemmerde, a weapon 'amply sufficient to have done this deed', and moreover one which could be disposed of without trouble. . . .

There were some treasury notes in a vase upon the bedroom mantelpiece, one of which, rather curiously, was marked or smeared with blood. This showed, said Hemmerde, that it had been handled by the murderer, and therefore the idea of theft could be utterly ruled out. 'And if you eliminate money,' counsel added, 'what are you left with? '

There had been a talk in the street on January 22nd between Wallace and the chess captain who had taken 'Qualtrough's' message. 'Can you tell me', Wallace asked him, 'at what time you received it?' About seven o'clock or thereabouts, the captain thought. 'Can't you get nearer to it than that?' said Wallace. 'It is of great importance to me.' Now why, demanded Hemmerde, why was it of great importance to him? The police at that time had certainly not told him that they thought that *he* was the person who had phoned. . . .

These, however, were secondary items, and Hemmerde was far too sensitive an artist to conclude such a bravura effort on a diminuendo. He had made a memorable speech and he meant to wind it up in memorable style.

He laid down the heavy black notebook which, according to his habit, he had used throughout both as symbol and mnemonic. Confronting the jury squarely, hands unencumbered for the comminatory gesture, he moved with a master's ease to his finale—a dazzling summary of the case he had presented.

The telephone call from the nearby box, the ostentatious and persistent quest for Menlove Gardens East, the trouble with the doors that 'evaporated' so opportunely, the prisoner's 'cold, collected air,' the mackintosh—all these weapons, so industriously assembled, were hurled upon the target in shattering succession.

The peroration was not uncharacteristic, nor unworthy. 'If you think that the case is fairly proved against this man, that brutally and wantonly he sent this unfortunate woman to her account, it will be your duty to call him to his account.'

13

During this long and gripping tour de force, Roland Oliver of necessity sat silent as his client. There was nothing he could do except possess his soul in patience. Now Hemmerde had finished; the evidence was beginning; henceforward the defender would come into his own.

But there was not to be a sudden and spectacular trans-formation. The procedure of the English courts did not admit of that. Whittling down the Crown case in cross-examination must precede any attempt to supplant it by your own, and in the Wallace trial, with its multiplicity of points, the whittling-down process was bound to be pro-longed.

The first consequential steps in this direction were taken when the chess captain came into the box.

This innocent instrument of a diabolical scheme had just been interrogated by Hemmerde for the Crown. He was not invited to give a direct account of his telephone talk with 'Qualtrough'; in the lack of proof positive that 'Qualtrough' was really Wallace (proof that would have determined the issue at one stroke) this would have infringed the hearsay rule. His evidence on the matter had had to be confined to the message he had passed to Wallace later on.

Oliver, though, representing the prisoner, could, if he thought it expedient, waive the rule's protection. This he proceeded to do with immediate advantage.

'I am interested', he said to the witness, 'in the voice that addressed you on the telephone. Could you reproduce the conversation for us, do you think?'

'I can give you an idea of it.'

'The part I am interested in particularly', said Oliver, 'is the part in which the voice told you about the business, whatever it was. Can you remember that?'

'Oh, yes.' The chess captain, unfamiliar with the rules that govern moves on the forensic board, may have been wondering why nobody had asked him this before. Willingly he got it off his chest. 'I told him that Mr Wallace was coming to the club that night; would he ring up again? He said, "No, I am too busy; I have got my girl's twenty-first birthday on, and I want to see Mr Wallace on a matter of business; it is something in the nature of his business."'

'Something in the nature of his business, coupled with a reference to his daughter?'

'Yes.'

The sting had been fully drawn from one of Hemmerde's sharpest strictures—that Wallace on the tram had talked about 'important business' when nobody had told him what 'Qualtrough's' business was.

Having made this neat score on a minor matter, Oliver passed to a much more vital point.

'You had altogether quite a conversation with the voice?'

'Yes.'

'You said it was a strong, gruff voice?'

'Yes.'

'And a confident one?'

'Yes; sure of himself.'

Then followed five of the most momentous questions ever asked and answered in a court of law.

'Was it a natural voice?'

'That is difficult to judge.'

'I know it is. But did it occur to you that it was not a natural voice at the time?'

'No, I had no reason for thinking that.'

'Do you know Mr Wallace's voice well?'

'Yes.'

'Did it occur to you that it was anything like his voice?'

'Certainly not.'

The definiteness of this reply carried extra weight because the witness had shown himself exceptionally scrupulous and disinclined to dogmatic assertion.

'Does it occur to you now that it was anything like his voice?'

The witness cogitated with a chess player's deliberation.

'It would be a great stretch of the imagination for me to say anything like that,' he said.

The reporters scribbled madly. The spectators raised their eyebrows. One or two found themselves impelled to glance at Hemmerde who looked straight ahead with majestic unconcern.

The whittling-down operations had got well into their stride.

14

They continued all through that day and the next. The regiment of witnesses—there were no less than twenty-six—called to make good that overwhelming opening undid in sum as much as they established. One Crown weapon after another that had seemed so mortal as it sped from Hemmerde's hand crumpled like paper and fell harmlessly away.

15

The second day ran specially well for the defence. It produced two witnesses of paramount importance—Mrs Florence Johnston and Professor John MacFall.

Mrs Johnston and her husband were Wallace's next-door neighbours. Circumstances had imposed on them not one but two ordeals: after the horror in the house that night came the undesired publicity and nerve rack of the trial. They stood up gallantly to both. Between them they drew a picture, unstudiedly graphic and palpably veracious, of the supposed murderer's arrival home.

Mr Johnston gave his evidence first. He was lucid, objective, manifestly unbiassed. He covered the ground so thoroughly—and so fairly—when examined by the Crown that Roland Oliver had few questions to put. But one useful point emerged in cross-examination: that Wallace, *with the Johnstons looking on*, had not fumbled nor pushed at the lock of his back door. If, as Hemmerde so strenuously suggested, he could have got in at any time, but was waiting for an audience, one might have expected some pretence of awkwardness to lend a little colour to his bogus protestations.

Mrs Johnston's tone was as sterling as her husband's, and her evidence-in-chief closely followed the lines of his. Oliver, though, detained her rather longer in the box. Maybe he had sensed what proved to be the fact—that she had the woman's observant eye for *people* as her husband had the male's observant eye for *things*.

Oliver asked her at once about Wallace's demeanour, which Hemmerde had termed 'extremely cold'.

'Before your husband left to fetch the police, did Mr Wallace appear to be suffering from shock?'

'Yes,' said Mrs Johnston, 'to an extent.'

'It is very difficult, isn't it, to judge what is passing in other minds?'

'Manners are so different, are they not?' replied the witness, thereby showing both sensibility and sense.

'But while you were with him did he break down?'

'Yes, twice; he put his hands to his head and sobbed.'

'That was before the police arrived?'

'Yes. If we were left alone he appeared as if he would break down, and he appeared to pull himself together when a great many were knocking about.'

'When the police came?'

'Yes.'

'He made an effort to control himself?'

'Yes.'

'Did you think', Oliver asked boldly, 'that there was anything suspicious about his manner from beginning to end?'

'No,' said Mrs Johnston firmly. 'I did not.'

That was at once concise and comprehensive. Good advocates do not stop to paint lilies at the wayside, and Roland Oliver immediately pressed on. He ascertained that, just before leaving her own home, Mrs Johnston had heard knocking on Wallace's back door—further support, this, for the defence's contention that Wallace was genuinely unable to get in. He ascertained too that Wallace, when asked in her presence by the police about the mackintosh, frankly and promptly declared it was his own—a valuable statement to have upon the record, as the police were now asserting that Wallace had been evasive.

Oliver then turned to this strange business of the mackintosh, and its singular position in relation to the body.

'Do you think it possible,' he asked, 'that Mrs Wallace

might have thrown it round her shoulders to go and open the front door?'

'That was my idea,' said Mrs Johnston.

'You had the idea, too?'

'It just flashed across my mind because it was a peculiar thing, a mackintosh.'

'I quite agree. Do you know that in fact Mrs Wallace had a cold?'

'Yes.'

'Did you know that she had seen the doctor for bronchitis?'

'No, but I knew she had been very poorly.'

These questions foreshadowed Oliver's theory of the crime; an alternative reconstruction to set up beside Hemmerde's and to pit against the surmises of Professor John MacFall.

16

MacFall was a very great expert. He instructed the students of Liverpool University in forensic medicine. He examined the students of four other universities in medical jurisprudence. He had been on the scene of the crime within an hour of its discovery; scientifically he had acquired the necessary data; now, facing the jury as he so often faced his class, he prepared to demonstrate exactly what had happened.

He had examined the body at ten past ten that night and observed the progress made by *rigor mortis*; from that he could deduce that death had taken place at least four hours before. (This, as a matter of fact, was a little awkward for the Crown, as they had already called the milk boy, who swore to seeing Mrs Wallace alive at half past six. But MacFall was unmoved; perhaps he placed more faith in *rigor mortis* than in milk boys. He stuck to his view, making only this concession—that there was a margin of error in *rigor mortis* calculations, which he fixed in this instance at an hour either way.) He had examined the blood marks on the furniture and on the walls; from them he could deduce that, at the moment of attack, Mrs Wallace had been sitting in an armchair by the fireplace, head inclined a little forward 'as if talking to somebody'. He had examined the bloodstains that were 'all over' the mackintosh; from them he could deduce that blood had 'spurted' on to the garment from *in front*. He had examined the blood clot in the water-closet pan; from that he could deduce that it had been spilt at the same time as the blood clot by the body. He had examined the position of the blows upon the head; from them he could deduce the murderer's mental state. 'I know it was not an ordinary case of assault or serious injury. It was a case of frenzy.'

Here was an exercise in the deductive faculty that would not have been scorned by Dupin or Sherlock Holmes. Much of it was highly detrimental to the prisoner. If MacFall was right, the murder had disrupted a quiet, homely talk with someone Mrs Wallace knew. If MacFall was right, the idea that Mrs Wallace wore the mackintosh was wrong. If MacFall was right, the blood clot reinforced Hemmerde's theory that the murderer had gone upstairs to wash.

It was a critical moment for his client when Roland Oliver got up to start a cross-examination which must rank among the best and most adroit of recent times.

He first took the witness's categorical assertion that the murderer, whoever he was, had acted in a frenzy. There was obvious capital to be derived from this.

'If this is the work of a maniac, and he is a sane man, he didn't do it. Is that right?'

MacFell knew, as Oliver did, that Wallace had been under

the usual observation, and that the experts held him to be of perfectly sound mind. He gave a canny answer.

'He may be sane now,' he said.

'It is a rash suggestion, is it not?' Oliver said sternly.

'Not in the slightest.'

'The fact that a man has been sane for fifty-two years, and has been sane while in custody for the last three months, would rather tend to prove that he has *always* been sane, would it not?'

The sarcasm was evident and justified. MacFall's response was the equivalent of a boxer covering up.

'Not necessarily,' he said.

'Not necessarily?'

'We know very little about the private lives of people or their thoughts.'

Oliver might have asked what sort of frenzy it would be that began at least twenty-four hours before it reached fruition. But he saved this for later comment; there were other, more vital, matters calling for attention.

The police had found three characteristic burn marks on Mrs Wallace's skirt, corresponding with the gas fire in the room. From that common ground, Oliver launched his attack upon MacFall's reconstruction.

'Those burn marks would indicate that the gas fire had been alight, would they not?'

'Yes.'

'The handle to the gas fire is on the right-hand side of it?'

'Yes.'

'And just above it is a gas light?'

'Yes.'

'Suppose a woman went into that room, lit the gas, and lit the fire, she would have to stoop down, wouldn't she?'

'Presumably.'

'If she did this with her back towards the doorway someone was on her right-hand side, he would be in a po tion to strike her as she rose?'

'He would.'

'And her head might very well be in the position in whic you have put it?'

'Exactly.'

In six questions the defence theory had been erected o MacFall's own foundation. It seemed as valid as his own. And it evoked, of course, an entirely different picture—that of a caller being admitted and brought into the parlour, perhaps on the pretext that he wished to leave a note. Such a request would not be startling to the wife of an insurance agent.

At this point Oliver reintroduced the mackintosh.

'If she had had it round her, and the gas fire was alight, and she fell when she was struck, so as to burn her skirt in the lit fire, don't you think it is quite possible that the mackintosh swung round on to the fireplace and caught fire?'

'No,' said MacFall, 'because there is no evidence of it being on her right or left arm.'

'Suppose it was round her shoulders, and she collapsed, do you not see the possibility of the bottom of the mackintosh falling into the fire and getting burnt too?'

'There is the possibility,' Macfall conceded.

'Her hair was pulled away from her head, all up?'

'Yes.'

'And the pad which had been under her hair was away from the body?'

'Yes, some inches.'

'Do you not see the possibility of someone having grasped her by the hair to pull her from the fire?'

'Yes.'

This again was completely successful. But while giving all credit to the advocate, one should not withhold it from the witness. MacFall was a theorist, but a fair-minded theorist; present him with a logical proposition and he would accept it without quibble.

Having established his own position, Oliver proceeded to advance upon MacFall's. The Professor had backed up, at least by implication, Hemmerde's postulate that Wallace wore the mackintosh.

'Whether clothed or whether naked,' Oliver asked, 'it would be necessary, would it not, that many splashes of blood would fall on the assailant?'

'Yes,' MacFall said, 'I should expect to find them.'

'The last blows being probably struck with the head on the ground, there would be blood upon his feet and the lower part of his legs?'

'I should expect that.'

'And the mackintosh would not come down below the knees, which would leave the legs from the knees downward exposed to the blood?'

'Yes.'

'And there would be blood on his face?'

'Yes.'

'And his hair?'

'Yes.'

'Would you agree that if blood gets below the finger nails it is difficult to get away?'

'It is difficult.'

'Would you agree it would be almost certain that the assailant would have blood under the finger nails?'

MacFall jibbed at this and cautiously covered up again.

'Not necessarily,' he said.

But Oliver held the initiative and declined to be put off.

'Supposing the mackintosh were placed under the body, the assailant would have had to lift the shoulder and the head to do it?'

'He would.'

'That would have involved getting himself heavily dabbled in blood, would it not?'

'Dabbled in blood,' MacFall agreed, 'but not heavily.'

The qualification, however fitting, hardly mattered. Oliver had achieved an advantageous situation. He had struck at MacFall's strongest points and carried them in triumph. Now he could strike at points where MacFall seemed weak.

'With regard to the time of death,' he said: 'When did you first think it was important?'

'Immediately I saw the body.'

'And you made a series of observations, first as to *rigor mortis*, and second, as to the condition of the exuded blood?'

'The blood is a help,' MacFall said, 'but it is not so definite as *rigor mortis*.'

'You put *rigor mortis* first. How many notes', Oliver asked offhandedly, 'did you make with regard to *rigor mortis*?'

'Practically none.'

'Can you show me one?' Oliver said pleasantly.

'No,' said MacFall, 'I do not think I can.'

'So you, being intent from the start on the importance of *rigor mortis* as to the time of death, have not made one note with regard to *rigor mortis*?'

This, of course, was no more than a debating point. The real issue over *rigor mortis* was joined with the next question.

'*Rigor* is a very fallible test as to the time of death?'

'Not in the present case of an ordinary person dying in health.'

'I suggest it is a very fallible factor even in healthy people.'

'Well,' said MacFall, 'it is, just a little.'

'And a powerful, muscular body will be affected much more slowly than a frail, feeble body?'

'Yes.'

'Was this not a frail, feeble body?'

'She was feeble.'

'Was she not frail?'

'She was a weak woman.'

'Frail?' Oliver insisted.

MacFall surrendered.

'Yes,' he said, 'she was frail.'

'Bearing in mind that this frail, feeble woman would be more likely to be affected by *rigor*, are you going to swear that she was killed more than *three* hours before you saw her?'

(Three hours before ten past ten, be it remembered, Wallace was already on the tramcar, chattering to the conductor about Menlove Gardens East.)

'No, I am not going to swear,' MacFall replied punetiliously. 'I am going to give an opinion, and I swear that the opinion shall be an honest one.'

It was a good answer; both honourable and engaging.

'Then what *is* your opinion?' the judge interpolated.

'My opinion was formed at the time that the woman had been dead about four hours.'

The witness could now be likened to a sitting bird.

'If she was alive at half past six,' said Oliver agreeably, 'your opinion is wrong.'

'Yes,' MacFall admitted. He could do no other.

The duel was nearly over now, with counsel unquestion-

ably gathering the honours. Only the blood clot still remained to be considered. Oliver suggested that it must have
dropped upon the pan at least an hour after the woman met
her death. MacFall thought not.

'Didn't it occur to you that someone who came in after
nine might have dropped that clot of blood upon the pan?'

'The possibility did occur to me.'

'Didn't you think that there was a chance that the police
had carried it there?'

'Yes,' MacFall said candidly.

Oliver sat down. He had realised the dream of every cross-
examiner. He had turned the chief expert for the Crown
into a witness for the defence.

17

Wallace is not one of the tidy cases. It has no single theme
round which the evidence revolves. It is a compound of
many parts, contributed from many sources, which build
up an effect not by unity but by mass. Frith's *Derby Day* is
perhaps its parallel in art. . . .

As the long line of prosecution witnesses passed in turn
through the harsh test of the box, Oliver was repeatedly
picking up small gains, which, in the aggregate, greatly
changed the picture. There was the Prudential Superintendent, Wallace's immediate superior, who said the normal
accounting day was Wednesday, and that anyone who knew
Wallace's habits or employment might expect him to have
the bulk of his cash at home on Tuesday night. There was a
police officer, the first upon the scene, who agreed that he
saw Wallace fingering the treasury notes, one of which was
smeared with blood—and this of course was after he had
touched the bespattered body. There was a locksmith who

had inspected the locks on both the doors; the back, he said, was rusty and opened upon pressure; the front was defective, with a worn and slipping latch. There was the City Analyst, who agreed with Roland Oliver that the burnt part of the mackintosh lay in *front* of the gas fire.

And, finally, there was the Detective Superintendent, whose cross-examination reached a climax in this fashion.

'You don't doubt, do you,' Oliver asked him, 'from your knowledge of this type of house, that the back kitchen was the sitting room?'

'Yes, it was.'

'And the parlour was kept for visitors?'

'Yes.'

'When a visitor comes in at the front door he is shown into the parlour, is he not?'

'I suppose so.'

'And the gas lit and the fire lit; that is the usual thing?'

'Yes.'

'What I am putting to you is that everything in that room was consistent with a knock at the front door, and the admission of someone, and the visitor being taken into the parlour.'

'It is quite possible,' the Superintendent agreed.

When the Crown evidence ended, early on the third day, the trial had assumed the shape that renders it unique. Any set of circumstances that is extracted from it will readily support two incompatible hypotheses; they will be equally consistent with innocence and guilt.

It is pre-eminently the case where everything is cancelled out by something else.

18

One small episode in the Crown case, deliberately excluded from our general scrutiny, must now be treated—as is appropriate—*in vacuo*. It was an episode without point, without bearing, without force; it defies connection with reasoning and logic; it detracts by its almost imbecile irrelevance from the dignity with which the trial was otherwise invested.

A constable was called to say he had seen Wallace, looking 'very distressed', on the day of the murder at *3.30 p.m.*—that is, at least three hours, on the Crown's own showing, before Mrs Wallace was savagely done to death. Asked what signs of distress he had observed, the constable replied that Wallace was dabbing his eye with his coat sleeve and appeared to him as though he had been crying.

'I wonder,' Oliver said, 'if it occurred to you that your eyes could water with the cold?'

The constable assented.

'And you might rub them?'

'Quite *possible*.'

'I suggest that you are mistaken in thinking that the signs you saw were signs of distress occasioned by committing a crime.'

'He gave me the impression,' said the constable, 'that he had suffered some bereavement.'

'If I were to call about twenty-five people who saw him that afternoon round about that time and they said he was just as usual, would you say they had made a mistake?'

The deepest of police instincts were aroused.

'I should stick to my opinion,' the constable said stubbornly. . . .

Put aside the possibility that the constable was mistaken. Put aside the possibility that he misconstrued what he saw.

Consider the time element alone. If this evidence was accepted, together with the inference the prosecution drew, Wallace went about the streets of Liverpool that day weeping over a crime that he was *going* to commit!

The notion is farcical, and I doubt whether Hemmerde relished the job of presenting such a witness. He was never afraid to criticise police follies, and one can imagine the blistering comment he would have made if this particular episode had occurred in a case which he had been trying in his capacity as Recorder of the city.

19

Oliver had abundance of material when he rose to introduce the prisoner's case. The Hanging Points had been blunted one by one. The telephone call, the trouble with the doors, the accused's demeanour, the riddle of the mackintosh—each had either assumed a different colour or shown itself open to a new and harmless inference. The garrulous quest for Menlove Gardens East alone retained its full initial force; but Oliver was to argue trenchantly that Wallace's enquiries, though prosy and *p*ersistent, came naturally from a man out in pursuit of business who did not want to return without profit or reward. If the jury would recognise that this possibility at least could not be excluded, by any rational assessment of the evidence the Crown's five Hanging Points had lost the power to hang.

But Oliver did not rest upon a negative defence. He counter-attacked with vigour, concentrating particularly on the limits set by time. If Wallace was indeed the murderer of his wife, he had a great deal to do that night before leaving the house. He had to make himself clean—hands, face, nails, hair—after a filthy and polluting deed. He had either to dispose of his blood-splashed, blood-smeared clothes, or—adopting Hemmerde's hypothesis—take off the mackintosh, go upstairs and dress. He had, presumably, to disarrange the bedroom. He had to wipe, secrete, and smuggle out the weapon. All this, together with the crime itself, must have been done in less than twenty minutes. No one disputed that. It was the Crown's case that Wallace had left home at ten to seven. It was the Crown's case that Mrs Wallace was alive at half past six.

Less than twenty minutes; even if the first blow fell with the milk boy's cans still clattering outside. Most improbable, Oliver said; most improbable that any man in so short a time could have accomplished so much with such thoroughness and success. Not a mark on his body. Not a stain on his clothes. Not a trace of a weapon anywhere.

If it was improbable in twenty minutes, it was clearly impossible in five or even ten. Oliver sought to narrow down the gap. As a preparatory step he put in the box the Professor of Pathology at Liverpool University, who drew from the evidence of *rigor* the conclusion that death might well have taken place after seven o'clock. Having justly pointed out that the Crown based the time of Mrs Wallace's last appearance on the word and recollection of a fourteen-year-old boy, Oliver proceeded to call three similar boys himself. One said that he actually saw the milk boy standing on the step in front of Wallace's house; this was two minutes after he had looked at a church clock and noted that the time was twenty-five to seven. The other two both swore that, on the night after the murder, the milk boy—by then no doubt the hero of the neighbourhood—remarked, in the course of conversation in the street, that he had seen Mrs Wallace at a quarter to seven.

Which of these lads was telling the truth? Who could

decide? And unless it could be decided, definitely and clearly, in favour of the milk boy and against his companions, could a verdict of guilty properly be found? On *ten* minutes? On *five*?

Hemmerde, in his otherwise exhaustive final speech, skated lightly and swiftly over this question of the time factor. He had already displayed power; now he displayed discretion.

20

In the last resort a prisoner is always his own chief witness. His influence on events cannot be gathered from the record. The jury try to mark, not only what he says, but what he *is*. They form an impression of the man himself which, whether true or false, may move them more than logic.

In the witness box Wallace lived up to all the descriptions given of his nature. He was quiet, gentle, unflustered and precise. His nerves were throughout under an absolute command which, independently of innocence or guilt, appeared remarkable for one in his position. Perhaps it was stoicism; perhaps it was callousness; perhaps it derived from ineradicable grief that made him await his fate without concern.

'Is there anyone in the world', Oliver asked him, 'who could take the place of your wife in your life?'

'No,' said Wallace, 'there is not.'

'Have you got anyone to live with now?'

'No.'

'Or to live for?'

'No.'

In the days immediately following the crime Wallace made numerous statements to the police. They were lengthy, they were detailed, and there was nothing in them he desired to change. 'I need not have called him,' declared Oliver rhetorically, and in the strict sense this was true. But expedience and *policy* could not be disregarded, and besides, there were several minor points that only Wallace himself could satisfactorily clear up.

They were put to him, these points, one after another. Why, if his usual accounting day was Wednesday, had there been so little money in the house that Tuesday night? 'I did not collect on the Saturday,' he said, 'because I was laid u*p* with influenza. . . . I paid ten guineas out in sickness benefit out of what I had collected up to then.' Why, if he was not trying to fabricate an alibi, did he take out his watch when talking to the policeman and call the latter's attention to the time? 'The policeman told me I could get a directory at the post-office up the road. . . . I realised that if it was a local post-office it was probably a mixed sort of shop, and if I left it till after eight it would be closed, so I looked to see what time I had to spare.' Why, unless prompted by consciousness of guilt, did he tell the chess captain, two days after the crime, that the exact time of the telephone call was of great importance to him? 'I had just come from the police station. Superintendent Thomas had given me the information that they had been able to trace the call to a call-box near my home. .   I felt that if I had left home at a quarter past seven, and the telephone call had been made at seven o'clock, and that the police up to then had believed all my statements to be true (and I had no reason to think otherwise), then that automatically cleared me of having sent the message.'

You believed—or you did not believe. You trusted—or suspected. But at least you did not have to search the void for explanations. Each item in the Crown case was meticulously met.

21

Hemmerde's questioning of Wallace was rigorous and close. He did not bully or harass him, as Muir had bullied and harassed Steinie Morrison, but the pressure he exerted can be fairly called relentless. It became apparent that nothing in the course of the hearing had shaken Hemmerde's conviction that Wallace was the culprit.

The cross-examination attained a rare level of technical accomplishment. Much of it was not designed to extract new information, but rather to restate and recapitulate the alleged improbabilities in the defendant's case. The telephone call, for instance; in a series of questions Hemmerde scoffed at the idea that the caller could have been anyone but the prisoner himself. The alternative, it appeared, was positively absurd.

'Of course,' he remarked, ' "Mr Qualtrough" had no means of knowing whether you would receive the message that night, because no one knew for certain you were going to be at the club?'

'Yes,' said Wallace. 'That is so.'

'Then without knowing you would even get the message, and without knowing you would ever go to Menlove Gardens East, he was waiting for your departure the next night?'

'It would look like it.'

'Did it ever occur to you that he would have to watch both doors, front and back?'

'No,' said Wallace simply. 'It did not.'

'You're a man of business instincts; you could hardly be a Prudential agent if you were not?'

'That is so.'

'You must have realised that he had not the slightest idea whether you got his message?'

'Yes, I did.'

'And in spite of that,' said Hemmerde incredulously, 'you go off to Menlove Gardens East?'

'Yes.'

'Not only could he not know that you would go, but he couldn't have known that you wouldn't look up a directory and find there was no such place?'

'No.'

'He would have to risk all that?'

'Yes.'

'And of course, you *could* have found out at once, if you *had* looked it up in the directory, where Menlove Gardens East was—or was not?'

'Yes,' said Wallace. 'I could have done.'

Hemmerde's share in this dialogue was manifestly brilliant. But one should not pass over the part played by the prisoner. The form of the questions must have tempted him to *argue*, to show that the medal looked quite different in reverse. He never once succumbed to the temptation. He answered always with the utmost candour and made no attempt at self-justification. The facts, he implied, would have to speak for themselves.

Occasionally Hemmerde seemed to catch him out. There was a dramatic moment early in the long interrogation when Wallace said he had never observed any blood upon his hands. 'Then,' said the prosecutor in pardonable triumph, 'no blood from your hands could have got on to those notes in the vase on the mantelpiece?' There were times when Wallace's evidence did not wholly correspond with one or other of his many written statements. There were 'discrepancies', too, in these statements themselves, but the judge was to put this in correct perspective. 'I have read through them very carefully,' he said, 'and I think it is wonderful that they are as lucid, accurate and consistent as they are.'

The scope of this comment might not improperly be extended to cover the prisoner's testimony on oath.

22

The fourth day of the trial was well advanced when, after hearing two impressive final speeches, Mr Justice Wright began his summing up.

Some judges, taciturn and unaspiring, here make their first real impact on the jury. Others, persistently voluble and assertive, merely pass from conversation into monologue. Wright could be placed in neither category. He intervened seldom in a well-conducted case; he made no effort to impose himself; but by the majesty of his mind and presence he occupied always an ascendant place.

There was nothing in Wright's career at the Bar to prepare him for the tasks of a Red Judge on assize. He had been a gifted specialist in commercial work, engaged on recondite disputes of admiralty and contract. His merits as a lawyer were admittedly outstanding, and he was now paying a brief call on the King's Bench Division in the course of a swift journey upwards to the House of Lords. His fame and his achievement were in the domain of pure intellect, and one might have supposed that the run of criminal trials, which demand from a judge other and broader virtues—imagination, worldly sense and human understanding—belonged to a sphere in which he would not excel. But the contrary was the fact. Wright was that infrequent and superlative phenomenon: a great lawyer who was also a great man.

The judge *directs* the jury on the law, and they are bound to comply with his direction. He does not direct the jury on the facts; he may, and often does, express his own opinion, but they have the legal right to disregard it. This is as it should be; if the jury is to be nothing more than the judge's rubber stamp there is no valid reason why it should be convoked. One could find it possible to wish that, in a great many cases, juries would show more independence than they do. But indictments for murder are in a class apart. The jury may entertain a personal belief that the prisoner is guilty on a capital charge. But should they not feel there *must* be reasonable doubt if a judge of massive and renowned ability indicates his view that the case is not made out?

Time and time again this theme recurred in Wright's incisive, luminous address.

He started with a solemn caution against prejudice. 'Members of the jury, you, I believe, are living more or less in this neighbourhood. I come here as a stranger, and know nothing about the case until I come into court or look at the depositions, and I need not warn you that *you must approach this matter without any preconceived notions at all.* Your business here is to listen to the evidence, and to consider the evidence and nothing else.' He followed this by reminding them that the evidence against Wallace was purely circumstantial, and explained in simple terms the test to be adopted. 'Circumstantial evidence may vary in value almost infinitely. Some is as good and conclusive as the evidence of actual witnesses. In other cases, the only circumstantial evidence which anyone can present still leaves loopholes and doubts   The real test of the value of circumstantial evidence is this: *does it exclude other theories or possibilities?* If you cannot put the evidence against the accused beyond a probability; if it is a probability which is not inconsistent with there being other reasonable possibilities; then it is impossible for a jury to say, "We are satisfied beyond a reasonable doubt that the charge is made out." ' By this, the correct test, the charge against Wallace failed, as Mr Justice Wright repeatedly implied.

He discussed the telephone call and asked: 'What is the reasonably certain evidence, substantially excluding other possibilities, that it was the prisoner who rang up that night?' Such data as they had, indeed, pointed the other way. '*It is difficult to imagine that a man like the chess captain, in a conversation so prolonged, would not, even if the voice had been disguised, recognise the prisoner's voice if it was the prisoner.*' He referred to the conversation between Wallace and the chess captain two days after the crime had been committed: '*It would be very dangerous to draw from that any inference seriously adverse to the prisoner.*' He advised them to dismiss the blood clot from their minds: '*It is difficult to see how it has any connection with the murder.*'

As the judge approached the major issues, he was equally penetrating and forthright. 'If the prisoner was the murderer, what time had he available? That is the most vital part of the whole case. You will have to consider whether the narrow limits allowed, possibly of not more than ten minutes, would be sufficient. . . . There was a lot to do, and twenty minutes afterwards he was found, apparently completely dressed and apparently without any signs of discomposure, on a tramcar twenty minutes' journey from his home. . . . It does not follow that he did not do it, *but you have to be satisfied that he did do it.*' Again: 'How did he get rid of the wea*p*on in the time open to him? The only possible place where he could have dropped it on his way, an open space between the house and the tram, has been combed, and the drains have been searched, but no trace can be found of it. . . . I do not say it is impossible for a murderer under these circumstances to have disposed of a weapon, but *when you are considering whether it is brought home to the prisoner, you must carefully consider all these aspects.*' Again: 'If he was going quite honestly to search for Mr Qualtrough in Menlove Gardens East in the hope of getting a useful commission, then no doubt he would have probed the matter to the bottom. . . . *It is no use applying tests to evidence if none of them really excludes the possibility of the prisoner being innocent.*' And again: '*It is not at all impossible that he might have been so upset at the moment as to have had a difficulty in overcoming the friction of the two locks.*'

The regular frequenters of the court—solicitors, officials, lawyers' clerks and pressmen—nodded knowingly to each other as the judge's charge progressed. No mincing matters; no beating about the bush. His lordship clearly thought it would be improper to convict, and he was telling the jury so in terse and pithy terms.

'However you regard the matter, the whole crime was so skilfully devised and executed, and *there is such an absence of any trace to incriminate anybody as to make it very difficult to say*—although this is a matter entirely for you—*that it can be brought home to any one in particular.*'

Judicial guidance was never more explicit. The news seeped out and spread along the corridors; Wallace'll get off; he's summing up for an acquittal

The jury remained out for just over an hour. One marvels that they dared return to court at all. But their fathers had perversely convicted Mrs Maybrick, and now these representatives of a more enlightened epoch jealously preserved the Liverpool tradition.

23

Wallace in 1931 *possessed* a remedy denied to Mrs Maybrick in 1889. There was the Court of Criminal Appeal.

The Court of Criminal Appeal—which generally consists of three King's Bench judges—exercises only defined and limited powers. It does not re-try cases. It does not, as a rule, examine any evidence unless already tendered in the lower court. It does not put itself in the position of a jury; it is not enough for the three judges to say : 'Had we been asked, we would have found a different verdict.' (In effect the Court said that about the trial of Steinie Morrison; Steinie's appeal was nevertheless dismissed.) The Court is a court of law rather than of fact; it will quash a conviction on a purely legal point (inadmissibility of evidence, misdirection by the judge), but it will not otherwise interfere with a verdict unless it is unreasonable and against the weight of evidence.

Since its inception in the year 1907 the Court has allowed hundreds of appeals on the ground that a verdict was against the rules of law. It has allowed appeals but seldom on the ground that a verdict was against the weight of fact, and until 1931, in a case of murder, never.

Wallace was to create that precedent. After a two days' hearing, in which Oliver fought magnificently to save his client's life, the Court delivered judgment with dispassionate formality. 'Section Four of the Criminal Appeal Act of 1907 provides that the Court of Criminal Appeal shall allow the appeal if they think that the verdict of the jury should be set aside on the ground that it cannot be supported having regard to the evidence. The conclusion at which we have arrived is that the case against the appellant, which we have carefully and anxiously considered and discussed, was not proved with that certainty which is necessary in order to justify a verdict of guilty, and therefore it is our duty to take the course indicated by the Section of the Statute to which I have referred. The result is that this appeal will be allowed and the conviction quashed.'

And so William Herbert Wallace was set free—free to return to Liverpool, where he was ostracised and hounded; free to resume his employment, where he was mercifully transferred to inside work; free to retire for refuge to the country, where two years later he died, solitary, broken, a victim of despair.

24

'The great fascination of Wallace,' said Agate, 'is that the case of both sides is unanswerable.'

'And, therefore,' I said, 'you would agree with the Court of Criminal Appeal?'

'Certainly.'

'And the likelihood of Wallace being guilty is no less, but also no greater, than that of his being innocent?'

'Of course.'

'Very well,' I said, 'let us adopt—as we ought to adopt—the theory of his innocence. Somebody else, then, did this dreadful thing. Somebody else invented Mr Qualtrough; somebody else invented Menlove Gardens East. And this somebody else has got away with it completely. He killed that woman in her own house, in a populous district, with her neighbours at home next door—and vanished into space. Possibly, probably, he is still alive. What sort of a person, now, do you think he'd be? A clerk? A writer? A civil servant? A priest?'

'A genius,' said Agate flatly. 'A brutal, bloody fiend—and a genius.'

'I wonder if he reads the stuff that's written on the crime,' I said, 'and sometimes talks about the case among his friends.'

'That', said Agate sombrely, 'is the most shocking thought of all.'

LIZZIE BORDEN

1

THE charge against Lizzie Borden was inconceivable. That was the enduring strength of her defence. No matter how cogent the evidence, no matter how honest the witnesses, how could anyone credit the prosecution's case? That a woman, gently bred and delicately nurtured, should plan a murderous assault upon her stepmother; that she should execute it in the family home with such ferocious and demoniac force that the victim's head was smashed almost to pulp; that, having gazed upon her sickening handiwork, she should calmly wait an hour or more for her father to return; that she should then slaughter him with even greater violence so that hardened physicians shuddered at the sight; that neither loss of nerve nor pricking of remorse seemed to follow in the wake of such unnatural butchery—this was a tale that not merely challenged but defied belief. It was like asking one to accept the testimony of others that a horse recited Shakespeare or a dog had solved an anagram.

2

Everything combined to make this strain upon credence almost insupportable. At the eighteenth century's lowest moral ebb, some slatternly wanton such as Hogarth drew might have done these murders in a fetid slum, and still relied on incredulity giving the most unthinking jury pause. But this was not the eighteenth century; it was 1892. It was no strumpet of the streets who faced her trial, but the well-respected daughter of a well-respected man. And the setting of the scene was not Gin Lane or Seven Dials but Fall River, Massachusetts, deep in the heart of puritan New England.

Fall River at that time was a pleasant enough place, about the size of modern Cambridge, and not unlike a University town in its strong sense of community. People took close interest in other people's business. The leading citizens and chief officials were known by sight to all. Town matters wagged more tongues than national politics, and Fall River natives recognised as aristocracy, not the remote Four Hundred of New York, but the old Yankee families dwelling in their midst.

To this local élite belonged the Bordens, with Andrew Jackson Borden at their head. He was a prosperous business man and banker who, through a union of acumen and avarice, steadily increased his considerable wealth. He chose to live, however, in rather modest style. His first wife having died when he was forty, he presently wedded one Miss Abby Gray and, with her and the two daughters of his former marriage, took up residence in a house on Second Street. It was a narrow house standing in a narrow garden, hemmed in by other houses on almost every side, with its front door only a few feet from the traffic and bustle of a much frequented thoroughfare. In a sense, nothing was lacking: downstairs had a sitting room, a dining room and a parlour; upstairs had a guest room and a dressing room for Mrs Borden besides a separate bedroom for each of the two girls. But there was space without spaciousness, convenience without luxury, and both inside and out the house was unimposing if one remembered that this was the abode of a rich man.

In August 1892 the Bordens had been living there for about twenty years. Andrew was almost seventy. His wife was sixty-four. Miss Emma was forty-one. Miss Lizzie was thirty-two.

Before Miss Lizzie reached the age of thirty-three, this sedate and unexciting gentlewoman had made her name a lasting household word.

3

To all outward appearance the Borden house harboured a tranquil and contented household. But the façade was deceptive. Behind its look of blank correctitude lay deep antipathies and painful tensions.

The causes, though various, were intimately allied. There was the unattractive nature of the master; with his niggardly ways and autocratic temper, old Andrew inspired dread rather than affection. There was the classical aversion to the presence of a stepmother; the second Mrs Borden, though amiable and harmless, could not engage the goodwill of Andrew's daughters. And as the latter grew up, their bitterness developed in the shape of jealousy and squabbling over property—jealousy that sprang from already strained relationships, squabbling that shadowed those relationships still more. The time came when Miss Lizzie, sharper-spoken of the sisters, pointedly dropped the appellation 'Mother' and adopted the formal 'Mrs Borden' in its stead.

The division in the family intensified and hardened. As years went by, Miss Emma and Miss Lizzie evolved a technique to avoid their parents' company. Downstairs in the common rooms some contact was inevitable, but they contrived to reduce this to a satisfactory minimum by altering the times at which they took their meals. Upstairs it was much simpler. By bolting a single communicating door, the first floor could be split up into independent parts, one served by the front stairs, the other by the back.

On both sides of this door the bolts were permanently drawn.

4

The Massachusetts summer is uncomfortably hot. That of 1892 was no exception to the rule, and Fall River sweltered through those long July days during which dogs are reputed to go mad.

Late in the month Miss Emma left for Fairhaven, where she had arranged to spend a holiday with friends. At the same time Miss Lizzie paid a visit to New Bedford, but was back again at home before the week was out. In the sultry, stifling nights that followed her return, four people slept at the house on Second Street: Miss Lizzie, the old couple, and the servant, Bridget Sullivan, who occupied a room on the attic floor above.

On Wednesday, August 3rd, the four increased to five. Uncle Morse, a brother of the late Mrs Borden, arrived un-expectedly to stay a night or two. He found Andrew and his wife a little out of sorts; whether through the heat, or through some less obvious cause, in the previous night both had been seized with vomiting, and, though better, were still not free from physical malaise. Lizzie, too, they told him, had been similarly affected, but in that divided and disservered house Uncle Morse was not to see his niece till nearly noon next day.

By then any thought of this mild indisposition had vanished in the stress of far more terrible events.

5

August 4th, 1892, is a memorable date in the history of crime.

At the Borden home, where the grisly drama was to be

enacted, the morning opened normally enough. The older people were all early risers, and seven o'clock found them sitting down to breakfast, prepared and served by the young Irish maid. The sun climbed swiftly into a clear sky; the air was heavy with the heat of many weeks; all signs portended, rightly as it proved, that they were in for another scorching day. All the more reason to perform one's chores before the torrid blaze of afternoon.

By nine o'clock Uncle Morse had left the house to visit relatives elsewhere in the town. By nine fifteen Mr Borden had set out on his round of business calls. Mrs Borden had got a feather duster and was occupying herself with her household duties.

Meanwhile Miss Lizzie had made her first appearance. At nine o'clock she came into the kitchen where the servant Bridget was washing up the dishes. Bridget asked her what she fancied for her breakfast, but Miss Lizzie didn't seem to fancy very much. Having helped herself to a cup of coffee, she sat down to drink it at the kitchen table.

When the dishes were finished, Bridget took them to the dining room. There Mrs Borden was assiduously dusting. She had noticed that the windows had got dirty and asked Bridget to wash them as her next domestic task.

Bridget decided to wash the outsides first. She got a brush and some cloths, filled a pail with water, and went out through the side door, which she left unlocked.

Mrs Borden stayed inside. So did Miss Lizzie. The sun beat down with pitiless persistence and a drowsy silence fell upon the house.

6

At the partition fence Bridget stopped for a gossip with the maid next door. Then she started on the window-cleaning, working her way methodically round the house. She naturally looked into each ground-floor room in turn. She saw nobody in any.

The outside washing took perhaps an hour. Bridget then went back into the house, carefully locking the side door behind her. The Bordens were fussy about things like that, being morbidly fearful of robbers and intruders.

Everything was quiet; no one was about. Upstairs, taking it easy, Bridget enviously thought; best thing to do, on a broiler such as this. Conscientiously she started on the inside of the windows. .

At a quarter to eleven there was a noise at the front door; fumbling with a key and rattling of the lock. Must be Mr Borden. Bridget dropped her cloths and ran to let him in.

She found the front door not only locked but bolted. As she struggled to get it open so as not to keep the master waiting, somebody behind her laughed out loud.

Bridget glanced over her shoulder. Miss Lizzie was standing at the top of the staircase, a few feet from the open door of the guest room. What moved her to mirth at that particular moment must ever be a theme for speculation; whether it was the spectacle of a flustered Bridget, or whether it was some hilarious secret of her own. . . .

When Mr Borden was finally admitted, Miss Lizzie came downstairs.

'Mrs Borden has gone out,' she volunteered. 'She had a note from someone who is sick.'

Her father made no comment. It was hotter than ever, and he had still not shaken off the after-effects of that mysterious illness. His walk round town had tired him more than usual. He went into the sitting room to rest.

Bridget was now doing the windows in the dining room. Miss Lizzie joined her there. She brought in an ironing board, put it on the table, produced some handkerchiefs and commenced to iron.

For a space the two women worked away in silence. Then Miss Lizzie asked a casual-sounding question.

'Are you going out?'

'I don't know,' Bridget said, energetically polishing, 'I might and I might not.'

'If you go out,' said Miss Lizzie, 'be sure and lock the door, for Mrs Borden has gone out on a sick call and I might go out too.'

'Miss Lizzie, who is sick?' the maid enquired.

'I don't know. She had a note this morning; it must be in town.'

The windows were finished. Bridget withdrew into the kitchen, where she washed out the cloths. Presently Miss Lizzie followed her.

'There's a cheap sale of dress goods on down town,' she remarked. 'They are selling some kind of cloth at eight cents a yard.'

'Well,' Bridget said, 'I guess I'll have some.'

But at the moment Bridget did not feel inclined for out-of-doors. She had been up since six and kept hard at it ever since. A lie on the bed would make a nice mid-morning break. . . .

In her attic box, Bridget yawned, stretched herself and relaxed. On the sitting room couch old Andrew, spent by his exertions, fell asleep. Once again the house lay in the stillness of that drowsy quiet.

7

The alarm was given fifteen minutes later.

Bridget, day-dreaming beneath the baking roof, heard

her name called somewhere far below. Even at that distance, though, she caught the note of urgency. She jumped up at once and called out to know what was the matter.

'Come down quick,' Miss Lizzie's voice floated up through the house. 'Come down quick; Father's dead; somebody came in and killed him.'

Dumbfounded and mistrusting her own ears, Bridget ran down the back stairs as fast as she could go.

Miss Lizzie was standing close to the side door. Bridget made as if to go into the sitting room, but Miss Lizzie checked her—perhaps to spare her feelings.

'Don't go in. I've got to have a doctor quick.'

Doctor Bowen lived opposite. Bridget flew across the road, leaving Miss Lizzie sole guardian of the dead.

The doctor arrived and went straight into the sitting room. He was to describe what he saw there later on the witness stand. 'Mr Borden was lying on the lounge. His face was very badly cut, apparently with a sharp instrument; it was covered with blood. I felt of his pulse and satisfied myself that he was dead. I glanced about the room and saw there was nothing disturbed; neither the furniture nor anything at all. Mr Borden was lying on his right side, apparently at ease, as if asleep. His face was hardly to be recognised by one who knew him.'

8

The news spread like wildfire. As police and officials hurried to the house, a crowd of gapers packed the street outside, eager for any sight or sound connected with calamity.

Dr Bowen had to force a passage through this throng when he came out of the gate. He had covered Andrew Borden's body with a sheet; there was no other service he could usefully perform; now, at Miss Lizzie's personal request, he was going to the post-office to telegraph Miss Emma. Mrs Borden, he had gathered, had gone upon some errand, and all they could do was wait for her return. Poor woman, Dr Bowen thought, as he watched the gathering thicken; wherever she is, she'll hear the tidings soon enough.

He dispatched the telegram and gloomily made his way back towards the house. As he entered a neighbour of the Bordens caught his arm. Her face was grey and her hands shook uncontrollably.

'They have found Mrs Borden,' she said huskily.

'Where?' asked the doctor.

'Upstairs,' said the neighbour. 'In the front room.'

It was Miss Lizzie's suggestion that had prompted them to search; 'I'm almost positive,' she said, 'I heard her coming in.' It was Bridget and the neighbour who discovered Mrs Borden, lying lifeless and mangled on the guest room floor. Her body was growing cold, and the blood which enveloped her mutilated head had already become matted and practically dry.

The doctors concluded that when Andrew Borden died his wife had already been dead more than an hour.

9

If the case had stopped short there, if no charge against anyone had ever been preferred, Massachusetts would still have gone through weeks of ferment. If some hobo, some outcast, had been taxed with the crimes, his trial and the verdict determining his fate would have furnished all America with months of keen discussion. But when, after seven days of correlating evidence, during which the incredible gradually took shape, Fall River police arrested Lizzie Borden, the case at once acquired an entirely different stamp. It transcended the limits of geography and fashion; its range in time was perpetuity, in space the globe.

10

The trial of Lizzie Borden, delayed by various formalities of the law, took place at New Bedford in June 1893. It lasted thirteen days.

English readers, recalling the farce at Monkeyville or the spirited court scenes filmed in Hollywood, might pardonably expect the Borden trial to yield its quota of slapstick and burlesque. On the contrary. From first to last, at all times and all levels, the proceedings were conducted with a native dignity seldom attained in any land or age.

Three judges sat upon the bench: Chief Justice Mason, Mr Justice Blodgett and Mr Justice Dewey. For the Commonwealth (equivalent of the Crown) was Hosea Knowlton, the District Attorney, aided and partnered by William Moody, a colleague imported from an adjacent area. George D. Robinson, a former Congressman and ex-Governor of the State, with Andrew Jennings and Melvin Adams made up the team engaged for the defence.

To the modern eye, which finds a whiskered barrister hardly less freakish than a bald musician, there would have been something richly comic in the fine display of fringe, moustache and beard visible on counsels' row at Lizzie Borden's trial. But the advocates who sported these adornments were far from comic figures. They were masters of their complicated craft: shrewd in tactics, dexterous in argument, keen in cross-questioning, eloquent in speech. The defence, while energetically contesting every point and seizing every benefit admitted by the rules, took care in doing so never to depart from the highest standard of forensic practice. The prosecution, while making no effort to conceal the reluctance and distaste with which they entered on the case, did not suffer this to influence or impede the effective discharge of their melancholy duty.

In contrast to the custom observed in English trials, junior counsel played a prominent part. They were not confined to calling a few unimportant witnesses; they shared the speeches, and sometimes the cross-examination. As Knowlton was reserving himself for later responsibilities, it fell to William Moody to open for the Commonwealth.

11

Moody's speech was diffidently phrased, as befitted a naturally modest second string. He had frequent recourse to the protective 'I believe' and to the half-apologetic 'We fix that as well as we can.' But there was no cause for diffidence in the evidence he outlined. Before he had finished it was clear to demonstration that the Commonwealth had only moved on very solid ground. Their case was widely as well as firmly based—on proof of motive, indications of design, circumstances pointing to exclusive opportunity, and acts by Miss Lizzie which (it could be argued) were only reconcilable with consciousness of guilt.

The motive broached, of course, was hatred of the stepmother, and concern for the destination of the father's substance. Counsel crystallised the bitterness that had inspired the former by referring to a slight but illuminating incident. It had occurred in the house on the morning of the murders while the bodies were still lying there in piteous quiescence. The Assistant City Marshal had arrived upon the scene, and in fulfilment of his office was questioning Miss Lizzie. 'When did you last see your mother?' he had asked. 'She is not my mother, sir,' Miss Lizzie had replied. 'She is my step-mother. My mother died when I was a child.'

To support their second proposition, that the prisoner was plotting and contemplating murder, the Commonwealth relied upon a curious conversation which had taken place between Miss Lizzie and a friend. On the eve of the catastrophe, while old Andrew and his wife spent their last night on earth entertaining Uncle Morse, Miss Lizzie went across town to see Miss Alice Russell, with whom for some time she had been on familiar terms. Miss Russell soon observed that her companion was depressed, and apparently a prey to morbid fears and fancies. 'I cannot help feeling,' she said, 'something's going to happen.' Miss Russell tried to dissipate this mood by cheerful logic, but Miss Lizzie stubbornly declined to be persuaded. 'Last night we were all sick,' she said. 'We are afraid we have been poisoned.   Father has so much trouble with men that come to see him, I am afraid that some of them will do something to him. I expect nothing but that the building will be burnt down over our heads. The barn has been broken into twice.' 'That', said Miss Russell soothingly, 'was boys after pigeons.' 'All right,' said Miss Lizzie, 'but the house has been broken into in broad daylight, when Bridget and Emma and I were the only ones at home. I saw a man the other night lurking about the buildings, and as I came he jumped and ran away. Father had trouble with a man the other day; there were angry words, and he turned him out of the house.'

Miss Lizzie's foreboding that 'something' was going to happen might have been premonition or sheer coincidence. But the Commonwealth, taking the conversation as a whole, invited the jury to accept a different view—that she was cunningly diverting suspicion on to others in respect of crimes she herself meant to commit.

The prisoner's opportunity of accomplishing both murders was plain and incontestable on the admitted facts. But the Commonwealth were able to take this a step further. It was not only that *Miss Lizzie* had had ample opportunity; was there any opportunity for *anybody else*? The other members of the household were ruled out; Emma was in Fairhaven, Uncle Morse was with a niece more than a mile away, Bridget at the time of the second murder was upstairs. If it was not Miss Lizzie, then it must have been an intruder. There had been no entry by force. And, assuming for the moment that someone could get in and out completely unobserved, where were the signs that anyone had done so? Nothing was disturbed. No property was taken. No drawers had been ransacked. Mr Borden's watch and money—more than eighty dollars—were left upon his person. What then was the motive prompting someone from outside? Was he perhaps one of those men Miss Lizzie spoke of to Miss Russell who had come to pay old Borden out after some angry clash? Then how came it that there was not the slightest evidence of a struggle? Old Andrew may have been asleep upon the sitting-room couch, but his wife would hardly go to sleep upon the guest-room floor. And yet, said Moody, 'the assailant, whoever he or she may have been, was able to approach each victim, in broad daylight, and without a struggle or a murmur, to lay them low'.

12

Motive fixed; design set forth; opportunity established. But there still remains the weightiest part of the prosecution case: the *behaviour* of Miss Lizzie that day and the days after. Upon three matters especially the Commonwealth pressed hard: one, the note from the unidentified sick person; two, the variations in Miss Lizzie's story; three, the burning of the light blue figured dress.

The business of the note is perhaps the most damning single point againt the prisoner. 'Mrs Borden has gone out,' says Miss Lizzie to her father, at the moment when he may go looking for her round the house. 'She had a note from someone who is sick.' There can be no denying that was what Miss Lizzie said; she admitted it herself when examined at the inquest. She had not, she deposed, seen the note with her own eyes, but Mrs Borden told her of it, without naming the sender. Hence her own statement when her father returned home—a natural passing-on of domestic information. But the Commonwealth would have none of it. 'That statement', declared Moody, 'we put forward as a lie; it was intended for no purpose except to stifle enquiry into the whereabouts of Mrs Borden.'

It is the grave and awful fact that neither note nor sick person ever came to light. The implications for the prisoner are appalling, and, try as they would, the defence could not avoid them. The Commonwealth, not surprisingly, came to elevate the note to the most vital place of all, and it formed the subject matter of a powerful passage in the long speech which constituted Knowlton's winding up. 'My learned associate said in opening that that statement was a lie. I reaffirm that serious charge. No note came; no note was written; nobody brought a note; nobody was sick. Mrs Borden had not had a note. *I will stake the case*', said the District Attorney, '*on your belief in the truth of that proposition.*

Little did it occur to Lizzie Borden when she told that lie to her father that there would be eighty thousand witnesses of its falsity. My distinguished friend has had the hardihood to suggest that somebody may have written that note and not come forward to say so. Why, Mr Foreman, do you believe there exists in Fall River anybody so lost to all sense of humanity who would not have rushed forward without anything being said? But they have advertised for the writer of the note which was never written and which never came. . . . The whole falsehood of that note came from the woman in whose keeping Mrs Borden was left by Andrew Borden, and it was false as the answer Cain gave to his Maker when He said to him, "Where is thy brother Abel?" '

Cain had answered, 'Am I my brother's keeper?' Lizzie Borden had not waited to be asked. 'Mrs Borden has gone out. She had a note from someone who is sick.'

Maybe she was more free from sin than Cain. Maybe she was just smarter.

13

That morning of August 4th, as person after person—the maid, the neighbours, the doctor and the police—learnt from Miss Lizzie's lips that she had found her father killed, each in turn was moved to ask her: 'Where were you?' It was not a query rooted in suspicion, but an instinctive reaction to something unexplained. Had she been out, had she repaired like Bridget to a remote part of the house, that she saw and heard nothing of the assault or the assailant?

Where were you? Miss Lizzie faced this question more than half a dozen times. Moody closely analysed her answers. To Bridget she had said: 'I was out in the backyard. I heard a groan, came in and found the door open and found my father.' To Mrs Churchill, first of the neighbours to arrive, she said: 'I was out in the barn. I was going for a piece of iron when I heard a distress noise, came in and found the door open and found my father dead.' To Dr Bowen she said: 'I was in the barn looking for some iron.'

To Miss Russell she said: 'I went to the barn to get a piece of tin or iron.' To one officer she said: 'I was out in the barn for twenty minutes.' To another she said: 'I was upstairs in the barn for about half an hour.' To a third she said: 'I was in the barn and heard a noise like scraping.'

Now hunting for what are called 'discrepancies' is a favourite occupation of legal pettifoggers. Such gentry often may be heard to say that they have 'been through the Statements with a fine tooth-comb', and they proudly point out the results of their tooth-combing—some trivial variation of emphasis or phrase. But statements made at different times by a really honest person hardly ever exactly correspond. Conformity is the offspring of deliberated art.

This consideration would not be ignored by able, upright men like Moody and his leader. Their criticism was thus not primarily directed at the variations catalogued above. They took a more effective point—that later, when the flurry of that day had passed and Miss Lizzie produced a full, detailed account, she departed in a genuinely essential particular from what she had said in her earlier replies. Three times at least in those first hours of confusion she had told of hearing some kind of a noise; a groan, a 'distress noise', a noise like something scraping—but at any rate a sound that had attracted her attention, drew her back into the house, and so led to the discovery. But 'as enquiry', Moody said, 'began to multiply upon her, another story came into view. . . . It is not, gentlemen, and I pray your attention to it, a difference of words here. In one case the statement is that she was alarmed by the noise of the homicide; in the other case the statement is that she came coolly, deliberately, about her business (from the barn), looking after her ironing, putting down her hat and *accidentally* discovered the homicide as she went upstairs.'

However ingrained one's detestation of 'discrepancies', one must concede the valid premise underlying this. In the upheaval following on the murders, the barn and the backyard may have seemed interchangeable and twenty minutes much the same as half an hour. But could you mistake how you had first made the discovery—whether a noise had sent you in already apprehensive or whether the hideous spectacle burst on you unawares? Could you forget whether the first alarm attracted eye or ear?

Unless Miss Lizzie was a liar and much worse, the answer is: you could.

14

The murders were committed on a Thursday. It was not till the next Sunday that Miss Lizzie burnt the dress.

There was no attempt at concealment or deception; no surreptitious happenings beneath the cloak of night. She acted quite openly, in daylight, before witnesses. For an innocent woman, her behaviour was extraordinarily naïve; for a guilty one, it was extraordinarily stupid—or, as in the tales of G. K. Chesterton and Poe, extraordinarily clever in its very ostentation. For Miss Lizzie had been warned to pick her steps with care. On the Saturday evening the Mayor of Fall River had expressly informed her that she was now under suspicion.

It was the following day, a little before noon. Alice Russell, who at this time was staying in the house, came down from the upper floor and went into the kitchen. There she found both Miss Lizzie and Miss Emma. The latter was busy washing dishes at the sink. Miss Lizzie was standing at the far end by the stove. She had a dress over her arm.

As Miss Russell came in Miss Emma turned her head and said to her sister: 'What are you going to do?' 'I'm going to burn this old thing up,' replied Miss Lizzie. 'It's all covered with paint.'

She proceeded forthwith to tear it into strips.

There were several policemen on duty in the yard who could easily see in any time they chose to look. Miss Russell was so conscious of the equivocal effect created by this scene that she urged her friend at least to stand back from the window. 'I wouldn't do that,' she said, 'where people can see you.' Perhaps this remark took Miss Lizzie by surprise. At any rate, she did step a little out of vision—and placidly went on with the destruction of the dress.

The police, as Moody pointed out, had already searched the house and examined every garment to see if it was stained. They had found none marked with paint.

If the Commonwealth could have proved beyond a per-adventure that the dress Miss Lizzie burnt upon the stove was the dress she had worn on the morning of the murders, they would have prised loose the chief plank in her defence. *Not one who saw her on that convulsive morning had observed any blood upon her person or her clothes*, though—out of convention rather than necessity—neighbours had un-hooked her dress, fanned her face and rubbed her hands. It was even more remarkable than in the case of Wallace. Wallace—on the assumption, for this purpose, of his guilt—had the house to himself while he washed and changed his clothes. He had to be quick, but he was safe from inter-ruption. If Miss Lizzie committed these two sanguinary crimes ('the assailant would be spattered', said the prosecu-tion expert) she would also presumably be bound to wash and change. But she must have done it *twice*—and each time at the risk of being come upon by Bridget before all the traces of blood had been removed. And even if she ran that risk and, by the yardstick of success, justified her daring, how did she dispose of the incriminating clothes? After the second death, when the time margin was so narrow, they could only have been hidden somewhere in the house.

There lay the significance of the light blue figured dress which the prosecution sought to prove was the robe of homicide. But this was precisely what they could not do. Their witnesses disagreed among themselves about the dress Miss Lizzie wore upon the crucial day. Mrs Churchill said one thing, Doctor Bowen said another, and neither Bridget nor Miss Russell could recall the dress at all.

None the less, and notwithstanding its contradictory features, the Sunday morning episode in the kitchen was not one calculated to allay suspicion.

15

If, upon purely circumstantial evidence, you invite a jury to convict someone of murder, you must be ready with the answers to all their unspoken questions. Moody had dealt with 'What for?' There still remained 'What with?'

Murders like these are not done with the bare hands, nor with any light and pocketable weapon. From some of the wounds on Andrew Borden's head the length of the inflicting blade could be accurately fixed. It was three and a half inches, and it had fallen with the weight of a hatchet or an axe.

Where was this fearsome and death-dealing instrument?

It had not been abandoned at the scene of the crime. The murderer, therefore, had taken it away. Was it likely, Moody asked, that an intruder would have done so—that he would have run out with his bloodstained weapon into the sunlit street? Or did probability point to an inmate of the house, acquainted with its resources for concealment and disposal?

In the cellar, in a box upon the chimney shelf, the police had discovered a hatchet's head. The handle had been broken off, and the fragment that remained was covered with a coarse white dust of ashes. The blade of this hatchet had been measured. It was exactly three and a half inches long. .

Here once again was deep suspicion that fell short of proof. The Commonwealth were appropriately reserved. 'We do not insist,' said Moody, 'that these homicides were committed with this hatchet. *It may* have been the weapon.' He paused. 'It may *well* have been the weapon.'

16

With force, and yet with moderation, the case against Miss Lizzie had been placed before the court. Moody's was a sound professional performance, and his distinguished leader looked on with approval as he began a final recapitulation.

'Gentlemen, let me stop and see where we are. The Commonwealth will prove that there was an unkindly feeling between the prisoner and her stepmother; that on Wednesday, August 3rd, she was dwelling upon murder, predicting disaster and cataloguing defences; that from the time when Mrs Borden left the dining room to the time when the prisoner came downstairs an hour later from this hallway which led only to her chamber and that in which Mrs Borden was found, there was no other human being present except the prisoner at the bar; that these acts were the acts of a person who, to have selected time and place as it was selected in this case, must have had a familiar knowledge of the interior of the premises and of the whereabouts and habits of those in occupation. We shall prove that the prisoner made contradictory statements. We shall prove that Mrs Borden's was the prior death. Then we shall ask you to say whether any reasonable hypothesis except that of the prisoner's guilt can account for the sad occurrences on the morning of August 4th.'

The opening was over and so was the morning session. The court did not sit that afternoon. Members of the jury were otherwise engaged, exercising a privilege coveted by millions. In State-provided transport and accompanied by officials, they went off to Fall River to inspect the Borden home.

17

Next day the witnesses got into their stride, and defender Robinson got into his.

The ex-Governor was a jury advocate of natural talent and mature experience. He knew the world; he gauged people astutely; he had a flair for methods of approach. His mind was subtle, his expressions simple; he not merely understood others, he could make others understand.

In the Borden trial, his most important cross-examination was that of Bridget Sullivan, the Irish maid. It could hardly have been bettered.

Bridget was not by any means a vulnerable witness. She was neither fool nor knave. But, like most human beings, she. was susceptible to suggestion and subject to mistake. Discreetly Robinson made his own suggestions; relentlessly he exploited her mistakes.

He began by seeking Bridget's help in challenging the idea that the Borden family was rent asunder by ill-feeling. How far he could go with this could hardly be foreseen, and it is worth observing how every question tests or prepares a foothold for the next.

'Did *you* have any trouble there?' he asked.

'I?' said Bridget. 'No, sir.'

'A pleasant *place* to live?'

'Yes, sir.'

'A pleasant *family* to be in?'

'I don't know how the family was,' said Bridget, 'I got along all right.'

This was a slight setback. It might even be a warning. Robinson explored with a sure but gentle touch, like a surgeon who comes upon some dubious obstruction.

'You never saw anything *out of the way?*'

'No, sir.'

Good; if she never saw anything 'out of the way' one might be a little bolder and more definite.

'You never saw any *conflict* in the family?'

'No, sir.'

Excellent; one could go the whole hog now, and put it into terms the jury couldn't fail to grasp.

'Never saw any *quarrelling*, or anything of that kind?'

'No, sir,' answered Bridget. 'I did not.'*

So far so good. The girl had seen no open wrangles. But Robinson wishes to take it a stage further, and dispel any belief in a purely passive feud. He tackled Bridget about the allegation that Miss Emma and Miss Lizzie held aloof from family meals.

'Didn't they eat with the family?' he asked.

'Not all the time.'

Robinson took this reply and turned it upside down.

'But they did from time to time, did they not?'

The meaning was the same but the effect had been changed. It was like substituting 'half-full' for half-empty'

---

* Those interested in the technique of cross-examination will find a detailed analysis of this passage in an appendix.

'Yes, sir,' Bridget said, somewhat doubtfully, and added, 'Most of the time they didn't eat with their father and mother.'

Counsel met her insistence with the utmost ingenuity.

'Did they get up as early as the father and mother?'

'No, sir.'

'So they had their breakfast later?'

A logician would have jibbed at the word 'so'. But George D. Robinson had the measure of his audience. The Borden jurymen would not be conversant with the fallacy of *post hoc propter hoc*. Absences from breakfast were credibly accounted for.

'And how was it at dinner?'

'They were sometimes at dinner,' Bridget said. 'But a good many more times they were not.'

'Sometimes they were out?' Robinson suggested.

'I don't know where they were; I could not tell.'

Bridget was digging in her heels. A whole string of gains may be sacrificed by ill-timed im*p*ortunity. Smoothly the advocate altered his direction.

'Did you ever hear Miss Lizzie talk with Mrs Borden?'

'Yes, sir; she always spoke to Mrs Borden when Mrs Borden talked to her.'

'Always did?' repeated Robinson, making certain they had caught it in the recesses of the jury box.

'Yes, sir.'

'The conversation went on in the ordinary way, did it?'

'Yes, sir.'

'How was it this Thursday morning after they came downstairs?'

Bridget wrinkled her forehead.

'I don't remember.'

'Didn't they talk in the sitting room?'

'Yes.'

'Who spoke?'

'Miss Lizzie and Mrs Borden.'

'Talking calmly, the same as anybody else?'

'Yes, sir.'

This enabled Robinson to make a bigger throw.

'There was not, as far as you know, any trouble that morning?'

'No, sir,' said Bridget. 'I did not see any.'

In this phase of the questioning relations were quite amicable. It would not have suited Robinson if they had been otherwise. But now a more acrimonious passage was impending.

The conception of a murderous intruder constituted a vital part of Robinson's defence. To account for the fact that between crimes One and Two an intruder must have remained upon the premises more than an hour, experiments had been carried out with the object of establishing that he could have concealed himself in a closet in the hall. But primarily he would have had to obtain access to the house; and this in practice was limited to periods during which the side door had been left unlocked. The more they were, and the longer, the better for Miss Lizzie.

Bridget, in direct examination, had fixed one; she owned to leaving the side door 'off the hook' while she was cleaning the outside of the windows. She agreed, too, with Robinson that, while she was engaged upon the windows in the front and while she was chatting to the next door neighbours' maid, the side door would be hidden from her view and—Robinson's words—'the field pretty clear for a person to walk in'.

All that was very well, but it was not enough. Robinson knew that a useful piece was missing. Earlier on the morning of the murders, Bridget had gone out, not to the front but to the yard; it would widen the scope for the conjectural intruder if she had left the door unhooked when she returned on that occasion. Many months before, at the inquest at Fall River, she had said she couldn't tell whether she did or not. With Miss Lizzie on trial for her life, Bridget had somehow recollected. 'When I came back from the yard,' she had asserted, 'I hooked up the side door.'

Robinson did not propose to let this matter pass. Every minute that the side door might have been unhooked was precious. Before she left the stand the girl was going to retract.

He picked up a bulky set of papers. It was a transcript of the evidence at the inquest.

'Do you think,' he said, and there was the faintest undertone of menace in his drawl, 'do you think you have told us today just as you told us before?'

'I have told all I know,' said Bridget.

'I don't ask you that.' The tone suddenly sharpened. 'What I want to know is whether you have told it today just as you did before?'

'Well, I think I did,' said Bridget, a shade taken aback. Mr Robinson had seemed such an easy, pleasant man. 'I think I did, as far as I remember.'

'What did you do as to the side door when you came in from the yard?'

'I hooked it.'

'Did you say so before at the other examination?'

'I think so.'

'Do you *know* so?'

Bridget wavered.

'I'm not sure,' she said.

'Let me read and see if you said this.' He read aloud very

slowly and distinctly. ' "Question : When you came in from the yard did you hook the side door? Answer : I don't know whether I did or not." Did you say so?'

'Well, I *must* have hooked it because——'

'That isn't it.' Robinson cut in without ceremony. 'Was that the way you testified?'

'I testified the truth.'

'I don't imply that you didn't.' It was indeed Robinson's whole point that she did; that the truth about the hooking of the door had been given at the inquest and not at the trial. 'I merely want to know if you recall testifying over there at Fall River that you couldn't tell whether you hooked the door or not?'

But it stuck in Bridget's gullet.

'It is *likely* I did hook it, for it was always kept hooked.'

Robinson's face was very stern.

'Do you positively recollect one way or the other?'

'Well,' said Bridget, scared but obstinate, 'I *generally* hook the side door.'

'That isn't what I asked.' The ex-Governor was peremptory. 'Did you hook it or did you not?'

'I know I *must* have hooked the door for I always——'

'That isn't it. Did you hook it or did you not?'

Bridget gave up.

'I don't know,' she said. 'I don't know whether I did or not.'

The spectators took a deep breath. Ex-Governor Robinson's frown relaxed. He looked almost affable again as he passed on to the next question.

18

At the luncheon breaks and afternoon adjournments jurymen poked each other in the ribs. That ole Guv'nor Robinson; he puts it across; there an't no flies on him. But the jury were out of court when he put it across best and when the absence of flies was most conspicuous. For Robinson's triumphs at getting evidence in were surpassed by his triumphs at keeping evidence out.

There was, for example, Mr Eli Bence.

Mr Eli Bence had a simple tale to tell. He was a drug clerk at a Fall River pharmacy. On August 3rd, sometime in the forenoon, Miss Lizzie, whom he knew, had come into the shop. She had asked for ten cents' worth of prussic acid—required, so she said, for cleaning sealskin furs. 'Prussic acid, my good lady', Mr Bence had replied, 'is something we don't sell without a prescription from a doctor. It is a very dangerous thing to handle.' Miss Lizzie had departed without her prussic acid.

The very name of this substance conjures up unnatural death; one might as well use the word 'poison' and be done. A picture of Miss Lizzie trying, *without success*, to purchase prussic acid on the day before the murders might easily provoke a prejudicial train of thought. Had she turned from one method of killing to another—from the inaccessible poison to the handy household axe?

Her defenders could not afford to sit back unconcerned while the ground was prepared for this damaging idea. If there was any way of stifling it, stifled it must be. So Mr Bence had barely settled on the stand, having got little further than announcing his full name, when George D. Robinson rose from his place with a general objection to the witness being heard.

This objection, argued of course in the absence of the jury, was based upon two points. First, that prussic acid had harmless as well as harmful uses; 'it is an article', said Robinson, 'which a person may legitimately buy.' Second, that the attempted purchase could have no conceivable hearing upon murders with an axe—'and that is all we are enquiring about here.'

Moody, for the Commonwealth, faced this submission squarely. (It might be thought that Moody, as Knowlton's junior colleague, was doing rather more than his fair share of the work. But it would seem that a rough division had been mutually agreed; Moody was to open the case and argue points of law, Knowlton was to cross-examine and make the final speech. And in the trial of Lizzie Borden, as will presently appear, the final speech on each side assumed paramount importance.)

The Commonwealth spokesman seized at once on Robinson's last point—that the prussic acid episode did not prove, or tend to prove, that the defendant committed two murders with an axe. Quite right, Moody said; the evidence is not being offered for that purpose. It is meant to show intent, to demonstrate premeditation, to cast a revealing beam of light upon the prisoner's state of mind.

For Robinson's other point, the Commonwealth were well armed. They had brought to court a furrier and an analytical chemist to say that prussic acid was not used for cleaning furs. 'I can conceive', said Moody, 'of no more significant act, nothing which tends to show more the purpose of doing mischief than the attempt, on an excuse which upon this proof was false, to obtain one of the most deadly poisons known to human kind.'

The judges conferred. They agreed with the Commonwealth where a layman might have hesitated—that proof of attempts to procure an instrument of murder might be introduced as evidence of intent even though the murder charged was subsequently effected with an instrument of quite a different kind. But they were doubtful where a layman might have felt no doubt at all—whether prussic acid could not be put to uses neither noxious nor medical.

They decided to hear the furrier and the chemist. These experts duly testified, and, while the jury still kicked their heels outside, there followed a long and whispered consultation between judges and counsel, who moved forward to the bench. There was much wagging of expository fingers and sceptical shaking of celebrated heads. It was noted that those concerned for the Commonwealth looked grave, while those for the defence looked inwardly exultant.

When at last the advocates returned to their seats, the judges proceeded to give a joint decision. There was insufficient proof to satisfy the court that the acid could not be used for an innocent purpose.

The poison evidence would therefore be excluded.

19

If Robinson had fought hard to keep out Eli Bence, he fought harder to keep out . . . Lizzie Borden.

Miss Lizzie had already given evidence on oath—at the inquest, to which she had been summoned by subpœna. There, under Knowlton's cross-examination, she had proved an obstinate but unconvincing witness. The contradictions in her story were rife and absolute; the explanations few and often incomplete. She had been downstairs in the kitchen when her father returned home; no, she had been upstairs, sewing on a piece of tape; no, she remembered, she had been downstairs after all. She had gone out to the barn to find a sinker for a fish line; she had not been to the barn before for possibly three months; she didn't know what made her choose that special, fateful moment; she had stayed up in the barn for a space of twenty minutes; it was a very hot day and the barn was dreadfully close; no, of course she wouldn't stay there any longer than she need. How long would it take to find the sinker—three minutes, or four? No, it took her ten. And the remaining ten, Miss Borden? She was just looking idly through the window of the barn, eating three pears she had brought in from the yard. . . .

These and a score of other jarring incongruities made Miss Lizzie's testimony a danger to herself. It had been the clinching factor that had led to her arrest, and now the Commonwealth were tendering it at trial to be read out to the jury as evidence of her guilt.

But again her leading advocate entered an objection. Miss Lizzie's inquest testimony, he claimed, was inadmissible.

The rule relating to and governing such matters rested on a long line of American authorities. All really depended on the status of Miss Lizzie when, in obedience to the fiat of the law, she appeared at the inquest and submitted herself to questions. Was she then a perfectly free agent, an ordinary citizen, called to help the coroner determine cause of death? If so, even though she may have been under suspicion, her testimony was 'voluntary' and admissible. Or was she already in effect an accused person, called less to help the coroner than to answer for herself? If so, any statements made by her would not be 'voluntary' and could not be employed against her at the trial.

The inquest concluded on August 11th. Miss Lizzie was arrested later the same day. Until that moment she was, by presumption, free, but Robinson argued that the contrary was the fact. For three days past the City Marshal of Fall River had had in his pocket a warrant for her arrest. During the whole of that period she was under observation by police detailed for the purpose and stationed round the house. She

was not cautioned before she gave her evidence. Her request
for counsel at the inquest was refused. 'In other words, the
practice that was resorted to was to put her really in the
custody of the City Marshal, beyond the possibility of any
retirement or release or freedom whatever; keeping her with
a hand upon the shoulder, covering her at every second,
surrounding her at every instant, empowered to take her
at any moment, and under these circumstances taking her
to that inquest to testify. Denied counsel, not told that she
ought not to testify to anything that might tend to criminate
herself, she stood alone, a defenceless woman, in that attitude. 'If that is freedom,' Robinson exclaimed, 'then God
save the Commonwealth of Massachusetts.'

Moody's reply was vehement and scornful. How, he asked,
could an undisclosed warrant, of which the woman had no
suspicion whatsoever, bear upon the exercise of her will
when she appeared as a witness at the inquest? Where was
there a grain of evidence to show that her liberty was re-
strained for an instant until the end of her examination?
What authority had been quoted, could be quoted, to justify
exclusion of such testimony unless the person testifying was
actually under arrest? Moody attacked Robinson with almost
spiteful sarcasm. 'I say of what my friend is pleased to call
his argument: it is magnificent but it is not law.'

Law or no law, Robinson gained the day. 'The common
law', said the Chief Justice, 'regards substance more than
form. It is plain that the prisoner at the time of her testimony
was, so far as relates to this question, as effectively in custody
as if the formal precept had been served. We are all of
opinion that this is decisive, and the evidence is excluded.'

This did not debar Miss Lizzie from telling her story to
the jurymen afresh. In Massachusetts, unlike Britain at that
period, prisoners were permitted to give evidence if they

wished. But Miss Lizzie did not intend to avail herself of this privilege. One encounter with Mr Knowlton was enough.

20

With the acknowledged leading lady unwilling to perform, Miss Emma Borden became the star of the defence.

Here was indeed a most serviceable deputy. She could give much of Lizzie's story without running Lizzie's risk. She could tell the jury almost all her sister could have told about the prelude, the background, and the sequel to the crimes; but because on August 4th she had been away at Fairhaven, she could not be cross-questioned about the day itself. The substitution of the elder sister for the younger was a neat and effective tactical device.

According to the best theatrical tradition, Miss Emma's entrance was deliberately delayed. When at long last the Commonwealth rested (on the tenth day, in defiance of the scriptures) the defenders first released a little swarm of witnesses each of whom contributed some item of his own. One, who lived just behind the Borden home, had heard a curious 'pounding' on the night of August 3rd. Another, who had passed the house early on the 4th, had seen a young fellow hanging round; he was pale and 'acting strangely'. A third, walking by a little later in the morning, observed an unknown man leaning up against the gate. Such evidence was flimsy, not to say remote, but shrewd George Robinson perceived a latent value in composing this sketch of an alternative assassin.

The jury spent some hours among these fanciful conjectures. When the big moment arrived, though, and Miss Emma took the stand, they were instantly plunged back into the cold harsh world of fact.

Miss Emma, whatever nervousness she felt, rose to the requirements of her exacting rôle. Her timing was precise. She described how her father always wore a single ring; how it had been given to him years ago by Lizzie; how it was the only jewellery he ever wore; how it was on his finger at the moment of his death and how it was still upon his finger in the grave. She described how thoroughly the police had searched the house and how Miss Lizzie never made the least objection. She described how her sister burnt the dress on Sunday morning, and said that *she, Miss Emma, had prompted her to do it.* 'The dress got paint on it in May when the men painted the house.   On Saturday, the day of the search, I went to the clothes press to hang up my own dress. There was no vacant nail. I searched round to find a nail and noticed this dress. "You've not destroyed that old dress yet," I said to Lizzie. She said: "I think I will," and I said: "I would if I were you." '

Miss Lizzie would certainly have done it far less well. George Robinson himself could not have done it better. The telegraph systems tapped it out across the world; the sister has come out strongly on Lizzie Borden's side.

21

In a long trial for murder, as day follows day and witness follows witness, even the participants may temporarily forget the agony of decision that awaits them at the end. They may become so immersed in the interplay of advocates, the interpreting of laws, and the balancing of issues that these processes come to appear ends instead of means—means by which twelve can arrive at a conclusion which will spell for one either liberty or death.

The completion of the evidence reawakens apprehension.

As the last of many witnesses passes from the stand, the minds of all in court are increasingly preoccupied by hopes or fears of the fast approaching verdict.

At this stage the verdict can sometimes be foreseen. Not so, however, in the case of Lizzie Borden. The clash was less one of *fact* than of *construction*, less a matter of which witness you accepted than which counsel. It was a battle of barristers for command over the jury, and the outcome of that battle had yet to be decided.

22

Other things being equal, recent impressions are bound to be the strongest. That is why advocates contend for the last word. In the Borden trial the last word lay with Knowlton, because of the evidence that had been called for the defence. Robinson had to precede his opponent, with all the disadvantages attached to that position.

In his introduction to the transcript of the trial—an essay that stands high in the literature of crime—Mr Edmund Pearson compares Robinson with Knowlton, and does not conceal his preference for the latter. It is true that Knowlton was animated by the loftiest sentiments and the noblest ideals. It is true that he spoke majestic prose with a splendid rhythm and an almost biblical ring. It is true that Robinson, by contrast, was homespun and colloquial, with both feet firmly planted on the Massachusetts earth. None the less, I am convinced, he was the better advocate and had the astuter mind. He possessed what, for want of a better word, one may call courtcraft; he attuned himself exactly to the mental pitch prevailing; he neither preached to nor lectured nor apostrophised the jury, but *talked* to them about the case as a neighbour might at home.

Along these lines and within these limits, his final speech was a real forensic feat.

It is evident that throughout he kept in mind not only the logic of facts and of events, but the way the jury could be relied upon to *feel*. He began by playing on their natural reluctance to believe that a woman could have carried out these crimes; 'it is physically and morally impossible.' He traded on the human love of jeering at the police : 'They make themselves ridiculous, insisting that a defendant shall know everything that was done on a particular time, shall account for every moment of that time, shall tell it three or four times alike, shall never waver or quiver, shall have tears or not have tears, shall make no mistakes.'

Beside these matters of emotional propensity, he swept into place the one solid piece of evidence that told heavily and positively in favour of his client. 'Blood speaks out, though it is voiceless. It speaks out against the criminal. Not a spot on her, from her hair to her feet, on dress or person anywhere. Think of it! Think of it for an instant.'

Having laid this foundation of artistically commingled hypothesis and fact, Robinson turned to the prosecution's case. He took the points against him one by one, and in plain, familiar words, with nicely managed raillery, made all—or nearly all—appear paltry or fallacious.

'Why do they say she did it?' he enquired. 'Well, in the first place, they say she was in the house.' Already it sounded far less good a point than when it had been termed 'exclusive opportunity'. Robinson added to the ground so quickly gained. 'She was in the house. Well, that may look to you like a very wrong place for her to be in. But . . . it is her own home. I don't know where I would want my daughter to be than at home, attending to the ordinary vocations of life, as a dutiful member of the household.'

The jury pouted their lips sagely. No doubt about that; she had a right to be at home. No, sir; couldn't say she was to blame for being at home.

Next, the Commonwealth had talked about a motive. Why, Robinson demanded, did they set great store on this? 'If a person commits a murder and we know it, there is no reason to enquire for what reason he did it. If he did it, then it does not make any difference whether he had any motive or not. . . . In this case the motive is only introduced to explain the evidence, and to bind her to the crimes.' And what sort of motive had they ultimately proved? They had shown that, from five or six years ago, Lizzie did not call Mrs Borden 'Mother'—Lizzie, who was indeed her step-daughter, and was now a woman thirty-two years old. They had stressed her correction of the Assistant City Marshal: 'She is not my mother, sir; she is my stepmother.' Robinson's comment on this was superbly opportune. He re-called to the jury 'a well-looking little girl' who had given some minor evidence on behalf of the defence. 'Why, Martha Chagnon, that was here a day or two ago, stepped on the stand and began to talk about Mrs Chagnon as her stepmother. Well, I advise the City Marshal to put a cordon around *her* house, so that there will not be another murder there. Right here, in your presence, she spoke of her step-mother, and Mrs Chagnon herself came on the stand after-wards, and I believe the blood of neither of them has been spilled since.'

It was the kind of illustration that a country jury loves: concrete, local, about people they had seen. They pouted again and shook their heads a little; didn't seem much in the stepmother business either.

The Wednesday evening talk between Miss Lizzie and Miss Russell—styled by the Commonwealth 'evidence of design'—was dismissed by Robinson as hardly worthy of discussion. 'There are a good many people who believe in premonitions. . . . Events often succeed predictions through a mere coincidence . . . . You all recollect that Miss Lizzie's monthly illness was then continuing and we know from sad experience that many a woman at such a time is unbalanced, her mind unsettled and everything is out of sorts and out of joint.'

'We know from sad experience.' It was another clever touch. The family men looked back into their own domestic lives, and the whole jury glowed with superior male strength.

The lawyers and reporters listening to the speech, who were well acquainted with George Robinson's quick wits, had never doubted his ability to score whenever circumstances offered the tiniest of openings. But they waited with deep interest to see how he would handle a matter in which they discerned no opening at all : the matter of the note 'from someone who is sick'.

The defender did not dodge the point; he could not if he would. And if it made the weakest part of a very powerful speech, no possible blame can be attributed to him.

'A person may say,' he said : ' "Where is the note?" Well, we should be very glad to see it. Very glad.' Nobody could doubt that this sentiment was sincere. If the note had materialised, it might have proved decisive. 'Very likely Mrs Borden burned it up. But then they say nobody has come forward to say they sent it. That is true. You will find men living perhaps in this county who do not know that this trial is going on, don't know anything about it, don't pay much attention to it; they are about their own business; don't consider it of consequence. Sometimes people don't *want* to get into a courtroom even if a life is in danger.'

Robinson's manner was as confident as ever, but the content of his argument now wore a little thin. The jury looked puzzled. His grip on them was loosening. Up to now they had gone all the way with Guv'nor Robinson, but they didn't feel happy with this talk about the note. Did it make sense? They tried to imagine what they would have done themselves—the test that he was always asking them to apply. Would *they* not have known that the trial was going on? Would *they* have hung back, if it meant somebody's life? But there wasn't really time to think the problem out; Robinson was moving on to another, better point.

The Commonwealth had charged his client with inconsistent statements. 'The others tell us she said she went out to the barn. It's the police that tell us how long she said she stayed there. It takes Assistant Marshal Fleet himself to get the thirty minutes. You see him. You see him.' He pointed to this officer sitting there in court, stiff as a ramrod, haughty as a dowager, obsessed with his own distinction and importance. 'You see him,' said Robinson, like an enthusiastic teacher taking his pupils round a zoo, 'you see the set of that moustache and the firmness of those lips.' The moustache bristled, the firm lips set still tighter. 'There he was in this young woman's room. . . . This man Fleet was troubled. He was on the scent for a job. He was ferreting out a crime. He had a theory. He was a detective. And so he says: "You said this morning you were up in the barn for half an hour. Will you say that now?" Miss Lizzie said: "I do not say half an hour. I said twenty minutes to half an hour." "Well," says Assistant Marshal Fleet, "we will call it twenty minutes." ' Robinson's voice grew higher in derision. 'Much obliged to him. He was ready to call it twenty minutes, was he? What a favour that was! Now Lizzie has some sense of her own, and she says: "I say from twenty minutes to half an hour, sir." He had not awed her into silence. She still breathed, though he was there.'

Assistant Marshal Fleet had no option but to listen, and the jury could savour his discomfiture in safety. They chuckled with delight at the slights he was enduring. That ole Guv'nor Robinson had them back again in thrall.

Robinson now ranged to and fro on ground that was congenial: the burning of the dress (where Miss Emma lent him strength), Miss Lizzie's supposed attempts to tempt Bridget to town ('If she had undertaken these deeds, think you not she would have sent Bridget out on an errand?'), the Commonwealth's uncertainty about the murderer's weapon. Nor did he forget to offer his own theory. 'The side door, gentlemen, was unfastened from about nine to eleven. . . . Bridget was outside talking to the next-door girl; she couldn't see the side door when she was there. Lizzie was about the house as usual. What was she doing? The same as any decent woman does. Attending to her work, ironing handkerchiefs, going up and down stairs. You say these things are not all proved'—Knowlton had stirred restlessly—'but I am taking you into the house just as I would into your own. What are your wives doing now?'

The jury felt homesick. They were suddenly out of this oppressive, crowded court; they had ceased to be the centre of the waiting world; they were back there on the farm, with a cool breeze blowing and the missus putting on a good New England meal.

'What are your wives doing now?' Robinson's voice wound its way into their thoughts. 'Doing the ordinary work around the house, getting the dinner. Well, where do they go? Down cellar for potatoes, into the kitchen, here and there. You can see the whole thing. It was just the same there.

'Now suppose the assassin came there and passed through.

Where could he go? He could go up into that bedchamber and secrete himself to stay there—until he finds himself confronting Mrs Borden. Now what is going to be done? He is there for murder; not to murder her, but to murder Mr Borden. And he knows that he will be recognised, and he must strike her down. A man that had in his mind the purpose to kill Mr Borden would not stop at the intervention of another person, and Lizzie and Bridget and Mrs Borden, all or any of them, would be slaughtered if they came in that fellow's way.

'And when he had done his work, and Mr Borden had come in, as he could hear him, he could come down. Bridget was upstairs, Lizzie outdoors. He could do his work quickly and securely, and pass out the same door as he came in.'

Robinson had very nearly finished, but, like most master advocates, he had nursed and husbanded his most dramatic stroke.

Steadily he gazed upon the close-packed jury box. His tones were level and imperative.

'To find her guilty, you must believe she is a fiend. *Gentlemen, does she look it?*'

The speech had gone full circle. 'Is it possible?' 'Does she look it?'

They looked, and saw Miss Lizzie with her high, severe collar; her modestly groomed hair; her long, slender hands and her sharp, patrician features; her unmistakable air of being, above all else, a lady

They looked at her, and her advocate had played his strongest card.

23

To Knowlton this was the most difficult and disagreeable case of his career. Having placed his own evidence squarely before the court, having closely cross-examined the opposition witnesses, he must have been tempted to exert himself no further. A short and colourless concluding speech, from which it would appear that he was loath to press the matter, presented itself as the least unpleasant course.

But Knowlton was a man of rectitude and principle; his personal inclinations did not influence his conduct. As a government official he owed a duty to the public. It was a primary part of that duty to ensure that criminals did not escape their just and proper punishment. He believed, with some reason, that he had a strong case, and that it would be a dereliction of his high responsibility to neglect any lawful means of capturing the jury.

As Robinson sat down, amid that buzz of tongues which bursts forth uncontrollably on the slackening of tension, Knowlton slowly rose, like a man oppressed with care, and resolutely started on his grim, ungrateful task.

He grappled at once with the greatest of his difficulties. 'My distinguished friend says: "Who could have done it?" The answer would have been: "Nobody could have done it." If you had read an account of these cold and heartless facts in any tale of fiction, you would have said: "That will do for a story, but such things never happen. . . . It was an impossible crime." But it was committed. Set any human being you can think of, put any degraded man or woman you ever heard of, at the bar, and say to them "You did this thing," and it would seem incredible. And yet—it was done; it was done.'

He particularly deprecated Robinson's suggestion that the murders could not have been committed by a woman, and permitted himself a few general observations on the temperament and nature of the female sex. 'They are no better than we; they are no worse than we. If they lack in strength and coarseness and vigour, they make up for it in cunning, in despatch, in celerity, in ferocity. If their loves are stronger and more enduring than those of men, their hates are more undying, more unyielding, more persistent.' In disdainful phrase he struck at a main obstacle to cool-headed decision. 'We must face this case', he said, 'as men, not as gallants.'

Through the twelfth afternoon and through the thirteenth morning, Knowlton continued his remarkable address; gravely exhorting, patiently explaining, impeccable in literary style and moral tone. His thesis was twofold: that Miss Lizzie's story was in itself incredible; that anybody else could have done it was impossible. It was beyond credence, he declared, that on that sweltering day she went up to the barn, 'the hottest place in Fall River', and there remained all the time that Bridget was upstairs. It was beyond credence that, upon discovering her father, she had not fled from the house to the safety of the street; 'she did not know that the assassin was not there; she did not know that he had escaped'. It was beyond credence that the murder of Mrs Borden could take place without Miss Lizzie seeing or hearing anything unusual; 'if she was downstairs she was in the path of the assassin, if she was upstairs only a thin deal door separated her from the crime'. It was beyond credence that a dress that had been good enough to keep through May, through June, through July, and into August should, innocently and by sheer coincidence, be destroyed twelve hours after she had heard of the suspicions. It was beyond credence that a mysterious assassin should know he would find the side door open at the exact time he desired, should hide in closets where there was no blood found, should come out when there was no opportunity to come out without being seen by all the world, should know Bridget was going upstairs to rest when she didn't know herself, should know

Lizzie was going to the barn when she couldn't have told it herself, should know that Mrs Borden would be upstairs dusting when no one could have foreseen it. 'What is the defence to our array of facts? Nothing; nothing. It is proven, Mr Foreman; it is proven.'

No passage in his speech was more impressive in its thoughtfulness and stunning in its horror than that in which he sought to analyse Miss Lizzie's motives. The order of the crimes, he said, supplied their key. He reversed Robinson's theory that the woman met her death through coming upon and recognising a murderous intruder who had got into the house to lie in wait for Mr Borden. 'No,' said Knowlton, 'it was Mrs Borden whose life that wicked person sought, and all the motive we have to consider bears on her.' And whatever might be said about old Andrew, except for Miss Lizzie (and the absent Miss Emma) his harmless wife had not a single foe. 'There may be that in this case,' said Knowlton very solemnly, 'that saves us from the idea that Lizzie planned to kill her father. I hope she did not. I should be slow to believe she did. But it was not Lizzie Borden who came down those stairs, but a murderess, transformed from the daughter, transformed from the ties of affection, to the most consummate criminal we have read of in our history. She came down to meet that stern old man. That man who loved his daughter, but who loved his wife too, as the Bible commanded him. And, above all, the one man in this universe who would know who killed his wife. She had not thought of that. She had gone on. There is cunning in crime, but there is blindness in crime too. She had gone on with stealth and cunning, but she had forgotten the hereafter. They always do. And when the deed was done, she was coming downstairs to face Nemesis. There wouldn't be any question but that he would know the reason that woman lay in death. He knew who disliked her. He knew who couldn't tolerate her presence under that roof.'

As a work of abstract art, this speech of Knowlton's has surpassing merit. The language is choice, the mood exalted, the reasoning taut and deep. It is excellent to read. But the study is one place, the courtroom is another, and the best advocacy seldom makes the best literature. The jury, simple folk that they were, may well have found George Robinson more comprehensible. They may have felt more at home with his less august style.

Before he ended, Knowlton made a brave attempt to lift the issue of the trial on to a spiritual plane. 'Rise, gentlemen,' he cried, 'to the altitude of your duty. Act as you would be reported to act when you stand before the Great White Throne at the last day. . Only he who hears the voice of his inner consciousness—it is the voice of God Himself—saying to him "Well done, good and faithful servant," can enter into the reward and lay hold of eternal life.'

This peroration has real grandeur. It puts to shame George Robinson's humble 'Gentlemen, does she look it?' But one wonders which stood uppermost in the minds of the jury as they sat in their little private room deciding Lizzie's fate.

24

By five o'clock that afternoon it was all over. Miss Lizzie had been acquitted in a tempest of applause. With her faithful sister Emma at her side, she was on her way home to celebrate her vindication. George D. Robinson, well pleased with himself, walked away from court amid the cheering of the crowds. Only in the office of the District Attorney Knowlton and Moody sat apart from the rejoicings. They alone, perhaps, were at that moment capable of beholding the Borden trial through the eye of history.

25

Miss Lizzie lived thereafter for four and thirty years, with every indication of an easy conscience. She had inherited a comfortable fortune which she placidly and soberly and decently enjoyed. She never married. She occupied herself— as she had formerly done—with a variety of charitable works, and in her will she left thirty thousand dollars to a society for the prevention of cruelty to animals.

Her death let loose in public a flood of speculation that had gone on in private ever since the trial. Students of crime and detection endlessly debate: was the Borden verdict right?

Others remember Lizzie for a different reason. A catchy little jingle, probably written before she was acquitted, has linked itself imperishably with folk and nursery lore.

Lizzie Borden took an ax
And gave her mother forty whacks,
When she saw what she had done
She gave her father forty-one.

Students may argue about her as they please. In the wide world that is her epitaph.

APPENDIX

(*See page* 227)

ROBINSON's aim is clear. He achieves it with the last question of this sequence, when he gets Bridget to agree that she never say any 'quarrelling, or anything of that kind'. But he dare not ask this baldly, without careful preparation, because he cannot foresee the terms of her reply. Supposing she says, in response to a blunt query, 'Miss Lizzie and Mrs Borden quarrelled all day long.' His cause will then be far worse off than if the matter had not been raised at all. So he needs to approach the question circumspectly, advancing only one step at a time, and at every stage leaving channels of escape which he can use without grave loss of face.

He starts with just one hard fact to work from. Bridget has been in the Bordens' service for close upon three years. That dictates the form of his first question.

'Did *you* have any trouble there?'

If Bridget says 'Yes,' Robinson can retort, without fear of contradiction, 'But you *did* stay there three years,' and then, accepting the danger signal, ride off to some less inflammable topic with a specious air of having scored a point. If Bridget says 'No'—as she does—he has strengthened his hand, improved his position, and gained a better sight of the ground ahead.

It does not take him very far. But it enables him to venture next on a question that appears superficially a mere rephrasing of his last. In fact, though, by an almost imperceptible change in stress, it is designed to bring him closer to his target.

'A pleasant *place* to live?' he asks.

251

This imports the idea that not only were things all right for Bridget personally, but the Borden household was all right in general. And yet he can be fairly certain that Bridget will say 'Yes' to this after her affirmative reply to the previous question. The two sound so alike. If, surprisingly, she does say 'No', Robinson's escape is open as before, but with additional virtue—'But you stayed there three years *and* you never had any trouble.'

This, however, does not arise. Robinson safely collects another 'Yes'.

Now he comes to the most delicate *point* in the sequence. He must ask, however broadly, about the family themselves. He has, it is true, buttressed himself by the two preliminary questions, but this is the danger spot, and he knows it.

'It was a pleasant *family* to be in?'

Bridget's answer raises a problem. A downright 'Yes' would have brought the advocate almost home. A downright 'No' would have driven him from the trail; it would have been far too dangerous to press her further. Robinson would have made off under cover of a volley of safe questions. ('Pleasant enough to make the place pleasant, eh?' 'Pleasant enough to stay three years with, eh?' etc.)

But Bridget's reply is enigmatic. 'I don't know how the family was,' she says. 'I got along all right.'

Is this to be taken at its face value? Or is she hinting that there were family dissensions and that she kept out of them? Robinson has gone a long way now; he does not want to withdraw without his prize. But the utmost care is called for.

The next question, so artless in appearance, packs into its small compass a lifetime's experience and skill.

'You never saw anything out of the way?'

'Out of the way' is exactly right. Respectable girls—and

Bridget is a very respectable girl—do not describe places as 'pleasant' where 'out of the way' things occur—as Robinson will, if necessary, remind her. But Bridget gives no cause.

'No, sir,' she says.

Now he is practically secure. If any quarrelling is mentioned, they are ordinary, everyday domestic quarrels, quarrels that could not be considered 'out of the way'. He can go straight forward.

'You never saw any conflict in the family?'

Even if, contrary to expectation, Bridget should say 'Yes', Robinson is well protected. But Bridget says 'No' and he reaches his goal.

'Never saw any quarrelling or anything of that kind?'

'No, sir.'

And few of the spectators are aware that they have heard a little gem of the cross-examiner's art.

11924568R00148

Printed in Germany
by Amazon Distribution
GmbH, Leipzig